WHERE THE OCEAN MEETS THE SKY

Barbara Stevenson

Luna Press

PUBLISHING

First published by Luna Press Publishing, Edinburgh, 2020

Where the Ocean Meets the Sky. *First published in Beyond Realities 2015, 2015.*
The Happy Tree. *First published in The Secret Attic Anthology, 2009.*
Step Inside. *First published in The Puffin Review E-Zine Issue 10, 2014.*
Dry Rot. *First published in Williwaw, An Anthology of the Marvellous, 2015.*
Zuri Mtu. *First published in The Breve New Stories, Issue 1, 2015.*
The One-armed Bandit. *First published in Beyond Realities Vol. II, 2016.*
Mimo Santos. (original to this collection)
Giacomo's High Doh. (original to this collection)
Zeitgeist. (original to this collection)
Duck Soup. (original to this collection)
By the Light. (original to this collection)

www.lunapresspublishing.com
ISBN-13: 978-1-911143-93-2

Thanks to Francesca T Barbini and Luna Press Publishing, for the opportunity to bring together this anthology of fun, friendship and imaginary crocodiles.

Contents

Where the Ocean Meets the Sky

'Pull her hard to starboard,' the mate called.

'Hard to starboard,' the hand said.

'We'll crash into the rocks, sir.' The midshipman grabbed the wheel.

'Captain's orders, hard to starboard,' the mate said.

'That's not hard to starboard,' the midshipman said. 'It's quarter to nine.'

The mate turned to look at the captain. The hands on the tall, wooden grandfather clock that was propped against the main mast, lashed to it with ropes, showed the time was fifteen minutes to nine. On cue it croaked out the first three lines of the Westminster chime.

'As you were, sailor,' the mate said, swinging his arms behind his back to twiddle with his thumbs. The ship scraped past the outcrop of rocks. 'What course are we on?'

'You don't know?' The midshipman's voice sounded like a tomcat hissing, which didn't surprise the mate. The midshipman had ginger fur, ten centimetre long whiskers and a battle scar on his striped tail.

'How should I know? I only boarded ten minutes ago,' the mate said. 'I was starching my beard ready for our passing out parade when I got the message that your ship was short-staffed.'

'Not so bad that we need a naval college moron to guide us,' the midshipman said.

'Watch your tongue, sir. I could have you court-martialled for insub … insubor … cheek.'

The midshipman ran his tongue over his left hand and washed

behind his ear.

'Don't do that when I'm addressing you,' the mate said. 'Where are the rest of the crew?'

'There's just you, me, the hand and Captain Clock,' Midshipman Tom said. 'But you can hardly ask the captain to chip in with the men.'

At that the ship's hand burst into a fit of giggles.

Tom groaned. 'We'll be late for the Infanta's tennis tournament now.'

The hand was rolling so hard on the deck that the ship listed. The mate was caught off balance and stumbled towards the midshipman. Tom leapt aside as the mate - all six-foot-two and fourteen stone of him - crashed into the grandfather clock. The wood creaked and the hour hand slipped to dangle over the six.

'I'm terribly sorry, Captain.' The mate saluted.

'Roc ahoy,' Tom said.

'Steer round it,' the mate said.

'It's a roc, not a rock,' Tom clarified.

'It can't be. They only exist in poems and picture books,' the mate said.

'Ordinarily yes, sir,' Tom agreed, 'but they will leave the pages, if there is something worth dying for.'

'Nothing is worth dying for.' The mate ducked as the huge bird cruised over his head.

'We've got nothing on board,' Tom said. 'We did have a present for the Infanta, but there was an accident.'

'It was a parrot and he ate it,' the hand said.

'I didn't eat it; it fell into my mouth,' Tom said. He grabbed a mop lying on deck and waved it at the bird.

'What are we going to do?' the hand asked.

'With the captain incapacitated, you will have to assume command,' Tom said, turning to where the mate had been.

'Sorry, what did you say?' While the hand was throwing rubber ducks at the giant bird, the mate had retrieved his mobile phone and was hanging from the side railing with his arm outstretched.

'What are you doing?' Tom said. 'Taking a picture for your mum?'

'This is going directly onto social media,' the mate said. 'It should get loads of hits.'

'You can't do that,' said the hand.

'It isn't against regulations,' the mate replied.

'No, but the reception is rubbish here,' the hand answered.

'Even from the top mast?'

'Perhaps you two humans could discuss broadband later.' Tom jumped as the canvas from the main sail was ripped from the ropes by the roc's beak and came crashing down.

'Watch it,' the mate shouted. 'Repairs don't come cheap.' The sun reflected from the screen of his phone, bouncing a shaft of light into the bird's eyes. It gave a squawk to deafen the nearby humpback whale and swooped down to seize the phone from the mate's hands.

'I think it wants a selfie,' the hand said.

'Quick, while it's distracted,' Tom signalled the mate and the hand to assemble beside him. 'If we all three tug on the wheel, the ship will turn sharply and the roc will fly smack, bang into that rock.'

'That should give it a headache,' the hand observed.

'Ready?'

'Wait,' the mate said.

'What is it?' Tom hissed.

'It's heading for the captain. Unhand him, you beast.'

The bird ignored the mate's frantic hand-flapping and gripped the grandfather clock in its claws. It wrenched the captain free of the ropes then rose into the air with three magnificent flaps and flew off.

'I think it's gone,' Tom said.

'But it has taken the captain,' the mate replied.

'It is only a clock, you know,' the hand said.

'A broken one at that,' Midshipman Tom stared at the mate.

'It could be mended,' the hand suggested.

'Cheaper buying a new one,' said Tom.

'That is not the point.' The mate was almost in tears. 'We are speaking about the ship's captain. What will people say when we arrive in port without him?'

'I wouldn't worry what others say,' Tom said. 'People are always saying catty things about me.'

'That's because you are a cat,' the hand said.

'I shall ignore that remark because we are friends,' Tom huffed. 'I wouldn't take it from anyone else.' He flexed the tips of his fingers to protract sharpened claws.

'Let's not argue,' the mate said. 'We need to rescue the captain.'

'No, we don't,' Tom said.

'You mean a quest?' the hand said. 'We will be legends.'

'I hate quests,' Tom said. 'Especially dangerous ones, where somebody dies.'

'Wouldn't you risk your life for your captain?' the mate asked.

'No. Besides, you said nothing was worth dying for.'

'That was ten minutes ago,' the mate said.

'I'm in, sir.' The hand stood beside the mate.

'See, the boy has more spunk than you, officer,' the mate put a hand on the hand's shoulder.

'I'm a girl, actually,' the hand said.

'Really?' The mate removed his hand.

'Able Sea-girl Becky Buchanan,' she saluted.

'I'm delighted to meet you, Becky. I'm Ship's Mate George Wilton-Watt, or I will be when I officially pass out. My father was Captain Willoughby Watt and my grandfather was Rear Admiral Cloudesly Watt.'

'You've got a Rear Admiral in the family?' Becky was impressed.

'Please, we don't want you passing out too,' Tom said. 'If the introductions are over, can we go to the Infanta's tennis party as planned?'

'Not before we've rescued our captain,' the mate was unflinching.

'But you've only been hired for an hour to guide us into the harbour,' Tom argued.

'An hour will be long enough,' the mate said.

'He's just gutted because he can't be captain,' Becky whispered to the mate.

'I heard that and it's not true,' Tom said.

'We don't have time for squabbling,' said the mate as he

marched towards the bow. 'Midshipman, set a course for the beast's lair.'

'Aye, aye sir.'

Tom turned the wheel as Becky sprung into action to haul the main sail into position.

'I'll be below if you need me,' the mate said. He wobbled to the top of the narrow stair leading to the captain's cabin and stopped to pull his stomach and chest in before trying to descend.

'Land ahoy,' the hand called.

'We can't have arrived already,' the mate said.

'You've only got forty five minutes left on your contract,' Tom said. 'We had to fast forward.'

'Are you sure this is the roc's lair? It looks like the Infanta's palace.'

'They are close neighbours,' Tom said.

'They had better be or I'll have you arrested for insub… in … su … disobeying orders,' the mate finished.

'That isn't very nice,' Tom said. 'We are all friends on this ship.'

'It's a friend ship,' the hand agreed.

'I forgave Becky for calling me a cat,' Tom explained.

'What about the captain? Isn't he a friend?' the mate asked.

'Technically, he isn't on the ship,' Becky said.

'And we can be friends without risking our lives,' Tom offered.

'Nobody is going to die,' the mate said.

'We will, at some point,' Becky mused. 'We're not immortal.'

'Of course, we will all die at some point,' the mate agreed.

'Except the captain,' Becky reminded him. 'He's already dead wood.'

'If I die, we are not friends anymore,' Tom said, pointing a claw at the mate.

'You can't say that,' Becky said.

The midshipman curled his lip, then grinned. 'Forty minutes now. We'd better get ashore before you have to report back to HQ.'

'It would be nice to have a long term position,' the mate mused. 'With time to get to know people.'

Tom mumbled something about a double-edged sword, but

nobody answered.

'Should I fix the landing ramp?' Becky asked.

'We can leap ashore from here,' Tom said. His back was arched, ready to spring.

'We're not all cats,' the mate complained, before realising his mistake. 'I'm sorry, I didn't say that.'

With a swish of his golden tail that hit the mate on the nose, the midshipman leapt from the vessel onto the pier.

The hand dragged a plank across the deck and manoeuvred it over the side. 'You first, sir.'

'This way,' Tom said as he met the others, now resplendent in white shorts, a white sports top and a sleeveless V-neck sweater. He swished a tennis racket in the air.

'We are going to the roc's lair,' the mate said.

'Won't your white clothes get spoilt?' Becky asked.

'If my clothes get spoilt, what does it matter what colour they are?' Tom said.

While the hand worked out the logic of Tom's remark, they headed up a steep path towards a magnificent, milk-white palace perched precariously on an overhanging cliff. Two mounted sentries guarded the gates.

'Are they what I think they are? Becky asked, looking at Tom.

'You could say they are more centauries than sentries,' Tom agreed.

'We have come to rescue our captain.' The mate puffed out his chest and stepped forward to greet the guards.

'We are expected.' Tom winked.

'Of course. The guests are assembled at the marquee.'

'Guests?' asked the mate.

'For the tennis tournament, sir,' the centaur explained.

'Tom?' said the mate.

'Well, I admit this is the Infanta's palace, but the roc will be here. He wouldn't decline an invitation.'

The gates were opened and the crew were directed into a tiled marble courtyard. A man approached wearing a tweed jacket, plus fours and green woollen socks that looked like they were straight from the loom. He was balancing a shotgun under his right arm.

'Tom, old man,' he greeted the midshipman. 'Are you here for the tennis?'

'Defending my title,' Tom said. 'If I win, it will be seven in a row and I get to keep the trophy.'

'The grandfather clock. Spiffing.'

'There will be no time for games. We are looking for the roc,' the mate said. 'I believe he is a neighbour of yours.'

'A roc?' The gentleman looked perplexed.

'A large bird with fearsome teeth and daggers for claws,' the hand said. 'If it pierces you with its eyes, your bones burn to ashes and, at the touch of a feather, your skin turns to ice.'

The mate and Tom shivered.

'You mean Bertie?' the gentleman said. 'Good man. I play golf with him on Sundays. He is probably terrorising the children or setting fire to barns. You could ask his housekeeper. That's her, beside the cheese.'

'The mouse?' Tom said.

'You think she looks like a mouse?' the man rubbed his chin. 'I have heard people mention the likeness. Don't see it myself.'

'She is about five centimetres tall, has a long tail, mouse fur and whiskers,' Becky said.

'Yes, but calling her a mouse would be like calling Tom here a cat. Ha!' the lord said. 'Must shoot off now.'

'I should speak with the roc's housekeeper. I have a way with ladies.' Tom twirled his whiskers.

'And mice,' Becky added.

The housekeeper was sweeping crumbs of cheese under a chair when Tom leapt up. She jumped back and dropped her broom.

'I hope I didn't frighten you,' Tom purred. 'I was just thinking how delicious you look, with your skirts swaying like that.'

The mouse blushed. 'I bet you say that to all the mice.'

'Not at all.' Tom licked his lips.

'Tom has to go,' Becky interrupted. 'He's due on court to open the tournament. He is the reigning tennis champion.'

The mouse fluttered her eyelashes. Tom was about to lift her in his paws, but Becky poked him in the chest. 'We'll meet you later,' she said. 'After we've seen the roc.'

'The roc? Yes, I would love to stay, but my opponent awaits.' Tom bowed to the housekeeper and darted off.

'What business have you with Sir Bertie?' the housekeeper asked.

'He has something belonging to us: a grandfather clock,' Becky said.

'The roc is a mythical beast. What need does he have for telling time?' the housekeeper wondered. 'You don't mean the music box he brought home this morning, do you?'

'The music box? Yes, that's it!' Becky smiled.

'Have you come to mend it? The roc is heartbroken he can't get it to sing.'

'Yes,' the mate said, before the hand could answer. He was puffing as he reached them. It had taken him some time to join the hand. The Infanta had waylaid him and insisted on a round of croquet. He had thought it only proper to allow the Infanta to win, but she had insisted on a re-match. 'Do you know where it is?'

'It is in Sir Bertie's private study. I'm only allowed in every second Wednesday to clear the bones and grimy bits of sinew that stick in his teeth.'

'Too much infor …' The mate grabbed the hand's hat and held it over his mouth.

'You will need to get the key from Sir Bertie,' the mouse said.

'Where is he?' Becky asked.

'It's his day to take the pensioners to the bridge,' the housekeeper answered. 'He shouldn't be long. There aren't many pensioners left.'

'I play a little bridge on my days off,' the mate said. 'Perhaps I can make up the numbers.'

Becky gave the mate a nudge, 'I don't think they are playing cards.'

Before them was a river that widened where it met the sea; high above it, in the distance, a shadow hovered several hundred feet above a suspension bridge. Dangling from the beast's legs was a tiny, struggling speck. As they watched, the roc released its grip and the speck dropped like a falling star, knocked against the bridge and rebounded into the water.

'I see,' the mate said. 'What exactly is the point of this game?'

'It's not a game,' said the housekeeper. 'The skull is cracked open on the bridge and the brains are then easier to pick out.'

'Maybe we should come back on a Wednesday,' Becky said.

'There is another way into the study,' the housekeeper said. 'If you can climb.'

The mate coughed and looked at the hand.

'Tom is the one for serious wall climbing,' Becky said.

'Is there a ladder to the study?' the mate asked.

'Or a fixed fire escape?' the hand added.

'You can climb up Punzel's hair,' the housekeeper offered.

'Punzel?' said the mate and hand together.

'The roc's ward. She's normally very prim and proper but, once she's drunk a few bottles of wine, she'll let her hair down.'

'Do we have any wine, sailor?' the mate asked.

'Only rum, sir.'

'That will do,' the housekeeper said. 'I have to go now. I serve the barley water between sets.'

'Thank you,' the mate said. He turned and handed the hand her hat. 'Get back to the ship and fetch the rum. I'll find this Punzel girl.'

'Aye, aye sir.' Becky replaced her hat and a congealed glob of half-digested bangers and mash slopped down her hair.

'Sorry.' The mate clenched his teeth.

Punzel was brushing tags from her twenty metres of hair when the mate found her.

'Allow me to introduce myself. My name is George ...'

'Whatever. Do you know who is winning the tennis?' Punzel interrupted.

'No, sorry.'

'It's probably the cat. He wins every year. Boring.' Punzel yawned.

'I guess he's good at tennis.' The mate shrugged.

'I'm rubbish at games, but I do know how to brush hair,' Punzel said.

'You get lots of practise, I'm sure.'

'What is that supposed to mean?' Punzel lowered her brush and took an aggressive step towards the mate.

'Nothing. Why, here's the hand with the rum rations.' The mate backed off.

'About time. I haven't had a drop to drink for hours.'

The hand was staggering under a crate of rum. She dropped it at the mate's feet.

'Careful, you might break something,' the mate and Punzel said, then stared at each other. Punzel helped herself to a bottle and cracked it open with her teeth. The alcohol was downed before the mate could even ask if she wanted a mixer. Punzel burped and reached for another bottle.

'I'm glad you like our rum,' the mate said. 'Perhaps you would be so kind as to do a teeny, weeny, ickle, peedie little favour in return?'

'Like what?' Punzel stopped drinking.

'We need to get into the roc's study to steal …' the hand began.

'Mend …' the mate corrected.

'… to mend the grandfather clock,' the hand finished.

'The music box, she means,' the mate said. 'We want it to be ready when Sir Bertie gets back from the bridge.'

'That's nice of you,' Punzel said.

'We're nice people,' said Becky.

'So you'll help us?' the mate asked.

Punzel choked on the rum. 'I didn't say that. Nobody goes in the roc's study without his permission. Not if they want to come out alive.'

'But if you were to go to your room and lean out the window, your hair might dangle down,' Becky said.

'And you would hardly notice if the lad here climbed up it,' the mate added.

'She's a girl,' Punzel said.

'Of course. I was forgetting.'

'She's got breasts bigger than two stuffed chickens,' Punzel said.

'Has she? I didn't notice,' the mate turned bright crimson.

'You're kind of cute when you do that, Georgie. Tell you what, if I can kiss your cheeks, I'll let you both climb up my hair.'

'Very well,' the mate said, drawing his face closer.

'Not those cheeks.' Punzel smiled to show a mouthful of broken teeth and pus.

The mate's crimson face turned green.

'I'll look away,' Becky said.

Ten minutes later the hand was clambering ahead of the mate up Punzel's hair to the window of the roc's study. There was no glass in the frame so they heaved themselves in.

'I guess the housekeeper hasn't been in for a while,' the hand said, holding the tail of her shirt to her nose.

'What is that?' the mate asked.

'Don't ask. It may once have been attached to some vital organ.'

They squelched across the floor, slipping on layers of jellied offal. Pickled eyes watched them from bottles on the shelves.

'Can you see the captain?' The mate had his eyes closed.

'Over here,' Becky called.

'Is he alive?' the mate said.

The hand put her ear to the clock. 'Barely ticking.'

'Get him to the window,' the mate ordered.

'I can't - he's taller and heavier than me.'

'It's a matter of technique,' the mate said. 'I'll show you.'

'No need. Look who's behind you.'

The mate felt the draught from the roc's wings as it came to rest on the window frame and turned slowly to face the beast.

'Ah good, you've got my phone,' the mate said, spotting the device in the roc's claws. 'Perhaps I could have it back?'

The bird raised its neck and bellowed out a raucous roar.

'Keep it. I need an upgrade anyway.'

The roc stuck out one wing to block the mate's escape.

'We tried to fix your music box, but I'm afraid we'll need to take it to our warehouse for repair,' the hand said.

'We don't have the body parts here,' the mate said.

The bird hopped off its perch, knocking the mate to the floor.

His new uniform was splattered with blood and bile. The beast advanced on the hand, making pecking gestures. Becky backed towards the door.

'Steady on,' the mate said, as he climbed to his feet. 'We weren't the ones who broke it.'

'Actually, you were,' Becky said.

'It's probably still under guarantee, so you won't have to pay,' the mate said.

The roc kicked the mate, sending him sprawling back into a pile of rotten fingers. The hand clawed at the door, willing it to open.

'Punzel, can you hear me? We need help. Now!' she called. The roc's beak hurtled towards her. Becky darted out of the way. 'Mrs Mousekeeper? Is anyone there?'

The roc pulled its beak from the door and took aim again. The hand closed her eyes. Before the roc could strike, the door swung open, sending Becky sprawling across the room. She grabbed the roc's tail to prevent herself falling out of the window.

'Am I missing the fun?' Tom said, entering the room.

The roc cocked his head to the side and made a cooing noise. Becky helped the mate to his feet and they scrambled behind Tom.

'Come on, let's go,' the mate urged.

'What about the captain?' Becky said.

'I'm afraid he's a goner.'

Tom moved towards the captain, taking care not to get any mess on his tennis whites. The roc had its eyes fixed on the object Tom was carrying.

'This old music box is broken,' Tom said. 'We can dispose of it free of charge and in exchange we can replace it with a brand new, mega shiny, working model.' He signalled to the hand to move the captain, then set the tennis trophy in its place. 'Listen to this.' Tom twirled the hands of the clock he had just won. The chime rang out and the roc danced a jig.

'Excellent moves, Sir Bertie,' Tom said, backing out the door.

The mate was already at the stairs, with the hand struggling to pull the captain after her.

'Allow me,' said Tom.

'What, you are actually going to do some manual work?' Becky said.

'Not at all.' Tom raised his claws to his mouth and gave a whistle. Before the last note squeezed out, three mice were scrambling round the hand's legs. More joined them until the corridor was a blanket of brown fur. Between them they lifted the captain and marched towards the stairs.

'I have a way with mice,' Tom said.

'Let me guess,' said the hand, scratching her head in an exaggerated manner, 'you threatened to eat them?'

'I asked for a little favour.'

'You call entering the roc's house and removing his grandfather clock a little favour?' the mate said.

'Well, they are only little chaps,' Tom said.

Behind them, they could hear the clang of the new grandfather clock chiming, followed by a thud as the roc practised his pas de chat. The mate sucked through his teeth. 'Just as well you won, Tom.'

'It was never in doubt,' Tom retorted. 'Pity I'll have to win the tournament another seven times before I can keep my prize.'

'You saved the captain, that's what matters,' the mate said.

Tom was about to reply, but they had reached the ship and the mice were waiting for instructions on where to deposit the captain. Tom sprang on board to direct them and they managed to shuffle the clock against the main mast.

'Excellent job, chaps,' said Tom, and dismissed them.

The hand had to quickly step aside to avoid being knocked into the water by a wave of fleeing rodents. She joined Tom on the deck, but the mate remained dawdling on the pier.

'Aren't you coming, sir?' Tom called.

'My work is finished,' the mate said.

'There are still four minutes left,' the hand said.

'Or longer if you go by the captain's time-keeping,' Tom added.

'Well, I suppose I should sign off properly,' the mate said, straightening his uniform before stepping aboard. The hand secured the captain to the mast and they all saluted.

'Good work, men,' the mate proclaimed. 'I'm proud to have

served with you.'

'The captain is in position, but he is still broken,' Tom said. 'We need a new commander.'

'Surely you will stand in?' The mate screwed his hands in his pockets.

'The crew would prefer you,' replied Tom.

'I don't mind who is captain,' Becky said before Tom stamped on her toes.

'You did say you would like a permanent position,' Tom said.

'Why yes. I would be honoured, if nobody minds,' the mate responded.

The captain, of course, said nothing, and Becky was too busy hopping around the deck to object.

'Welcome aboard, captain,' Tom saluted. 'The ship is ready for her next adventure.'

'Very good. Pull her hard to starboard.'

'Hard to starboard it is, sir.'

The Happy Tree

It was Green Earth Week. Don't ask me who comes up with this corn. I'm not hot on global warming, but I'd done enough crazy things not to jump at the offer of publicity. It was that or upholding my vegan principles in a creepy-crawly jungle.

The promo was for public figures to plant a tree for posterity, in the hope that Joe Public followed seed. A bangle of ex-girl band hipsters, two soap extras and an Olympic athlete had signed up. Having come third in a reality TV game show, guested on a morning chat show and appeared on kids' telly dressed as a rabbit, my five minutes of fame had over-run its decency level. No lucrative prime time deal materialised and I had returned to my nine to five job. This was manna from above.

'We'll record you planting a maple in May' the producer said.

Maple comes as syrup in bottles. I would look a wally planting a plastic tub. Besides, I live in a second floor flat with no window box.

'Great,' the producer said when I told her. 'You'll be an example for urbanites. Everyone can do their bit, no matter where they live.'

I was to plant a seed in a designer pot with "Green Earth Week" blazoned on the side. Not even Aunt Jenny would pay to watch me stick a half-chewed apple seed into a carton of compost and recite potty poetry written for the occasion, but if one viewer to the north of Kathmandu tuned in for one second…enough said.

I gnawed through four apples, three oranges, five plums, a grapefruit and a partridge in a pear tree in the run-up to filming. I had a pile of seeds and pulled one out for the programme. I was wearing an orange vest top, so I told the flown-in audience I was planting an orange.

'What would your dream be for the world?' the presenter asked.

I wasn't expecting that. I 'ummed' for a second. My dream was to make it big in Hollywood, but that wasn't what the organisers wanted. The presenter smiled and I remembered my gran saying that being happy didn't cost the Earth.

'I dream of happiness growing on trees,' I said. 'On this tree.'

'That is a beautiful thought,' the presenter said, with not a smidgen of sarcasm.

There was a moment like a solar wave kissing earth's hardened shores, a glimpse beyond the barricades, before the autocue came up with my line of poetry and I stuck the seed into the pot with a Shakespearean flourish. I flunked the verse and didn't realise until watching the playback. The producer thought it was the best part and didn't cut it. My sister came around to watch and she was in fits.

'What have you done with the celebrity?' Jess asked, looking around. 'You haven't killed it?'

The pot was on the windowsill. The window looked onto the street and the blinds were kept down.

'Aw, isn't she cute,' my sister said.

'It isn't a baby.'

To my surprise, a needle-thin shoot was sprouting from the soil, complete with two button leaves. They were smiling at us.

'I didn't think oranges were pink,' Jess said.

The plant was indeed pink - an anaemic salmon, but not green.

'It could be a pink grapefruit?' I said. For no reason, I grinned back at the seedling.

Jess filled a glass with water and sprinkled the plant, laughing as she baptised it 'Lily'. The twig bobbed like a Hawaiian dancing girl as the water splashed around it. We hadn't started on the bubbly, I swear.

Two weeks went by and my citrus was a joy to behold. It leapt up twenty centimetres and branched out to fill the pot with marvellous, pink foliage. And the fragrance wafting across my room – close your eyes and you'd breathe in a tropical paradise washed by an azure sea.

I held a party to mark my twenty first birthday. It was well after two in the morning when there was a banging on the door. More friends arriving I hoped, but peeking through the spy hole I made out two stern-faced coppers. The real McCoy, not Fraser and Tom messing around. I opened the door. My downstairs neighbour Grumpy Glenda was squashed between the PCs.

Disturbing the peace, public nuisance, noise pollution.

'What a delightful plant. It smells like my gran's apple pie,' the first policeman said.

'Hey, it's grooving to the music,' his colleague added.

'You're welcome to join.' I invited them in.

'Just for an hour or three,' Glenda said. 'I'll get my husband. Luke loves a boogie.'

Glenda and I have been mates ever since.

I wore one of the pale mauve flowers on my jacket when I went into town. Everybody smiled at me. Problems melted like Polar icecaps. I got a job as a dancer in a local club. The bank manager agreed an extra large overdraft - interest free - and the shop assistant gift wrapped my crisps. The bus driver had change galore and the babies on the bus stopped crying. The marketing potential was ginormous. Pounds, dollars and euros clicked in my eyes as I unlocked my door.

There was one catch. Although Lily produced a multitude of sturdy, sweet-smelling blossoms, ever more to please me it seemed, none germinated to produce viable seeds. I Googled the internet. Lily was either a sterile hybrid or lacking a partner for cross-germination. I planted the remaining mouldy seeds in my jar, but none grew.

I wrote into a gardening magazine and received a diagrammatic information sheet on how to propagate cuttings. I followed the instructions, investing in agars and rooting solutions, but instead of growing new plants, Lily was left sadly mutilated.

After a month of trying for a baby, Lily developed a blue spot on her lowest leaf. Jess noticed it first.

'What have you done to Lily?'

'Is she pot-bound?' I said, remembering an article in the gardening magazine.

I re-potted Lily three times, but the situation got worse.

'What about a mineral deficiency?' Jess was never short of ideas.

I dowsed the plant in miracle fertiliser. The spot became an ugly patch and the leaf fell off. Another leaf turned blue and shrivelled. My happy plant was dying.

The end came mercifully fast with the last leaf dropping off on New Year's Eve. Jess cried, but I was glad. I couldn't stand the rancid odour of rotting carbon oozing from the pot. It was worse than Uncle Joe's socks. A droplet of sap wept from the last twig before the stump toppled over. My tree had enjoyed its minutes of glory. Green Earth Week hadn't been a success. The climate wasn't right. There were no plans to repeat the event. I thought about keeping the pot as a souvenir, but cleaning it out put me off. I tossed everything in the wheelie bin before Jess came up with a ludicrous funeral service.

I put it down to Lily being a freak mutant, brought about by pouring unwanted carrot soup into the pot. It gave us fun for a while, but everybody knows, like money, happiness doesn't grow on trees.

A landfill site several miles away.

A homeless tramp hobbles about the dump. It is raining and a chill wind pierces his ancient Mac. His bones haven't thawed from the night before. He bends, a string of vituperations dribbling from his blue lips, and then... smiles.

Budding from the clay soil, machéd-newspaper mountain and layers of detritus is a fragile pink stem, growing in soft focus before the tramp's methylated spirit soaked eyes. He points and his cough becomes a chuckle as the plant offers up its vibrant cerise leaves. A rainbow glimmers through the thunder clouds, caressing the coral pink branches. A bud forms setting a cascade of silver-pink blossoms giggling into bloom. The tramp holds his sides, doubles over in hilarity then leaps three feet into the air tossing his arms wide. An explosion of glittering sparkle projects millions of tiny, shimmering seeds into the breeze to drift far, far away.

Step Inside

Whitened fingers gripped the steering wheel as the cab driver slammed his foot on the brake. Tyres screeched. The smouldering of rubber choked out the reek of urban smog as the car skidded and walloped into the sidewalk. A hundred dollars worth of damage to the street lighting. The driver scrambled from the wreck and hot-footed it down the alley. He kept a wife and five kids in Puerto Rico. There was no way he'd be subpoenaed as a witness.

The line of white-spatted, machine gun toting hoods were taking over the downtown bank. Fats Mulligan at the head, backed up by Billy 'The Babe' Kane and Domino Waller. All three were known to the Chicago PD – untouchable.

'Hey boss, what's with the kid?' Domino said, spotting the pale-faced High School student striding behind them.

'It's okay Dom he's one of us - for now. Guard the door Pete. Yell if the cops come.'

'Looks like he could do with a good meal,' Billy laughed. 'He's scrawnier than a Milwaukee mule.'

Peter Simpson, fourteen years old, but not yet sprouted, did as he was told. His heart was clawing his rib cage in a bid to escape and something in his head was performing cartwheels. This was the first time he'd tried it. It seemed to be working, but what had he got himself into? Were they using real bullets or Hollywood dummies?

Inter Action Boxes – IABs - were the rage. Everyone had one, except Marty whose parents ate vegetables and read books. To the initiated they were television upgrades where pressing the red button did heaps more than selecting which game to view. Peter stepped inside the mega-screen and here he was in 1920s Chicago.

Next time he'd remember to dress the part.

From the oak door of the bank he could see the yellow light. The manual instructed users to press the yellow button when they wanted to exit. Since it was his first time he wouldn't stay long, besides he had football practise at six. The police siren echoed round the high-rise buildings. Pete let out a yell to warn Fats and the gang. That was his bit done, it was time to go.

Billy's fingers trembled on the trigger. Fats and Domino stuffed dollar bills into their jute sacks three times faster than their fingers could cope with. Ten dollar notes scattered over the floor. Pete could see one of the clerks, teeth chattering, watching where they fell.

'The cops are here,' Pete yelled again. 'Shouldn't you be scarpering?'

'You scared?' Billy grinned. Baby-face he might look, but when he opened his mouth his teeth were black.

Pete shook his head then gulped. The yellow light had gone.

It stated on page five, paragraph four of the multi-lingual instruction pamphlet that it was inadvisable to change channels when someone was 'interacting'. A weight in Pete's guts told him that was what had happened.

Billy skipped in front, prodding Pete with the barrel of his gun. 'Where're you going buddy?'

'I need air.' Pete pulled at his school tie. Billy pushed him back inside the bank.

'You're with us til the end kid.' He grinned at Fats. 'Can we shoot the place up boss?'

'Sure, we're through here.'

Billy let loose, scattering bullets round the room with manic ease. Pete closed his eyes. He wished he could close his ears and nose. He didn't want to know if the blonde cleaner and the bald accountant ducked in time. His feet moved fifteen to the dozen with no input from his brain as he knocked past Domino. Outside, the area was cordoned off. Strobe lights bombarded his eyeballs. Sirens blared and a loud mouthed sergeant was screaming down a megaphone. Pete ran full tilt into the chest of a blue-shirted cop. The impact winded them both. As he fell back, blottoed, Pete was sure he could see his dad being led away in handcuffs by two

British Bobbies. He could hear his dad protesting.

'If you will let me explain, constable, I stepped into the IAB, my first time, to sit front row with the audience watching Miss Universe. The camera switched angles before I could get my leg over. I was falling into the pool. I had to grab something.'

All eyes fell to the canary yellow bikini bottoms held in evidence by the first policeman. Pete's dad's face burned. In the background Miss Arctic Circle was being consoled by the presenter.

'Pete, what are you doing here?' Ron Johnson was wearing a navy jersey over his white school shirt. Someone had pinned a Chicago police department badge onto it, but he looked less like a cop than Pete was Bugsy Malone.

'I think I've done something wrong,' Pete said. 'The yellow light has disappeared.'

'Mine too. I've been here for yonks. The cops think it's a hoot, but they're looking after me. The grub's not bad.'

'Did you see my dad?' Pete asked.

'No, but I've seen my mum - several times. Who needs parents? Last time she was on Errol Flynn's charger dressed in Lincoln green. She's always dreamed of being Maid Marion.'

Their conversation was cut to the quick by a shower of bullets speeding at them from camera five.

'Holy Mo-ses.' Ron froze.

Pete grabbed his arm and dragged him behind the nearest police car.

'This is the fifth time we've done this scene,' Ron said. 'Repeats.'

The police were driven back as Fats and his boys advanced, guns blazing. As Pete gagged on the smoke one of the cops shielded him from the shrapnel with his forty-four inch chest. The gunshot died and the policeman hauled Pete clear of the car. The lingering smell of stale tobacco on the cop's breath clung to Pete. He had to get out.

Another cop took Ron by the ears. They got clear seconds before the car burst into flames.

'Look,' Pete called, sweat dribbling down his forehead. 'There's the light.'

'Can't see nothing.'

'Follow me.'

He heard the wail of a vintage fire engine, but Pete didn't look back. Leaping towards the yellow glow, he struck the button with his left foot as cleanly as he would a penalty for his team. He landed back through the television screen, smacking his nose on the far wall of the room. Gasping for breath, it took him a minute to notice his father on the sofa, head in hands.

'What's up dad?'

'The television was plugged in, the green light was showing. What was I to think? You'd got the IAB working. You know I'm useless at that sort of thing.' Mr. Simpson sighed. 'After a day at the office I didn't want to watch a dumb gangster movie, not with Miss Universe on the other side. Do you think anyone saw me?'

'No more than ten million.'

His dad looked like he would burst into tears. Pete had other worries.

'Where's Ron? Didn't he come through with me?'

His dad didn't answer, but it was clear his friend wasn't in the room. Pete glanced at the screen. The scene had changed to a nightclub. A short man was surrounded by feather boa clad girls, arguing with the club manager. Pete rubbed his eyes. It was Ron, forcing a fat cigar up the manager's left nostril. He reached for his mobile and pressed the call button to Ron's house. Mrs. Johnson answered, her voice flustered. Three days with Robin Hood had taken its toll.

'No, we haven't seen Ron for days. I thought he was staying with you.'

'He's in the IAB. You have to change channels.'

'Now? Charlton Heston's about to star as El Cid.'

'Now. He's in the gangster movie, channel fifteen.'

Pete switched the phone off before Mrs. Johnson could make excuses. Sophisticated technology wasn't meant for adults. That went for his dad too.

'Dad, don't you think I should keep the IAB in my bedroom.'

His dad lifted his head. Pete forestalled the refusal. 'You wouldn't want mum to watch the re-run of Miss Universe, would you?'

Dry Rot

The customer is not always right.

According to the manager, what I should have said was, 'of course we shall adjust the dress free of charge. It will be delivered to your door this afternoon by personal courier, in time for your party. Please accept complementary vouchers to compensate for your trouble. We value your custom and strive to please.' What I actually said was more like, 'we warned you your fat behind would need several sizes more than you insisted on ordering. Now you've damaged a hand-made silk dress beyond thought of repair and we shall debit your store card accordingly.'

I was told to leave without passing 'go'. My P45 would be in the post. I hated the job anyway, but it paid the bills. I couldn't rely on Tim doing that any more. He walked out on me the previous week after he strolled into the garage and caught me French kissing his brother. Joe was a mechanic and had come over to replace a wheel on my Mini.

'I was just saying 'thank you',' I told Tim.

He accused me of deliberately causing a puncture in my front tyre, just as I knew what I was doing when I filled it with diesel instead of petrol the week before. I didn't need excuses to see his brother. Besides, an innocent smooch didn't mean I was cheating on him. What is it with guys? Tim said I had to get my act together or we were finished.

Stuff him.

On the way home I stumbled into a blind tramp and his mange-ridden mutt taking up half the pavement. His cap was overflowing with silver and gold. Pound coins and fifty pences.

Parasite. It made my blood rise and I kicked his cap. My toe caught it nicely and the cap rose in the air and went sprawling across the street. The money rolled into the gutter and under the wheels of the traffic. The blind man didn't realise what was happening, but the dog growled at me.

'That beast should be put out of its misery,' I said.

A woman in the crowd agreed with me, but most of the passers-by stopped to recover the money and put it back in the hat. One man wearing a punk T-shirt fished in his wallet for an extra fiver to give the tramp. I walked on.

A weekend at a country hotel and spa was just what I needed to clear my head. It was a perfect autumn morning, a nip in the air and coloured leaves scooshing under my wellies. I strolled through the oak wood down to the burn, kicking the damp leaves underfoot. My gran used to warn me about tree sprites and wood nymphs getting up to mischief with unsuspecting walkers. Good for them. I wanted to be a wood sprite. Either that or a traffic warden.

The water bubbled over the stepping stones. Only a fool would think of trying to cross. A fool with slippery soled boots whose mind was on other matters and who wasn't looking where they were going. You could say I was lucky to skid off the first stone beside the bank and not the moss covered boulder in the middle where the water was knee-deep. The stone wobbled and my left leg jerked in the air. My arms waved like windmill blades as I struggled to regain my balance, but before the yell was out my mouth I had landed on my bahookie in a pile of mush. A puff of dust rose from the leaves, damp earth and toadstools that had cushioned my fall. I tapped my chest to stop myself choking.

Nothing was bleeding or broken, not even my pride since no-one saw my tumble. I got to my feet and wiped my hands down the side of my jacket. There was already a mud stain on the back of the material. My leg throbbed as I hobbled home and I imagined a black and blue bruise beginning to tint my thigh. What I needed was a luxury sauna in the hotel spa followed by green tea and cakes. Lots of cakes. The hotel towels were good, thick pile quality. I managed to stuff two of them in my weekend bag, knowing the maid would get the blame for snaffling them.

I had a job interview the following Wednesday, but with wind and hailstones bashing my window and my head being bombarded worse than the glass, I didn't have the energy to get up. My throat felt woolly and I couldn't get the taste of mushrooms out my mouth although I hadn't eaten any. I didn't like them. When I managed to stagger to the bathroom at about noon, the reflection in the mirror shocked me. My face was as pale as a ghost's behind and strands of hair were glued to my ears with saliva. I drew my fingers down my cheeks, hoping to rub a little colour into them. It felt like I was patting my sister's cat and there was a powdery residue between my nails. I scrubbed my hands and splashed my face. Droplets of water clung to what now seemed like a thin layer of fur on my skin. I rubbed vigorously for five minutes until whatever it was had gone and a rusty conglomerate was draining down the plug hole.

The incident gave me a turn. I needed tea and someone to talk to. I phoned a few friends, but they were busy at work or with prior arrangements. Eventually Beth told me outright that I was being snubbed. It was all amazingly childish. I'd been talking about someone we knew, having a giggle at her attempts to cover her acne and suggesting personal hygiene tips if she ever wanted a partner. How was I supposed to know she was suffering from some serious physical illness with social and mental complications?

'You are just a rotten cow,' Beth said. I switched the call off before she could finish and went back to bed.

The next day the fuzz was back, on the palms of my hands as well as my face. It scrubbed off, but left my skin red, puffy and painful. I went to the local pharmacy to get some cream.

'You'll need an anti-fungal,' the girl inspected my hand. 'It looks like thrush.'

I didn't think you could get thrush on your face and hands, but I took the cream and after a couple of applications it started to work. My skin was clear for a fortnight. The night before my next job interview I noticed a brownish stain under the arms of my white shirt when I was getting undressed for bed. The material reeked of soggy newspaper. A trip to the bathroom revealed little brown cobblestone nodules growing under my arms and between my thighs.

That's when I screamed.

It was easy to snap the tops off the nodules, it was like popping bubble wrap, but they left what seemed like stems sinking into my pores and spreading under my skin. I squeezed the tube of cream from the chemists until the last squelch was released. It didn't help. I needed something stronger. I arranged to see a female doctor.

'Brown nodules?' she said.

I undid my blouse, but she didn't bother to look at my skin before prescribing another brand of anti-fungal and telling me to warn my partner it could be contagious. The ointment smelt like newly laid tarmac, but I applied it three times a day as it said on the label, rubbing it in to the hard to reach places. It did lift the growths, but it took half my skin with it and left suppurative blisters that burst to release a thick yellow pus. My arms and legs were red, raw and angry. I was angry.

'You didn't tell me about the side effects,' I said to the doctor.

'It must be an idiopathic reaction.'

'I'm not the idiot here. I could sue, you know. I want a second opinion.'

'This is the NHS, not Harley Street. Let me take another look.' She rumbled in her cupboard for a magnifying glass while I undressed. 'Interesting. Very interesting. I've not seen anything like this before. Hold on a second.' She reached for a medical book on her shelf. The antique one with the battered leather cover that was really only there for show. A couple of sepia pages fell from the moth eaten binding as she leafed through it. 'I remember reading about a similar case in Brazil in 1894 when I was a student. The case was in 1894, I wasn't a student then. Anyhow, the boy was from a deciduous tribe that lived deep in the Amazon rain forest. It was a case of over-active sweat glands and leeches in the water. Here it is. Page four hundred and seventy, paragraph three. The doctor made a presumptive diagnosis of the three ems.'

'The three ems?' I gaped at her.

'I know, it sounds like a case for Sherlock Holmes,' she said. 'Mushrooms, mildew and mould.'

'What happened to the boy?' I asked.

'When they got the results from the samples sent to Rio for testing, it turned out only to be a severe case of ringworm.'

'You sound disappointed.'

'It's always nice to discover something new,' she said, jiggling in her swirling chair. 'And I would say you definitely have the three ems. Quite advanced, from the description in the book.' She turned the book round to show me some hand drawn illustrations of mushrooms sprouting from a person's hand. 'The lilac stems could almost make it wood blewit, apart from the smell. That is more reminiscent of a stinkhorn. Foul.'

I drew back. 'Gee, thanks. What do we do about it?'

'First, would you mind if I took some photographs? It will help with diagnosis and monitoring treatment.'

I let her take some snaps of the lesions.

'We should really get a professional medical photographer on the job,' she said.

'As long as you don't intend writing me up as a case for the Lancet.'

The doctor gave a nervous laugh. 'Try these tablets and come back in two weeks.' She put on thick gardening gloves before handing me the prescription.

I didn't wait the fortnight. After ten days white plaques that tasted of mouldy bread formed on my tongue. My gums were bleeding and my teeth wobbled in their sockets. My hair started falling out and was replaced by what my mother described as puffballs.

'Excellent with roast pork. Don't you like mushrooms?' The doctor was being a little too flippant. 'Sorry, just trying to lighten the situation while I get ready.' As well as protective gloves, she put on a full length disposable apron and covered her nose and mouth with a mask before examining me.

'Maybe I should see a specialist,' I said.

She reluctantly agreed to get me an appointment. 'It won't be until after the New Year, though.'

'But that is weeks away.'

'At least you've got an excuse to cover up at this time of year.'

Not helpful.

As I left I heard her spraying the room with aerosol. Apart from being unsightly, my skin was itchier than a dog with a double dose of fleas. I bathed in extra-strong deodorant, sprayed eau de Cologne on my clothes and only went out in the dark. I could feel roots crawling under my skin and through my veins. My fingernails and toenails were crumbling like wet sawdust and my hands were as crinkled as lichen. I couldn't sleep at night, but lay in bed with my legs throbbing. My blood was trying to battle through a web of hyphae. That's the word the doctor used. I looked it up online and read about mycorrhizae and symbiotic relations. It was all Greek to me. I blamed it on my fall in the woods. The spores from the woodland fungi had somehow got up my nose and into my system, but surely it wasn't natural for toadstools to grow on people.

While my family were Christmas shopping, going to parties and singing carols, I was at home, barely able to move. My joints had stiffened to tree trunks and my feet were amass with blobs of rubbery toadstools. I couldn't even find slippers to fit. I would have cried, but my eyes were dried up with silken threads of mould drooping from fronds on the lids. Visitors to the house would have mistaken me for the yuletide log, except I didn't have any guests. The only text messages were from the surgery telling me I was still on the waiting list to see an expert.

'You must have the perfect environment for growth,' the doctor said. I was getting quite familiar with her. I was at the surgery three times a week to have Debbie debride my caps with a scalpel. By this time the clinic staff had taken to wearing full protective space suits with a shatter-proof glass helmets before I was allowed in the building.

'What do you mean, the perfect environment?'

'Most fungi like a moist niche, like wet leaves or a rotten tree stump, where they can find enough nutrients to multiply.'

'Rotten?' I didn't like her use of the word 'multiply', but I let her go on.

'The ground, or in this case your skin, should be slightly acidic and it is important that the area is dark.'

'Dark?' I repeated.

'Fungi don't need to photosynthesis like green plants. They aren't really plants at all. Perhaps we should send an environmental officer round to your house to check for dry rot.'

'There's no need,' I said. 'Thank you.'

The answer had suddenly come to me. I had no job, no friends and no partner. My life was rotten and my heart was dark. I knew what to do to get rid of my affliction. My lips were chaffed and powdered with yeast, but I attempted to smile. I clonked myself from the chair and hobbled to the door like the tin man from the Wizard of Oz.

'I won't need to see the specialist,' I said. 'Merry Christmas.'

'Well, that is excellent news,' Debbie said, 'but I recommend you put your trousers back on before you go into reception.'

Duck Soup

'Carys and Chloe won't throttle us,' Dave said, trying to straighten the kink at the end of his tail. 'They play with us every day. We aren't rubbish.'

'Of course we aren't, but humans are fickle. One day they cry their hearts out because we've been put in the linen cupboard by mistake, the next they complain that we're dowdy because the bubble bath has faded our colouring. They rarely think of the consequences of their actions,' Donna replied.

Dave thought about consequences. He wasn't sure what Donna meant. 'Do you think they will lose interest in the Jeanie throttle?' he said.

'I doubt it. They are doing their bit for the environment. Everything has to be green these days.'

'We're yellow,' Dave said. He looked at Donna. 'Or orange.'

'I'm not talking about colour.'

'What then?'

Before Donna could explain, they heard the front door open. The twins had been arguing over their game of snap, but jumped up with a whoop, sending the cards sprawling on the floor.

'Daddy, can we play with the Genie Bottle?'

'It's not a toy, girls,' their mother said.

'Give me time to get my coat off,' Mr. Derwent answered. He hung it up then rubbed his palms. 'What will we zap today?'

'There are empty plastic tubs in the kitchen,' Mrs. Derwent said.

'We zapped those yesterday,' Carys said. 'Can't we try something different?'

'There's plenty of useless plastic in your play room,' Mr. Derwent said.

Chloe and Carys hurried into the room. Carys snatched a small bouncy ball and they ran out giggling. Dave and Donna heard scraping noises and the click of metal. Mr. Derwent spoke.

'Are we ready? What do we sing?'

'Genie Bottle, the ocean's best friend.' Both girls sang in unison with their father. Dave found he was humming along to the catchy ad jingle until a look from Donna closed his beak.

'You don't even know the words,' she snapped. 'It's Genie Bottle, not Jeanie throttles.'

'Ooh, the light has turned green,' Chloe squealed.

'Can I put the ball in?' Carys repeated the question several times, louder and faster, until her mother answered.

'Daddy will do it.'

The ducks heard the machine whirr into action. The girls "oohed" as the rotation rose to a crescendo.

'Ready? Wheee.'

'You are as bad as the children,' Mrs. Derwent said.

Gobble, click, munchety-crunch, tic-tic… plop.

'*Voila*, plastic into harmless water we can pour down the plughole,' Mr. Derwent declared. The girls cheered.

'My turn,' Chloe shouted.

'That's enough for now,' Mrs. Derwent said.

'I want a shot. Carys had hers.'

Chloe ran into the room. She stood in the centre and looked round, but was unable to choose an object. Her mother and father came in after her.

'What about that?' her father said.

From the shelf, Dave could see Chloe's lips pucker. She didn't speak. Her father stepped across the room and picked up a pink unicorn. Its mane was tangled and there were felt pen markings on the body.

'Not that.' Mrs. Derwent stepped in.

'It's grubby and there are plenty of others,' Mr. Derwent argued.

'That's Unicorn Zen. I spent three weeks trying to find it.'

'Then Santa brought him,' Chloe added.

Mr. Derwent sighed. He replaced the unicorn in the shoe box and picked up a toy car. 'Come on girls. Let's do our bit for the environment. Genie Bottle, the ocean's best friend.'

Carys sang with him, but Chloe looked at her mother and was silent.

Gobble, click, munchety-crunch, tic-tic… plop.

There was a longer pause before the *plop* and the final splash of water sounded like a sob.

'Gran gave the girls that car,' Mrs. Derwent said.

'An ugly piece of junk it was too,' her husband replied. 'If we're done here, I think I'll go for a jog before dinner. Have you seen my water bottle? I left it on the table.'

'It was made of plastic,' Mrs. Derwent answered. Mr. Derwent grunted.

The Genie Bottle was unplugged, but Dave was left shaking. His plastic heart was beating faster than a real duck's hearing a hunter's gun. 'What can we do?' His voice wavered. 'The Derwents are on a mission. They won't stop until there's no plastic in the house. I wish we were made of rubber, like bath ducks used to be.'

'Stop blubbing,' Donna said. 'It's evolution. There's nothing we can do about that.'

'I can see that plastic bags are bad, but how can we be a threat to the oceans?' Dave said after moments of thought. 'Ducks swim in them, don't they?'

'Some ducks do, but not bath ducks. Most ducks live on ponds.' Dave wondered how Donna knew that, but she had been sitting next to a book on Farmyard Friends for a week. 'What we need is a plan,' she decided.

'To do what?' Dave asked.

'To break the Genie Bottle.'

Dave wiped his tears. Donna could be scary at times, but she was a clever duck. She could read ABC and count 1 2 3 thanks to a friendship with a coloured brick. It occurred to Dave that he hadn't seen the brick for a few days, but he thought it wiser not to mention this to Donna.

Whenever she had an idea, Donna wobbled closer to the

edge of the shelf and Dave feared her excitement would send her tumbling beak first into the storage box below. He shuffled closer to the box of jigsaws to give her more room to think, but the dust made him sneeze. Donna told him to shush while she was thinking, but it was taking her a while and he moved to speak to a train engine with its wheels missing.

'Won't be long now,' the train chuffed.

'What won't?' Dave asked.

'The dark tunnel.'

'What dark tunnel?'

'The one with no way out.'

Dave bobbed his head, pretending to understand. He hadn't thought Donna was listening, but she turned on the engine. 'That is a defeatist attitude. We need to stand together.'

'It doesn't bother me,' the engine gloated. 'I'm made of wood.'

'Extinction affects us all,' Donna argued. 'First cartons, then broken toys. Soon it will be the dolls, the farm animals…' Her voice choked and tailed off.

'Wood doesn't go in the Genie Bottle, only plastic,' the engine said.

'Wood burns,' Donna answered with what Dave felt was a little spite.

'How do you intend breaking the plastic eating machine?' The engine retorted. He waited while Donna waggled her tail. 'You don't know, do you? You could push it off its shelf. That's how I lost my wheels. Every day for three months I pulled five animal wagons from the jungle to the zoo. The tigers clawed my paintwork and the elephants ruined my suspension. I wanted it over and was going too fast, lost my grip at the corner and slid off the table. My axels snapped and the wheels broke off. I was lucky the bogie wasn't damaged or I would have been tossed in the bin. One day Mrs. Derwent will get round to fixing me.'

'I don't think we could push the Jeanie throttle machine over the edge of the table,' Dave said. 'It's made of metal.'

'Wood, metal… that's it. You are a genius, Dave.'

'Am I?'

'Mr. Derwent warned the family never to put the wrong

materials in the Genie,' Donna reminded them. 'It screws up the workings, according to him.'

'Don't think I'm going to be your sacrifice,' the engine said.

Donna opened and closed her beak. She gulped, but didn't speak. Dave noticed a gleam in her bright blue eyes. Later, when the engine had turned its attention to the games compendium, she bent close to Dave and whispered. 'Do you think being zapped hurts?' Dave answered with a strangulated quack.

'Bath time, girls.' Carys and Chloe were playing with their dolls, sending them into space on a rocket made from the inner tube of a kitchen roll splattered with glitter paint, when their mother called. The twins groaned.

'We haven't reached Mars yet,' Chloe protested.

'You can play with your ducks in the tub. Where are they?'

Dave had edged closer to Donna so that his beak was full of plastic feathers. A hand reached up and caught him. Another took Donna by the neck.

'I want Donna,' Carys cried, abandoning her doll in space. Mrs. Derwent handed the duck to Carys. 'She feels heavy today,' Carys said.

'Don't be silly,' her mother answered.

The twins carried their ducks to the bathroom and got ready for their bath.

'Donna is swimming all lopsided,' Carys said, once they were playing among the bubbles. 'Look.'

Donna bobbed low in the water and her body tilted towards the left. Dave got to swim underwater in search of the missing bath sponge, which was usually Donna's job, but he couldn't enjoy the thrill. He was worried about Donna. When bath time was over and the twins were snuggled in their pyjamas, dressing gowns and slippers drinking hot chocolate, Mrs. Derwent examined the duck.

'What's up?' Mr. Derwent asked. His wife explained and Mr. Derwent took hold of Donna.

'Is it supposed to have a hole in its head?'

Carys giggled. 'That's where Ginger bit it.'

'He thought it was a dog toy,' Chloe said.

'It's had that for ages,' Mrs. Derwent said. 'It hasn't affected it before.'

'It's pretty grotty anyway. I think its time you had new bath toys.'

Carys clapped her hands and gave a squeal

'We could Genie zap Donna,' Carys said.

Chloe was holding Dave. Her fingers tightened round him. He was shaking, but Donna seemed calm. Her painted smile widened.

'You can't zap your favourite toy because it has a small notch,' Mrs. Derwent protested.

'It's mouldy old plastic,' Mr. Derwent said. 'How would you like bath crayons that let you draw pictures on your skin?'

'Cool,' Carys cooed.

Chloe slipped Dave into the pocket of her dressing gown. Donna was balanced on Mr. Derwent's palm, her head slanting at a strange angle. She was ceremoniously paraded towards the Genie Bottle plastic-zapping, ocean-saving monstrosity. Dave felt his cheeks moisten, but he heard Donna's words in his head. No blubbing. He didn't want to watch, but he needed to see Donna. He poked his head out from the pocket.

Mr. Derwent pressed the button and the machine purred into action. Dave imagined it was licking its lips. He closed his eyes as Donna was lowered inside.

Gobble, click, munchety-crunch, tic-tic...

Dave waited, but there was no *plop*. There was a crack, a hiss and a *bup, bup, bup* similar to the noise heard when Mrs. Derwent forgot to empty pockets before filling the washing machine. There was a spark, a puff of smoke and a burning smell before the machine ground to a halt.

'What's wrong, dad?' Carys asked.

'Something must have got stuck.'

'That looks like a glass marble,' Mrs. Derwent said, with a hint of delight. 'How did that get there?'

'I guess that's the zapping over,' Mr. Derwent said.

'Can I have Donna back now?' Carys held out her hands.

Mrs Derwent looked at the orange fluid seeping from the bottom of the machine. 'Do you want to tell her, dear?'

'Would you stop crying?' the engine moaned once Dave was back on the shelf. 'The water is ruining my varnish.'

'I'm not crying,' Dave answered in a high-pitched squeak that sounded like he had catarrh in his beak. 'I haven't been dried properly.' He sniffed and looked at the empty board beside him.

'They'll get the machine mended,' the engine said. 'Life goes on.'

Dave took a deep breath, wobbled an inch closer and pushed the engine over the edge.

Giacomo's High Doh

'Funny you should mention that,' Iorwerth said. He was lounging in a hammock drinking pink gin as his friends played croquet on the lawn and they didn't hear a word. He raised his voice. 'I said, I have a friend who is a Milanese tenor.'

'I've got a friend who is a Tenerifian milliner,' Jordy answered, swinging his mallet an inch above the ball. 'That was a practice shot.'

'It's Tinerfeño or Tinerfiña if your friend is a lady,' Jane corrected him. 'And that is your fifth miss.'

Jordy stuck out his tongue. It looped over the nearest hoop. With a swift flick, the hoop was lifted from the grass and swung back over his ball. 'I've run a hoop,' Jordy whooped. 'I get another turn.'

'That is cheating,' Jane complained.

'I am a pangolin. I can't help having a long tongue. You are being species-ist.'

Jane threw her mallet to the ground. 'I'm tired of this game. It's boring. Summer is boring when you have to spend it at home with… with…'

'Rare breeds?' Iorwerth offered.

'Jordy may be a rare breed, and getting rarer if he continues to cheat at croquet, but you don't even exist. No-one at school will believe me when I tell them my parents left me with a Welsh wyvern.'

'I'm not sure I like your tone, young lady,' Jordy said.

'And speaking of tone, did I ever tell you I have a friend who is an opera singer in Milan?' Iorwerth said.

Jane gave an exaggerated sigh.

'It just so happens he has sent me tickets to hear him sing at La Scala. It's a shame you don't want them.' Iorwerth finished his gin, slouched in a ball and wrapped his barbed tail round his nose to protect it from the sun.

'I've heard you and your friends sing,' Jordy said. 'I'd rather listen to a bunch of caterwauling tigers any time.'

'If you don't appreciate fine opera I shall return the tickets. Giacomo will be upset, but it can't be helped,' Iorwerth muttered from beneath his scales.

'Who or what is Giacomo?' Jane asked, stifling a yawn.

'Giacomo della Voce Celeste.'

'Giacomo della Voce Celeste, the world-renowned tenor? He is a friend of yours?' Jordy's tongue hung loose.

'That's what I've been trying to tell you. If I have to repeat everything, Jane's parents will be home before we get to Milan.'

'Can he really hit four notes above the normal range?' Jordy said.

'If you had agreed to go to the opera, you would have found out.'

'I didn't disagree. I said I would rather listen to caterwauling tigers, but since there aren't any around…'

'How are we supposed to get to Milan?' Jane interrupted. 'It's in Italy.'

'We fly, of course.' Iorwerth sat up and flapped his wings. The draught sent Jordy fluttering upwards into Jane's arms.

'Does anyone speak Italian?' Jane said, setting Jordy on the grass.

'I know how to hiss and puff in Italian,' Jordy answered. 'Would you like to hear me?' He didn't wait for an affirmative, but began prancing around the croquet hoops making weird noises.

'Do we have to take him?' Jane asked Iorwerth, holding a hand to her mouth so that Jordy didn't hear.

'I'm afraid so. Your mother did leave us both in charge of you.'

'She left me with my aunt.'

'And you said you'd rather stay with two scaly beasts rather than that old dragon. Voila.'

'Whatever. If we're going to Italy, I'm going to pack. I need a hat, sun cream and a copy of Vogue Italia.'

When they were ready, Jordy and Jane strapped themselves to Iorwerth's back and, with a bag in both wing claws, he took to the air. 'Would you like me to take the scenic route?' he asked.

'No thank you,' Jordy said before Jane could reply. 'The world is running out of beauty spots fast enough without help from your pestilent breath.'

'That's the fun part of being a wyvern. I can't hold my breath all the way to Italy.'

'You could try mouthwash.'

'Would you two stop squabbling,' Jane said. 'I'm trying to study this map. Once we're over the Channel, fly down France and into Switzerland, then over the Alps to Milan.'

'France? Switzerland? What sort of map are you looking at?' Iorwerth said. 'Just as well I have the route in my head.'

'What's wrong with my map?' Jane asked, turning it 360 degrees.

'Iorwerth navigates by the clouds,' Jordy explained. 'And he won't be flying over the mountains, he'll be going through them.'

'Won't that be dangerous?'

'Only if the trolls are having a barbeque.'

Iorwerth soared above the clouds and Jane and Jordy played "spot the cumulus giraffe", which Jordy won because he was the referee. Thankfully the trolls and gnomes were engaged in battle among themselves and they had a clear path through Mont Blanc/Monte Bianco. As they headed down towards Milan, Iorwerth was blinded by a flash of light.

'Lightning,' he warned.

'I don't think so,' Jordy said. 'I think it was a camera flash.'

Iorwerth groaned. 'We don't want to get snapped by the paparazzi. We'll never get to the opera if people think there's a dragon loose.'

'Jane, can you find somewhere on your map we can land without being noticed?' Jordy said.

'Look for a cathedral. If I land on the roof, people will mistake me for a gargoyle.'

'Got it, the Duomo. Take a right turn at the palace.'

'How will we get from there to the opera house?' Jordy asked.

'I've sent Giacomo a text,' Iorwerth said. 'He will send a car.'

Grey clouds obscured their touchdown on one of the cathedral spires. As promised, a yellow Lancia Flavia, complete with liveried chauffeur, was waiting to whisk them through the traffic to the opera house.

'This is the life,' Iorwerth approved.

'You'll have to sit in the back,' Jane said.

'But I was the one doing the flying.'

'You don't want anyone to see you. The back windows are blacked out.'

'I could sit in the front,' Jordy said. 'No-one would notice me. No-one ever does.'

While they were squabbling, the driver lifted their bags and dumped them on the front seat.

'I guess we all sit in the back,' Jane said.

The car stopped outside the theatre entrance and they got out. Posters advertised the upcoming performance of Verdi's Othello, with a life-sized Giacomo taking the title role.

'That is Giacomo,' Jane said, unable to hide her disappointment.

'He has been putting on weight,' Iorwerth gave the poster a poke. 'He always did have a fondness for fondant mice.'

'He's an owl,' Jane said.

'Not just any old owl. A grand, European, long-eared, singing owl,' Jordy explained. 'It is reported there are only two in existence.'

'Rumours shouldn't be believed. It's said there are none of me,' Iorwerth said. 'But grand, European, long-eared singing owls are rare. Giacomo doesn't want to start a family until his singing career is over.'

'That looks like him now,' Jane said.

An owl the size of a Shetland pony, painted with stage make-up and in theatrical dress, waved to them from the door of the opera house. He bounced through the central entrance arch and embraced Iorwerth, kissing his cheeks and squeezing most of the air from his lungs.

'Mio amico, I am delighted you could make it. Too-wit. I am

sorry I couldn't meet you in person. As you see, I have come from our dress rehearsal for the opening night.'

'We are very much looking forward to hearing you sing, sir,' Jordy gave a small bow.

'Ah.'

'Is there a problem?' Jane asked.

'No, no problem. Too-wit. Why should there be?' The owl spoke rapidly then gave a hoot and burst into tears. 'I am so sorry. I cannot sing for you. Too-woo. I fear I shall let my audience down.'

'Why? Whatever is the matter?' Iorwerth put a wing on his friend's shoulder.

'I have lost my voice.'

'It seems fine to me,' Jane said. 'A little loud, if anything.'

'Not my speaking voice, too-wit. My beautiful high doh – gone. Too-woo.'

'What happened?' Iorwerth asked. 'Can we help?'

'Too-wit, I am so glad you asked. I would hate to impose on you, my good friend.' The owl gave a weak smile. 'Come inside and I shall tell you what happened over a fine Lombardy spumante.'

Giacomo nodded to the doorkeeper who carried their bags inside. The others followed Giacomo through the foyer.

'Be careful not to slide on the polished floor,' Giacomo warned, a second too late. Jordy was pirouetting with the grace of "La Barbarina" until his gaping tongue caught around one of the columns and he ended up wound like a ball of string round the marble.

'I'm sorry, I had to bring him,' Iorwerth apologised.

Once Jordy was untangled, they made their way to a luxurious suite at the back of the building where attendants had laid out glasses of sparkling wine.

'I don't suppose you have a slice of that delicious chocolate and chestnut panettone I had last time?' Iorwerth asked one of the serving girls.

'Giacomo said you were coming, so I kept one back,' the girl answered.

'And the cassata and Florentine orange cake?'

'What is this about you losing your voice?' Jane asked before the conversation was sidelined into discussing continental confectionary.

Giacomo swallowed a mouthful of wine and wiped his beak before answering. 'Too-wit, two days ago, I accompanied some of the cast on a trip to Lake Garda. There was Maria, who plays Desdemona, Edoardo who plays Iago and Bogdan who is our understudy. Bogdan is from Sofia and Maria wanted to show him the lake by hiring a boat. If nature had intended me to go in the water I would have been a goose, but who has heard of a tenor goose? I would have had to drop to a baritone.' Giacomo sniffed before continuing. 'Edoardo and Bogdan were keen, so I foolishly agreed to go with them. I fear it is there I lost my high doh. Too-woo.'

'You caught a cold?' Jane said. 'Laryngitis?'

'No, no, too-woo. I lost my beautiful singing voice. It must have fallen over the side when I spread my wings to prevent Maria's feet from getting wet. That was Edoardo's fault. Too-wit. He insisted on rocking the boat.'

'Nothing to do with your weight…' Jordy muttered an aside.

'I don't get it,' Jane said. 'You can't drop your voice over the side.'

'I should imagine it is illegal,' Jordy agreed.

Giacomo's feathers puffed up and he was too flustered to explain. He pulled a spotted handkerchief the size of a boy's shirt from his top pocket and suppressed floods of tears. An attendant wheeled in a trolley with plates of fruit cakes and pastries. Iorwerth licked his lips, forgetting about his friend's plight as he stacked his plate with goodies and stuffed slices in his mouth.

'Remember we have to fly home,' Jordy said.

Iorwerth returned a half-eaten slice of tart, already covered in dragon drool. 'So, how can we help?' he asked.

'Too-woo, you are adventurers, are you not?' Giacomo said.

'Yes, but not divers,' Jordy responded. 'Nobody has asked us to find their voice before.'

Jane was trying to outdo Iorwerth in the number of cakes she could devour in a minute. After four her face turned green and she felt sick. 'Did your mother never warn you about the dangers of eating too much sweet food?' she asked.

'No,' Iorwerth replied, finishing the last slice of chestnut gateau before wiping his snout. 'Delicious. I don't suppose…?' The attendant shook her head. 'Pity.' He eyed the piece of chewed cake he had replaced.

'Too-wit, if you find my voice, Iorwerth, I will buy you every chestnut cake in Milan,' Giacomo said.

'Really? Then what are we waiting for? How do we get to Lake Garda?' Iorwerth sprang up. He was about to seize the remaining crumbs of cake, but Jordy's tongue beat him to it.

'I can have my driver take you there at once,' Giacomo said.

'Not so fast,' Jane cut in. 'We can't search the whole lake, find Giacomo's voice and hope to be back before the opening performance. We should speak with Maria, Edoardo and Bogdan. They may remember something which will give us a clue where to look.'

'I have already asked them,' Giacomo said. 'They remember nothing.'

'Something may come back to them, if we ask the right questions,' Iorwerth said. 'Where will they be?'

A crumb puffed from Iorwerth's mouth and landed on Giacomo's left wing. He pruned the feathers before replying. 'I believe Edoardo and Maria have left the theatre, but Bogdan is still rehearsing. Too-woo, he will be needed to sing my part.'

Fearing a further lake of tears, Iorwerth opened the door, preparing to go in search of Bogdan.

'Wait for me,' Jordy said.

'You haven't finished eating,' Iorwerth said snidely. 'The tiramisu doesn't quite have the je ne sais quoi of the chestnut panettone, but well worth sticking your tongue in.'

'It would have been nice to try the chestnut cake,' Jane said pointedly. She lifted the jug of wine, poured a glassful and was about to drink when Iorwerth stopped her.

'You are too young for that. Whatever will your mother say?'

'Nothing, because you told me not to tell her about you and Jordy.'

'Well… you don't have time. I need you to come with me.'

'Why? You didn't need Jordy's help.'

'Don't you want to help Giacomo?'

'Yes, but… fine.' Jane made her way to the door. Iorwerth was holding it open and she walked beneath his wing. He made to follow her, then returned to the trolley to gulp down Jane's wine before skipping out the door, licking the last drops from his whiskers. Jane knitted her eyebrows in disapproval, the way her mother did.

'If you are going to act like a grown-up, you can't play with us,' Iorwerth said. Jane made a face. 'That's better. In here.' He nudged Jane into a recess, behind the bust of a famous singer.

'What is this about?' she asked.

'Shh, not so loud. I don't want Giacomo to overhear.'

'He's in the other room,' Jane answered, 'Although I suppose he does have rather long ears.'

'He can hear a mouse think from five kilometres away, but when it comes to brains there isn't much room left in his head,' Iorwerth said. 'He's my friend and I don't want Jordy to mock him. Promise me you won't laugh at what I tell you.'

'I promise.'

'Giacomo burst from his egg with a voice that could part clouds, open the heavens and make the sun shine, but without a speck of self-belief. To give him confidence, his mother gave him a lucky charm and told him that was his voice – his special high doh. He was at an impressionable age, before his flight feathers developed, and he believed her. There has never been a day when Giacomo hasn't worn his mother's charm round his neck. I'm guessing it is this charm he has lost and without it he thinks he can't sing.'

'That's ridiculous.'

'You promised you wouldn't laugh.'

'I'm sorry. I used to believe in fairies and dra… Dracula.' Jane bit her tongue. 'This is dreadful. We have to find his charm.'

'We won't if it is at the bottom of Lake Garda. I can't remember exactly what it looked like, but one of the cast members might. With luck, we'll be able to replace it.'

'Good thinking, although I wouldn't have minded a trip to the lake.'

'We may still have to go there and pretend to find it in the water,' Iorwerth said.

'It would help if parents were honest with their children.'

'Tell me about it.'

Bogdan was prancing round the stage as they peeped through the door to view the auditorium.

'It's like a palace,' Jane whispered. She looked up. 'Are these the boxes? They look like stars, and look at that chandelier.'

'Business first. We can do the sightseeing tour later,' Iorwerth reminded her. They stood listening until Bogdan finished. Jane clapped politely.

'That was awful,' Iorwerth said.

'It sounded fine to me, but I don't know much about opera.'

'If you think that sounded fine, you don't know anything about opera,' Iorwerth answered.

'I think you'd better leave this interview to me,' Jane decided. Iorwerth muttered something she suspected her mother would not wish her to hear. Ignoring him, she squeezed through the half-open door and strode down the aisle to take a seat in front of the orchestra pit.

'Can I help you?' Bogdan asked in a superior tone that reminded Jane of the time she was caught trying to rescue her homework book before her English teacher marked the exercise she had done wrong.

'I would like to talk to you about Giacomo,' she said.

Bogdan gave a snort. 'That twit. You should have heard him at rehearsals. He sounded like a stuck pig.'

Jane thought she heard a dragon's hiss emanating from the back of the hall. 'I heard he had lost his voice, but hearing you sing... well, every cloud has a silver lining.'

Bogdan swaggered towards the edge of the stage. 'Really? Would you like my autograph, little girl?'

'Oh, yes please,' Jane said. She stood up and approached the stage. Bogdan pulled a quill pen from his pocket and looked for something to write on. There was no paper available, so he signed his name on the sleeve of Jane's blouse.

'Thank you.' Jane pretended to swoon. 'I shall never wash this blouse.' Her mother did the laundry, so it wasn't a lie. 'I've heard great performers are superstitious. Do you have any little rituals you do before going on stage?'

'Rituals?'

'I mean, do you wear lucky socks or touch wood or step on stage with your right foot forward?' She gave a titter.

'I see what you mean. Hey, are you a journalist?'

'I am editor of our school magazine.'

'If you misquote me, I'll sue.'

Jane pretended to laugh, but something told her Bogdan was serious. She looked behind her for inspiration and spotted a dragon-shaped shadow hopping from one leg to the other at the back of the hall.

'Sailors are superstitious,' she said, twisting the conversation the way she wanted. 'For instance, I believe it is bad luck to kill an albatross.'

'Bad luck for the albatross,' Bogdan joked. 'But there aren't any albatrosses in Milan.'

'That was an example. I was told Giacomo della Voce Celeste wears a lucky charm when he goes on stage.'

'Why do you keep talking about him? I thought this interview was about me.'

'It is,' Jane assured him.

'Well, the fool doesn't only wear it on stage, he keeps it close all the time. Even in bed – or so people say.'

'It must be very lucky. What does it look like?' Jane asked.

'It's a golden apple medallion on a silver chain, or it was.' Bogdan stopped to chuckle. 'He lost it. That's the reason he can't sing. He can't even put a foot on stage without getting jittery and breaking into a nervous sweat.'

'And roughly how big is it?' Jane asked.

'About the size of a walnut, with a little stalk, too-wit.' Bogdan imitated Giacomo's accent. 'It has a chip on the side where it got dented during a sword fight while he was playing Don Quixote. Can you believe this – it opens up playing Puccini's "One Fine

Day" to reveal a picture of his mother with a tear in her eye?'

'That's sweet,' Jane said. 'Well, I'd better let you get on with your rehearsal. Thank you again for the autograph.' She blew Bogdan a kiss as she scurried out, grabbing hold of Iorwerth at the door and dragging him away before he could blow a poisonous raspberry at Bogdan.

'If you hadn't pulled me back I would have ripped that sneering, troll-brained ispolin's vocal cords out.' Iorwerth swiped his tail against one of the columns. A crack crept up from the base.

'What did you call him?' Jane asked.

'An ipsolin. It's a Bulgarian dragon-slayer.' Iorwerth spat.

'At least he did tell us what we wanted to know about the charm.' Jane tried to placate Iorwerth before he caused further damage. 'I don't think we'll be able to find a suitable replacement.'

'Then we need to find the real thing.'

'Or work out a plan to convince Giacomo he doesn't need it,' Jane offered.

'What about his mummy's tears?' Iorwerth added. 'The acoustics in the hall are first-class. I heard everything.'

'Bogdan did describe the charm in great detail,' Jane said, going through the conversation in her head.

'Down to the chip on the side – ah – am I thinking what you're thinking?' Iorwerth cocked his head.

'I think so,' Jane agreed.

'We need a plan,' Iorwerth said. He gave a small leap, sending a tremor running along the hallway as he landed. 'I think I have one. We need to find Jordy.'

'First I need to find a laundry,' Jane said. 'This blouse is ruined and I don't have another one with me.'

'This is an opera house. There is bound to be a suitable costume in the wardrobe department.'

'We're in Milan, the home of fashion. I don't intend looking like Carmen or Madam Butterfly.'

'You would make a beautiful Juliet,' Iorwerth said.

'Doesn't she die?'

'Yes, but she dies beautifully.'

Jordy and Giacomo had finished the refreshments when

Iorwerth and Jane returned to the suite. Giacomo was regaling Jordy with stories of his various performances and the pangolin was curled up and dosing under his scales, trying not to snore. He uncurled when Iorwerth and Jane entered the room. Giacomo was demonstrating his love for an imaginary Juliet, 'o speak again, bright angel', and his outthrust wing bumped Jordy on the nose.

'Too-wit, I'm terribly sorry,' he apologised. 'It's not going to bleed is it? Too-woo, I faint at the mere thought of...' Giacomo fell to the floor at their feet.

'Find him a cushion and leave him there,' Iorwerth said. 'We have business better performed without him.'

'What business?' Jordy said. 'I thought we had to get to Lake Garda pronto.'

'Plans have changed.'

'We can't leave him lying here,' Jane said. 'If someone opens the door they'll trip over him.'

'And what about my nose?' Jordy sniffed.

'One at a time, please,' Iorwerth said.

Jane picked a napkin from the trolley and handed it to Jordy before bending down to help Giacomo sit up. 'Are you all right, sir?'

'I feel a little feather-headed.'

'Perhaps you should lie down in your dressing room,' Iorwerth suggested. 'We'll give you a hand.'

Jordy stepped forward to help Iorwerth get Giacomo to his feet, but the singer waved him off. 'No, no, too-woo. You may still have blood on your... your...' The thought of blood made Giacomo collapse again.

'Better get him to his dressing room before he wakes up,' Iorwerth said.

It took all three of them to safely deliver the owl to his room. Jordy went ahead to hold the doors while Iorwerth held Giacomo up by the wings. Jane did her best to stop his rather large head from lolling over. They managed to lay him out on his chaise longue and Jane threw a cover over him. Jordy poured himself a glass of water from a beaker on the star's dressing table. He took a swig and spat it out.

'What is that?'

Iorwerth gave the liquid a sniff. 'It smells like Giacomo's special mouthwash, made from the saliva of cockroaches and the gallbladder fluid of pink marshmallows.'

Jordy stuck out his tongue and flapped it several times before wiping it on the curtains.

'Then again, it could be Russian vodka,' Iorwerth admitted.

'Mama.' Giacomo gave a little moan and turned over.

'Mama is going to find your voice.' Iorwerth leaned over to whisper. 'Go to sleep now, and when you wake up you will be able to sing for your good friends tomorrow evening.'

Once Giacomo was safely seen to, Iorwerth, Jordy and Jane left the opera house and took over a corner table in a nearby café. Iorwerth examined the menu.

'What is the new plan?' Jordy asked. 'How are we going to find Giacomo's voice before he wakes up?'

Jane gave Iorwerth a nudge.

'Sorry, I was thinking about grilled perch with parsley and a delicious Hollandaise sauce.'

'No, not grilled and not Hollandaise,' Jordy replied. 'It has to be slow baked in a citrus and anchovy jus or, if you don't like that, capers and white wine.'

'Mmm.' Iorwerth licked his lips.

'Stop thinking about your stomach,' Jane ordered. 'We don't have time.'

'Spoilsport. We know where Giacomo's charm is.' Iorwerth said.

'You do?' Jordy said.

'Not exactly, but we know a man who does.'

'We think Bogdan has taken it so he can sing instead of Giacomo,' Jane explained.

'And you are going to get it back?' Jordy said.

Iorwerth grinned, showing a mouthful of footlong fangs. 'No. You are.'

'But… how… I mean…'

'Jane shall keep Bogdan occupied while you sneak into his dressing room and find it,' Iorwerth said.

'Can't someone else break in?'

'Someone is bound to notice me,' Iorwerth said. 'I am twenty foot tall and bright red.'

'Whereas you are small and insig…' Jane caught her word and swiftly changed it. 'Insightful.'

'What if it isn't in his dressing room? What if he has it on him?'

'Plan B. Jane will sneak into his costume and search for it,' Iorwerth said. Jane slapped his wrists. 'What's wrong with that? You were crawling all over him earlier.'

'That was an act.'

'You fooled me.'

'What will you be doing?' Jordy asked.

'I will be co-ordinating the mission.'

Iorwerth flexed his claws and Jane and Jordy realised it wasn't wise to argue with a wyvern. The waiter brought their drinks and they sat in silence until they finished them, then returned to the opera house.

'Good luck, chaps,' Iorwerth clapped a wing on Jane and Jordy's backs.

Jordy was dispatched to Bogdan's dressing room, but Jane remained in the foyer.

'Aren't you going to the auditorium?' Iorwerth asked.

'I have a better plan. Come with me.'

'Where to?'

'The wardrobe department.'

Jane rummaged through the racks and selected a fur coat which she arranged over Iorwerth's back. 'Don't worry, it isn't real,' she said.

'It smells of mothballs.'

'What are they?'

'Balls of moths, of course.'

Jane decided not to pursue the conversation. She handed him a pair of sunglasses. 'You'll need these too.'

'I don't understand,' Iorwerth said, positioning the specs.

'I'll explain on the way to the stage.'

Iorwerth grabbed a fedora and propped it at a rakish angle between his horns before following Jane out.

Bogdan was still rehearsing, but stopped singing as they entered the hall. 'The performance isn't until tomorrow… oh, it's you again. Do you want another autograph or a photograph?'

'No autographs; we want to listen to your rehearsal. You don't mind, do you?' Iorwerth smiled.

'Actually, I do. I hate an audience when I'm practising. I need "me time".' Bogdan waved them away.

Iorwerth imitated stamping on Bogdan's foot and Jane gave him a push. She smiled at Bogdan. 'My friend Iorwerth is a world-famous film producer from Follywood. You must have read about his latest project in the New Pork Rinds. Unfortunately he has to catch his flight home before the performance.'

'Did you say The New York Times?'

'Didn't I?'

'Perhaps I could make an exception – for your friend.'

'Iorwerth is searching for a new face for his next blockbuster – a musical about the life of Casanova.'

'Casanova – why that is me all "ova".' Bogdan burst into a little song and dance and Iorwerth's faux fur coat bristled. He ground his teeth together then stretched his lips into a grin. With an agile bound he leapfrogged onto the stage, sending Bogdan scuttling to the side. Before he knew it, the tenor had a dragon's wing on his back.

'You don't mind, do you?' Iorwerth said in a Californian accent. 'I need to be sure.'

'Sure of what?'

Iorwerth ignored the question as he moved his clawed hand towards Bogdan's chest, feeling for his top pocket. 'Ha…humm… .a…huh, huh.' His throat vibrated as he did so.

'Please, carry on rehearsing,' Jane called from her seat in the front stalls.

Bogdan reached for a top 'C', but over-reached the note as Iorwerth screwed a claw into his trouser pocket.

'Sorry my fault, cold hands,' Iorwerth apologised.

'Would you get off me!' Bogdan insisted.

'Certainly, I have found what I want. I mean, I have all the information I require.' Iorwerth stepped away from the singer.

Bogdan cleared his throat, but his voice had deserted him. He croaked what might have been lower G. 'I need my pastilles.' He stood waiting for someone to hand him the lozenges, but there was no-one from the stage crew in the hall. He gave a sigh and marched towards the wings.

'Wait until I am the star…' he grumbled. 'What am I talking about? I am the star.'

Iorwerth rejoined Jane and dangled the apple pendant in front of her. 'I knew my idea would work.'

'Your idea?'

'We should get it to Giacomo before Casanova realises what has happened,' Iorwerth said.

'He can hardly complain that we stole it from him,' Jane said. 'We can return the coat on the way.'

'I was getting used to it,' Iorwerth said. 'I always wanted to be a Vietnamese furry dragon.'

They returned the costume to the wardrobe department and made their way to Giacomo's dressing room. As they walked along the corridor they heard shouts, furniture being thrown and groaning.

'What's going on?' Jane said.

Iorwerth swallowed. Jane glared at him. 'Jordy,' they said in unison.

'I'd forgotten about him,' Jane said.

'Most people do,' Iorwerth agreed. 'That's why they're nearly extinct.'

Jordy was lolloping along the corridor towards them, with Bogdan close on his heels, waving a walking cane. He brought the stick down and Jordy dived beneath Iorwerth's feet to avoid being hit. Iorwerth put out a wing.

'Hey buddy, what is the meaning of this attack?' He put on his American accent.

'This… thing… is a thief. I found it in my dressing room, going through my property,' Bogdan complained.

'Indeed. That is dreadful.' Iorwerth turned to Jordy. 'What have you to say, you felon?'

'It was your idea,' Jordy answered. 'I told you it was stupid.'

Bogdan lowered his cane and put his hands on his hips.

'Don't listen to a word this rat says,' Iorwerth answered. 'He is clearly suffering from Scaly Rat Syndrome.'

'I've never heard of it.'

'The scales are the most obvious sign, but the disease affects the brain, making it impossible for sufferers to speak the truth. Luckily you can tell they are lying because their tongues grow. Stick out your tongue, rat.'

Jordy duly obliged, dribbling saliva on Bogdan's leather shoes.

'An advanced case.' Iorwerth shook his head. 'We need to get him to a doctor immediately.'

Jane had been standing back, but on cue she moved to pick Jordy up. 'He's burning with a fever,' she reported. Fanning him with her hand, she walked off.

'He took my lozenges,' Bogdan protested.

'Kleptomania is one of the side-effects,' Iorwerth agreed. 'We'll get him sorted though. Now, if I can be of any further service, you need only call.' He gave Bogdan a bow and bounced over him to catch up with Jane.

'He's got my charm.' They heard Bogdan wail as they increased their speed.

Giacomo was awake and sipping an Aperol with red vermouth on his sofa when they entered his room. He gave them a weak greeting. Jane put Jordy down and Iorwerth removed the charm from between his toes. Giacomo's eyes sparkled. He revolved his head three times then gave Jane, who was standing closest to him, a bear hug. A pool of tears gathered on her collar as he declared his never-ending gratitude.

'Tomorrow, I shall sing like a nightingale for you, too-wit,' he promised. 'I must get to rehearsals at once.' Giacomo flustered around the room for several minutes, examining every detail of his face in the mirror before leaving.

'Nobody understands me. Too-wit.' Jordy wiped his brow and assumed a theatrical stance. Jane laughed.

'I haven't been to the opera before,' she said.

'You might need these, too-woo.' He handed her a pair of ear muffs.

'You are both Philistines,' Iorwerth chided.

'I'm sorry, I was only laughing at Jordy,' Jane said. 'I can't wait to hear Giacomo sing.'

'Me neither – that's the reason I came,' Jordy agreed.

Iorwerth pouted for a moment then broke into a grin. 'I have even better news for you. Not only will Giacomo be performing, but I have used my connections to secure sabre-toothed sopranos, Amur altos and Bengal baritones. A whole chorus, in fact, of caterwauling tigers.'

Zeitgeist

It was 1990 and the prospect of relocating to Berlin for a year was awesome. Paisley town centre on a muggy Monday or 'Unter den Linden', Charlottenberg and the Ku'damm? It was a no brainer.

I worked for a PR company - a good one - and we had been chosen by none other than the Reverent McAllistar-Brean OBE to promote his high-profile launch of a charity helping orphans in Eastern Europe. McAllistar-Brean was our local bigwig philanthropist and orphanages were the in thing for big-wig philanthropists to do. He had business connections in Germany, so Berlin was the natural choice for his headquarters. New to the firm, I wasn't first choice for the assignment, but my ability to speak fluent German notched me up a grade.

Okay, so I got a grade D in my 'O' grades. I lied on my application form, but who doesn't?

This is all to explain why I enrolled on a crash course German top-up evening class. The group was as to be expected: a retired couple looking to spend quality time sharing a new hobby, a middle-aged nursery teacher panicking in case her brain became locked in cartoon mode, a mother whose adult daughter was nursing in Hamburg, myself and my friend Elinor who had been roped into accompanying me with promises of weekends clubbing in the German capital. Then there was Bix.

Bix was every mother's nightmare. Of no specific age - possibly mid-to-late thirties – he looked and acted like a Hell's Angel whose parole officer had borrowed (and crashed) his Harley. Greasy hair matted over his eyes, his jeans were torn in all the wrong places and he wore a custard cream leather jacket over his BO. You know the type – someone you dread standing behind you in the supermarket check-out queue as you know he's inspecting every purchase of tights, condoms and sanitary towels.

Elinor nudged me. 'Keeps copies of 'Loaded' under his mattress.'

'I'm betting he lives alone,' I said.

Elinor smothered a giggle. 'No, with his mum.'

We should have ended the conversation there, but I didn't want to be bested by my friend. 'So why is he learning German?' I asked.

'International terrorist.' Elinor had a fiendish imagination.

I laughed. 'He's probably not been further than the limits of his bus pass.'

Elinor gestured for me to keep my voice down, but I think he heard that. He was staring at us with dark eyes. Quickly we began paying attention to our tutor.

'Ich bin Lucy.' I faltered over the words in my strong regional accent.

The teacher grimaced, but answered, 'Sehr gut Lucy'.

It was no parting of the Red Sea when Bix cornered Elinor and myself on the way out the door.

'You're not in a hurry.' He wiped his nose on his sleeve. 'Some of the others are going for a drink to get to know one another and discuss the class. Want to come?'

No I didn't and I couldn't imagine any of the others agreeing, but Elinor was game for anything. Typically, it was only us in a run-down bar I hadn't known existed in a long-forgotten part of town near the Abbey. Bix bought the drinks and carried them over to our table from the bar. Being suspicious of what might have been slipped into the glass, I sipped without really drinking hoping our classmate wouldn't notice and become aggressively offended.

'Are you going to Germany?' I asked in support of polite conversation.

'Maybe.' He didn't seem interested in small talk. I studied the stained wooden table and sought ways of escape. My eyes were drawn to his fingernails. Black. Elinor spotted them too and curled her lip.

'Do you have any hobbies? Gardening perhaps?' I asked. My voice was stilted. I really didn't want him to answer. I didn't want to know, but that was the 'Open Sesame' to Aladdin's cave. His eyes widened – seriously, they began to glow like reddened coals – and his voice took on the silkiness of Vincent Price narrating Edgar Allan Poe. Names like Roger Bacon, John Dee and Aleister Crowley danced from his lips.

'Isaac Newton – he was a lad. I knew him before he got too good for his mates,' Bix boasted.

The others could have been his heavy metal pals, but naturally I'd heard of Isaac Newton. Not in the way he was describing, though. Alchemy, the philosopher's stone, secret elixirs, homunculi, immortality. The words merged into each other without meaning. Whatever macabre cult he was involved in, I didn't want any part of, but Elinor was hooked. She sucked it all in open-mouthed. I desperately wanted to go home, but I couldn't leave my best friend in the grasp of this weirdo. Not now that he was suggesting we should leave the safety of the bar and go on some sort of field trip. It was closing time and due to the vandalised street lighting, it was spookily dark. I had come out in my light jacket and the wind mocked me. I drew it tight round my chest.

'Where are we going?' I asked with increased agitation.

Bix laughed. 'Not far. I need to get some stuff first.'

Getting stuff meant pilfering a jam jar from a waste recycling box left out for collection.

'Best place to get them.' Bix chirped as if he thought I would need to know. 'They're clean that way.'

'Oh good.' I tried to make my sarcasm obvious. Elinor scowled.

'Hope that jacket isn't Prada, we have to squeeze through here.' Bix taunted.

In the dark I hadn't noticed where we were going.

'I am NOT going in there.' I froze.

'Not afraid are you? I thought you weren't superstitious.'

Beside me Elinor began humming that grotesque piece from Saint Saens that I knew from the television mystery programme.

'Shut up.' I slapped her forearm. She looked taken aback at

first, but then she blew a raspberry. Elinor was a non-raspberry blowing accountant. It was clear she had been drinking more than I thought.

Heaven knows how, but I was coaxed into creeping through the hole in the stone wall into the graveyard. There had been a burial ground here since the dark ages and it held more secrets than MI6 headquarters. There were no lights on in the neighbouring church, but the moon lit up the stones like a theatre spotlight. Brushing cobwebs from my hair I stumbled across a clammy monument to Jacob Mooney, died age ten months.

'Smothered by his mother,' Bix drooled in my ear. My heart skipped a beat. Bix's eerie laughed circled round my head and I wanted to run. My feet didn't move. There was a line of bats flying from the church gables, squeaking their way round the stones. The clawed wings and velvet bodies close to my face gave me the heebie jeebies.

'What's this great experiment you wanted to show us?' I asked. My teeth chapped like a blind person's stick.

Bix held a finger to his lips. I could see that not only were his fingernails black, they were also torn to the quick. Not bitten, but worn down. A night bird screeched overhead like in the Hammer horror films, but without the ridiculous hamminess. I began to cry.

'I want to go home.' I sobbed.

Bix, in his element, was having none of that. Somehow I wished he would just attack us and get it over with. He took a knife from his jacket and I screamed. Immediately a hand was over my mouth. Cold, earthy, evil flesh, too stinking to bite. Bix was breathing his fetid stench on the back of my neck.

'Do you believe in heaven?' He whispered.

I didn't, but wasn't sure if this was the right reply.

'Or hell?'

Hell? Yes I believed in that. I was living in it right then. I shook my head.

'Exactly.' I could see his cruel grin in the moonlight. 'You and thousands, millions, like you. People who die not believing in anywhere for the soul to go. They condemn it to wander the earth for eternity.' He chortled, coughing up phlegm. I could see Elinor searching under piles of earth. She had either been hypnotised by his twaddle or had been drugged. I suspected the latter.

'That is, until I catch it,' Bix finished.

Suddenly my mouth was freed and with the rarest of movements he swooped his jam jar behind my left ear, simultaneously slashing with the knife. Before I could scream again the jam jar lid was sealed in place.

'There, what do you see?' He demonstrated his catch with puerile pride. It could have been a butterfly or tadpole he was showing his teacher. I stifled a further sob. What did this madman want?

'A soul?' I ventured. My voice rattled. My hands shook. My knees knocked. All of me trembled.

'A soul.' He agreed with vigour. 'And what do we do with this soul?' He sounded like our German tutor. I was meant to recite the answer by rote, but had forgotten to do my homework.

'I don't know sir.'

'We eat it.' Bix leered offering me the jar. I retched.

I mean, of course there was nothing in the bottle, but he had me convinced I would be swallowing a dead soul. Elinor was now at his side, anxious that she should taste the delicacy. She grasped at the jar, but he pushed her away, snatching the glass to his chest.

'No, this one is mine.' He growled, raising the jar to his lips. 'This soul is a young one. Easy to catch and easy to mould. It will be used to renew my body. It will renew my life.'

What was he saying – that he was some sort of vampire sucking souls rather than blood? The man needed psychiatric help.

'How old do you think I am?' He rounded on me. 'Three hundred? Four hundred? Keep going.' He unscrewed the lid and flicked out a forked tongue. A halo of light shone directly in my eyes and an unholy screech pierced my ears.

The security guard shone his torch full in my face and I realised the ululation was my own. I hadn't believed any human capable of such a cacophony beyond the age of two. Elinor had fainted and lay peacefully on an upturned grave. There was no trace of Bix.

The sergeant at the station was unimpressed by our nightly

jaunt. We were old enough to know better, he reminded us and gave us a strict lecture on alcohol abuse, drug usage, trespassing, causing a public disturbance and whatever else he could find in his book. We stayed the night in the cells, but in the morning it was decided not to bring charges.

'Wasting police time,' the sergeant muttered as he showed us the door.

I hoped to keep the incident quiet, but news like that gets into print around here. I was humiliated to read of our 'abominable prank' in the local paper. Elinor laughed it off, but for me it meant the end of my chances of going to Berlin. Reverent McAllistar-Brean was a man of impeccable morals. He would never allow an employee with a dubious background to besmirch the name of his charity.

I was called in to head office. My immediate boss was there, pin-striped and solemn. The head of our division looked ashen-faced. An immaculately groomed and tailored gentleman was sitting in a revolving chair behind an over-sized desk. His back was to us and he was staring out of the window. I noticed the dog-collar and assumed this was the Reverent himself.

I began to apologise before anyone else could speak, babbling nonsense that no-one would believe. The chair swivelled noiselessly round. The Reverent smiled with a practised, patronising air.

'I think we can overlook this little matter gentleman. Miss Smith will be perfect for the project.' He handed my boss a file. His fingernails were black.

For over four hundred years old, the suave theologian was looking remarkably good. I smiled, knowing my job was secure. The Reverent Bix would certainly not want the Sunday tabloids to become interested in his little hobby.

It was only when I was on the flight to Tegel that my smile faded. All things considered, did I really want to be working for a ghoul?

The Secret of Mimo Santos

Whereas purveyors of fine chocolate are familiar with the island of Sao Tome, few have heard of its neighbour Mimo Santos, yet the cocoa beans grown on the side of the island's volcano are of such outstanding quality, monarchs would give up their realms to savour them.

That is, according to the chief executive officer of the Tantalising Chocolate Company™. On the grounds that such an island did not appear on their charts, the board were understandably wary of his decision to send a delegation to the island to secure sole trading rights. Their doubts were compounded when his psychiatrist recommended a long-term break in a residential institution; nevertheless, his niece Amanda volunteered to head an exploratory party, consisting of herself and the trainee doorkeeper Jack.

They flew to South Africa and their ship sailed from Cape Town.

'People say Mimo Santos doesn't exist,' Jack confided to Amanda as he served her hot muffins in her portside cabin.

'But for the sake of our venture, I have imagined that it does,' Amanda said. 'I have even added a fine library, which my uncle failed to mention.'

'Could you include a fine hotel?' Jack said.

'There is an inn and a tearoom.'

They sailed for two weeks, with Jack becoming ever more restless. 'We've been sailing for months and we haven't spotted a volcanic island yet,' he complained.

'All you need is belief,' Amanda assured him, sunbathing on deck with a pink gin.

The following day the lookout spotted land, and by midafternoon the waft of chocolate reached them. They berthed in the two-ship harbour of the only town on Mimo Santos. The crew secured the landing ramp and Amanda marched across, followed by Jack, who staggered under her bags. The port was bustling. Unemployed sailors eyed up companions for the evening, port workers spat tobacco, children ran after dogs and policemen in dark glasses strutted along the streets like extras from a cop series.

'Did you have to imagine quite as many police?' Jack asked.

'What are they up to?' Amanda said. She scurried after a pair of officers, but was brought to an abrupt halt by the heel of her left shoe snapping on the cobbled paving. She bent to pull it off and felt a rough hand on her shoulder. 'Do you mind, this is Armani.'

The officer grabbed Amanda's right hand and forced it behind her back. His partner took hold of Jack, lifting him off the ground by his collar.

'Unhand us at once,' Amanda said.

'FYI, her uncle is CEO of the TCC™, OK,' Jack added.

The letters volleyed back by the policeman showed he wasn't impressed.

'We've done nothing wrong,' Amanda insisted. 'We're here to purchase your cocoa beans. If you don't release us this instant, I shall make sure no-one buys your chocolate, ever.'

'Put that in your sausage roll and stuff it.' Jack stuck his tongue out.

The argument resulted in Amanda being handcuffed. Jack was secured by having his head locked in a firm hold beneath the policeman's elbow. This was poor decision making on the part of the police. As they marched to the town hall, the officer restraining Jack felt a mouthful of sharp teeth in his backside. Before he could react, Jack's knee was in his groin. He let go of his prisoner and Jack did not need the surreptitious eye flick from Amanda to vamoose into the crowd. The officers conferred before deciding to continue with one prisoner.

'What about my luggage?' Amanda protested, glancing at her abandoned cases.

'You won't need those where you are going,' the sergeant sniggered.

News of a stranger in police custody spread. Windows opened and faces appeared round street corners. A squashed mango hit Amanda on the nose and she had to swirl her hips to avoid being accosted by a flying snail. Once inside the town hall, the gates were shut fast and Amanda was ushered into a circular room with a wooden table taking up two-thirds of the floor. A bald, wrinkly-headed man was sitting at the far side of the table counting cocoa beans, sliding them across the polished surface as he did so. His nose was an inch from the table. He didn't look up. After a minute the police sergeant cleared his throat.

'Sir, we have apprehended the robber responsible for the theft of Orion.'

'Nine, ten, eleven…'

It took a moment for the charge to sink in. 'You said Orion?' Amanda queried.

'It's a star constellation,' the policeman answered. 'Rigel, Betelgeuse, the horse head nebula – you must have heard of it. Last night it disappeared from the sky and this morning you appeared.'

'I haven't studied astronomy, but I do know constellations don't simply disappear. Are you sure it wasn't hidden by the clouds?' Amanda said.

'There were no clouds, just a hunter-shaped hole in the sky where it should have been.'

'What makes you think I had anything to do with it?'

'Twelve, thirteen.' The bald, wrinkly-headed man came to the last of the cocoa beans. He stopped counting and bent below the table to reach for the object at his feet. 'We are about to find out,' he said, lifting the bundle and setting it on the table.

'What is that?' Amanda said. It looked like a three-way pile up between a dressmakers' work box, a pyramid of coconuts and a bidet. When it came to the overpowering scent it gave off, the bidet came out on top.

'It's a hat,' the man replied. He put a hand inside and pulled out the contents. 'I have here two cards with the words "yes" and "no" on them.' He demonstrated the cards. The word "yes" was written in red on one and the word "no" was written in blue on the other. 'I shall put them back in the hat.'

'Is this a magic trick?' Amanda asked. 'I'll be able to tell if there is any legerdemain. I have eagle-sharp eyes.'

'I shall ask the question. Is this the criminal responsible for stealing Orion?' The bald, wrinkly-headed man shook the hat and offered it to the sergeant. The officer rummaged around before picking out one of the cards.

'The answer is "yes",' the policeman announced.

'That isn't fair. You looked in the hat before you picked,' Amanda protested.

'We make the rules on this island, not thieving foreigners,' the policeman sneered.

'Guilty as charged,' the bald, wrinkly-headed man said.

'I object, your Honour. What sort of judicial system is this? I demand a fair trial with a jury,' Amanda said.

'It is our system.' The bald, wrinkly-headed man waved away her complaint.

'What is my sentence?' Amanda asked.

'A long one with complicated, subordinate clauses.'

'There has obviously been a misunderstanding. I had nothing to do with the loss of Orion, but I have connections. I can help you find it, if you let me leave,' Amanda bargained.

'You take me for a fool. You will sail off and we will never see you or Orion again. Guards, take her to the dungeons.'

The police officers jostled Amanda to the cells beneath the town hall. Water dripped from the stone walls, encouraging a wide growth of moss and fungi. The jailor unlocked her handcuffs before inviting her in. He locked the metal door with a jangle of his keys. Amanda rubbed her reddened wrists. She had an odd feeling of déjà vu, but to her knowledge she hadn't been in prison before. 'Perhaps it hasn't happened again yet,' she said to a rat gnawing a bone in the corner. She leaned her back against the wall and slid down to the floor, where she sat until she had counted to five hundred and ninety-two. Her scalp was itchy and she pulled at her hair, imagining a colony of biting lice tucking in to her head. 'What am I going to do?' she wailed. 'I could starve to death down here.'

'I don't think so. The rats are fat enough to last you until well after Christmas.' A voice sounded from above her. A slit in the top of the door had been drawn across and the jailor was staring at her. 'Not that you'll be here at Christmas.'

'Why do you say that? Has the bald, wrinkly-headed judge seen sense?'

The jailor laughed. 'That's the mayor. Expecting him to see sense would be like asking the Emperor – may he dine on chocolate for ever – to sleep in a caravan.'

'What Emperor?' Amanda asked. 'I didn't imagine one. Tell me more about the island.'

'I shouldn't, it's bad luck. Our cocoa harvests have failed this year. The beans rotted on the trees before they ripened. The Emperor – may he dine on chocolate for ever – needs a sacrifice to appease the chocolate-giving gods, or we will have no chocolate and die in poverty.'

'That is rotten luck,' Amanda sympathised. 'Nobody wants you to die in poverty, but is a sacrifice the best way to appease your gods?'

'Oh yes. You see, for the past thousand years the Emperor – may he dine on chocolate for ever – has thrown a cocoa bean into the mouth of the volcano every Saturday morning. It's a bind, ruins weekends away, but it is his one duty.'

'And that has satisfied the gods?' Amanda said.

'Yes, until three months ago.' The jailor assumed a hammy, horror movie voice. 'It happened overnight. Our plants became infected by a mystery illness. First the leaves grew hairs, which made them kind of cute, but then the black spots appeared and the fruit melted into blobs of gooey caramel before exploding. Poof.' He threw out his hands. Amanda had moved close to the door and a finger poked her in the eye.

'Poof, indeed. We need to find out about plant ailments. The library will help.'

'That's where the mayor found his book.'

'What book?'

'The one about a boy, a chocolate factory and magic stuff.'

'I've read that,' Amanda said. 'I don't see how it helped.'

'It didn't, but caught between the pages was an ancient parchment written in hieroglyphics. The mayor was able to translate them.'

'That was fortunate.'

'They told how a human sacrifice could placate the gods. The honour of being the sacrifice was offered to the Emperor – may he dine on chocolate for ever – but he's a generous chap and insisted someone else should take his place. No-one came forward. I didn't put my name in because of my lumbago. That's when the mayor had his brainwave. The sacrifice should be a prisoner. We got our offering and they got a chance to make up for their wrongdoing. A win-win situation.'

'But your cells have been empty since he made the proclamation,' Amanda guessed.

'No dog had even pooed on the pavement for two months.'

'I imagine being a sacrifice is a deterrent.' Amanda gulped. 'No, I shouldn't imagine. I'm the one in jail. I'm the one to be the sacrifice.'

'Tomorrow morning, before the cock crows three times, you'll be escorted to the mouth of the volcano where the Emperor – may he dine on chocolate for ever – will pour a cauldron of molten chocolate over you, then feed you to the volcano gods. It will be a glorious show.'

'Whoopee-doopee.' Amanda didn't share the jailor's enthusiasm.

'Have a pleasant night.' The jailor tapped his forehead and slid the shutter across. Amanda slumped against the cell wall, wondering what Jack was doing. No doubt the scallywag had stowed away on the first ship leaving port. To pass the time she counted cockroaches until it became too dark to distinguish the ones she'd already tallied.

'I spy, with my little eye, something beginning with "N",' she spoke aloud, looking round the cell. 'Nothing,' she guessed. 'Correct, your turn Amanda.' She fumbled for her pocket and drew out her handkerchief to blow her nose and dab her eyes. She wiped away the snot that attached to her eyelash. Talking to yourself was not good. It was one of the reasons her uncle had been advised to consult Dr. Sigmund. 'I don't want to die covered in molten chocolate,' she sniffed.

'Psst.'

'What? Where? Who's there?' Amanda scrambled to her feet. There was a hollow crack as she banged her head on the stone.

'It's me,' the voice said.

'Nanny?'

'No, it's Jack.'

'Oh, you sound like nanny. Have you brought my hot water bottle and bedtime cookies?'

'I'm the trainee doorkeeper, remember. You need to follow me.'

'Where are you?'

A hand gripped her ankle and she screamed. A beam of torchlight flickered from a hole in the cell floor. After a couple of blinks, Amanda made out the top of Jack's head. 'I can't go down there. My blouse will be ruined.'

'Would you rather be burnt in chocolate and thrown into a live volcano?'

'How do you know about that?' Amanda rubbed the back of her head, where a bump was forming.

'I'll explain once we're out of here.'

Jack's head vanished. Amanda hesitated then scrambled to the manhole and eased after him. She sniffed the rancid air. 'Is this the city's waste disposal channel?' she asked.

'It's a sewer.'

Jack crawled ahead along the drainpipe. Amanda caught a glimpse of his behind as he turned into a rat-ridden corridor smelling of sweaty socks, rotten eggs and dodo droppings. A hundred yards along, a shaft of light shone from the street above. Jack reached the spot and stood on his tiptoes to reach the manhole cover. By the time he had slid the metal grate back, Amanda was at his side.

'Give me a leg up,' she said. Jack cupped his hands to form a step and Amanda stuck a foot on them. He staggered back under her weight and the heel of her one good shoe snapped.

'At least you have a matching pair,' Jack consoled before Amanda could consider docking his wages.

She grabbed at the street paving to steady herself and her hands landed in a divot of dog dirt. Jack sniggered, but stopped when he realised she needed her hand to pull him out. Amanda swung suspended from the kerb for several seconds before Jack managed to shift his shoulder below her derrière and nudge her up. Above ground, she checked for broken nails and arranged her hair before realising Jack needed help.

'I'll need a steaming bath with bags of bubbles when we get back to the ship,' Amanda said, once Jack was beside her.

'We can't go back… to the ship. It's been taken over… by island guards,' Jack spoke in short gasps. 'After I escaped the police, I found the inn and had a glass of hot toddy by the fire. That's where I heard the town gossip. My first plan was to return to the ship, fight off the guards then sail home.'

Amanda's jaw fell. 'Without me?'

'I thought, since you imagined the island without Orion, if I could reimagine the island with Orion in the night sky and the cocoa plants healthy, all would be well.'

'But if you pictured the island even a teeny-weeny bit different,' Amanda held a hand in front of Jack's face and positioned her first finger a millimetre above her thumb, to make sure Jack knew what a teeny-weeny bit was, 'I would have been trapped in this imaginary hellhole forever.'

'I didn't think of that. Just as well I chickened out of retaking the ship and went for plan "B" – rescuing you.'

'Now we need a plan "C" to get out of here,' Amanda rubbed her chin. 'Thankfully, I wasn't head girl of my school because daddy paid for the new sports' emporium.'

'Your uncle supplied the tuck shop with chocolate too,' Jack put in.

'Tantalising Chocolate™,' Amanda said. 'But before I can think, I need a cup of herbal tea.'

They made their way to a back street café and found a table in the corner. The waiter was more intent on his notepad than their faces, but Amanda pulled her jacket collar over her ears and deepened her voice.

'Have you thought of a plan?' Jack asked.

'I have,' Amanda answered when the waiter departed.

'Where do we start?'

'My nanny showed me. You work your way from the outside in.'

'I'm not talking about the cutlery.'

'Oh, well neither am I.' Amanda cleared her throat. 'We can't escape, so we need to start by finding an answer to the problem of the dying cocoa plants.'

'I know more about Botany Bay than botany,' Jack said. 'We could find a book in the library.'

'The mayor did that. Unless we act, someone will be sacrificed tomorrow morning to appease the chocolate gods. Since I've escaped, I've a feeling it will be the friendly jailor.'

'I heard about the mayor,' Jack said. 'Nobody trusts him. The police force is his private army and he intends taking over the island to control the chocolate trade. The Emperor – may he dine on chocolate for ever – won't like that.'

'Why did you say that bit about the chocolate?' Amanda asked. 'I don't know.'

'Then please don't.' Amanda twiddled her teaspoon. 'We need to talk to this Emperor.'

'May he di…' A glare from Amanda cut Jack short, but resulted in a darker look from the man at the next table. He pushed his chair back. It took a moment for Amanda to realise what the unfinished sentence sounded like. 'Dine,' she said. 'My employee said dine.'

'On chocolate for ever,' Jack added.

Satisfied, the man resumed his dinner. Jack leaned over to whisper to Amanda. 'If we go to see the… you-know-who… he'll have us both fed to the chocolate gods.'

'We have to try,' Amanda said. 'My family are a family of triers.'

'Mine are liars,' Jack said. 'Or so my dad said, but he may have been lying.'

'Spare me the wit.' Amanda finished her tea and stood up. She tapped the shoulder of the man at the next table. 'My good sir, please tell us where the Emperor lives.' The man stuffed a forkful of pie in his mouth and munched. 'Did you hear me, you cloth-eared peasant? I asked where the Emperor lives.'

Jack pulled at her sleeve. 'You have to say "may he dine on chocolate for ever".'

'Doesn't that get tedious? Very well, where does the Emperor – may he dine on chocolate for ever – live?'

'In his palace, of course.' The man spat out crumbs as he spoke.

'And where might that be?'

'At the top of the volcano.'

'Which is expected to erupt any time,' Jack said. His voice quivered. 'I read that in a book on board our ship.'

'How can there be a book about an island I imagined two days ago?'

'I pictured one,' Jack said.

'Then picture the money to pay our bill,' Amanda answered.

They managed to slip out the window of the ladies' lavatory. When they were out of town, Amanda set a brisk pace to the bottom of the volcano. They were breathless before they put a foot on the mountain.

'Did you have you imagine the volcano so steep?' Jack complained.

'I was a fair distance away at the time. Things are larger close up.'

'We could imagine ourselves at the top,' Jack mused.

Amanda refused, not wanting to miss vital clues on the way. 'The climb will give us time to work out what we'll say to the Emperor.'

'If he's at home,' Jack said.

'My nanny told me to think positive thoughts,' Amanda said.

'I'm positive this trip was a bad idea. I thought it would be a jolly cruise leading to a fast track promotion, not sewers, blisters and girls' toilets.'

Looking round, they were less than six feet ahead of where they were two minutes previously, which wasn't far. Jack sat on a bank of earth and rubbed his ankles. 'I don't suppose you've got any chocolate?'

Amanda laughed. 'We are surrounded by cocoa plants and we don't have a square of chocolate to fight over.'

'The plants don't look happy,' Jack said.

'Plants don't have feelings. You have been spending too much time reading. Reading isn't good for you.'

'I wish I'd paid attention to biology lessons in school. My teacher used to say there was "seeing and seeing", or was it "weeing and peeing"?'

'Those are the same things. Your teacher sounds madder than uncle – oops, I didn't say that. Let's keep going.'

They found a burst of energy and at last they were through the trees and greeted by a ring of warm, dark smoke. Amanda spotted a viewing platform.

'You can see the whole island from here,' she said. 'There's our ship in the harbour.'

Jack joined her. 'How much further do we have to go?'

Amanda consulted her map.

'Where did you get that?' Jack asked.

'In the cafe, next to the leaflets about the rescue centre for man-eating lizards, fire walking courses for pyrophobics and holidays in Brighton. We are at the rim of the volcano.' She took a few steps, surveying the scene. 'I can't see a palace.'

'I can't see anything for smoke.' Jack rubbed his streaming eyes.

'It must be here some…' Amanda lay stretched out on the ground with her eyes closed. A gobstopper-sized lump was swelling on her forehead. Jack reached for her wrist to check her pulse. She slapped her palm over his hand.

'Stealing my Rolex?'

'You're alive,' Jack said, freeing his hand.

'Of course I'm alive. What happened?' Amanda sat up and felt her forehead.

'You took a step forwards, stopped and fell,' Jack said, 'Like this.' He raised his right leg in the air and took a step, landing a second later on the ground next to Amanda. 'I feel like I've walked into a brick wall,' he groaned.

'It is forbidden to walk on the Emperor's lawn.' A man dressed in a red fur coat decorated with yellow pompoms was running towards them carrying a wooden pole. He was wearing joke glasses with false eyebrows. They slipped down his nose towards the withering lines of his silver moustache and he paused to push them up.

'Where did he come from?' Amanda said.

Jack got to her feet and gave Amanda a hand up. They faced the stranger together. He had looked comical as he approached, but close up, he towered over them. The pompoms had spikes and his wooden pole had a spearhead attached. The point was sharpened and glistened in the sun. Amanda pushed Jack ahead.

'We've come to talk to the Emperor,' she said, poking her head over his shoulders.

'May he dine on chocolate for ever,' Jack croaked.

'Are you stupid? I said get off the grass.' The man poked the blunt end of his spear in Jack's tummy.

'Can you see any grass?' Jack whispered to Amanda.

'Humour him,' Amanda said. She gave a ludicrous grin and walked backwards, pulling Jack by his shirt. 'Are we off the grass yet?'

'That will do,' the man said. 'Didn't you read the sign?'

'We didn't see a sign.'

The man tapped the air with the spearhead. There was the sound of metal striking metal. 'It says keep off the grass in thirty-two languages.'

'It's invisible,' Jack said.

The man peered at them. 'Aha, you aren't wearing the spectacles. You are supposed to get spectacles at the town hall before you come up. I'm amazed you got this far without them.'

'What do you mean?' Amanda asked.

'The path is littered with booby traps, tripwires and pits. Invisible unless you are wearing the special glasses.'

'I don't suppose you've got a spare pair I could borrow?' Amanda said. 'I'll hand them in at the town hall on my way back.'

The man leant his spear against the invisible sign and fished around in the pockets of his coat. He managed to find a pair of specs. 'Will one of you wear the pair or do you want one glass each?'

'I'd better have them,' Amanda said before Jack could reply. She took the glasses from the man and balanced them on her nose. 'Oh, I see the wall now.' She turned her head and took a step back. 'Wow. That is some palace.'

'Can I see?' Jack reached out, but Amanda moved away.

With the glasses on, she could see a fantastic crystal fortress supported on stalagmite stilts that rose up in a semicircle from the rim of the volcano. There were towers and turrets, balconies and balustrades, cloisters and campaniles. The architect couldn't decide if it was a fortress, a palace, a monastery or a supermarket. The man in the red coat tapped the sign again. Amanda read the instruction to keep off the lawn.

'It's for your own safety,' the man said.

'So I see.' Sprawled on the immaculate lawn were five lions with multicoloured manes. 'Are those natural?'

'Rare rainbow heads, found only on this island,' the man explained. 'Do you have an appointment with the Emperor?'

'I'm afraid not. We only arrived this morning,' Amanda said. 'We have come about the cocoa plants.'

The man raised his spear and eyed them suspiciously. 'Who sent you?'

'We are representatives of the Tantalising Chocolate Company™. My uncle is the chief executive officer. He is the trainee doorkeeper on a fast track to the top.' Amanda tilted her head towards Jack, who was trying to sneak the glasses from her. 'It's a long story. If we could see the Emperor, we wouldn't have to repeat ourselves.'

'But you can see the Emperor,' the man said.

'Excellent.' Amanda clapped her hands. 'Can you take us to him?'

'I am the Emperor – may I dine on chocolate for ever. I enjoy nothing better than a long story, with a nice glass of red wine, cheesy nibbles and perhaps… I'm blabbering. Are there any crocodiles in your story?'

'No, I don't think so,' Amanda said.

'That's a pity.' The Emperor had made himself comfortable on a boulder, ready for the tale, but he got up and shook the hems of his coat. 'You'll have to return to the town and come back when there are crocodiles in your story. Goodbye.' He turned to leave.

'Aren't you're forgetting the three crocs we had to fight off in the harbour, miss?' Jack said, making sure the Emperor heard.

'You're right, Jack. I thought they were alligators, but no, definitely crocodiles,' Amanda answered.

'Three of them? In the harbour here?' The Emperor turned back. His eyes were glistening.

'Might have been more,' Jack said.

'Wonderful.' The Emperor danced on the spot. 'Come, come inside.' He waved them to follow him. 'I'll make tea, then you can tell me about it.'

'What about me?' Jack called as the Emperor and Amanda marched towards the invisible palace with their glasses on.

'Wait here,' Amanda ordered.

'Oh, that isn't a good idea,' the Emperor warned. 'The lions will be expecting their dinner in two minutes. The keeper is usually on time, but if he's a second late, the cats will make their own arrangements.'

'You'd better come,' Amanda allowed.

'But don't walk on my grass,' the Emperor reminded him.

Jack latched onto the bottom of Amanda's jacket and tagged behind as they made their way to the palace.

'Were they green crocodiles?' the Emperor asked.

'Well…'

'The green ones are the most vicious. They can snap a ship's hull with one swish of their tails.'

'I think they were green,' Amanda agreed.

'It's my fault,' the Emperor said. 'I hope they didn't damage your boat. I was bored one Wednesday and imagined what it would be like to be stuck on an island surrounded by green crocodiles. The next day they appeared.'

'That is a powerful imagination,' Amanda said.

'Why thank you.'

'We have that in common. My imagination has landed us in a spot of bother.' Amanda was about to launch into the story of the missing Orion, but the Emperor was quick to remind her they hadn't had tea. Ten minutes later, seated on a luxurious sofa and sipping Darjeeling from china cups, Amanda was able to proceed with her account. Every few sentences she paused to savour a sip of tea and Jack, who didn't have tea because he couldn't see the cup, interrupted the story to add another crocodile.

'I spotted a fire-eating, brown-snouted caiman in the sewers.'

'The sewers? When were you there?' The Emperor sounded shocked.

'He said the jewellers,' Amanda answered, not wishing to be sidetracked by the rights and wrongs of escaping from the dungeon. 'But about your cocoa plants, have you any idea why they are dying? Has anything changed on the island?'

'Not apart from Orion going walkabout. I put that down to the sudden change of seasons. Two days ago it was midwinter and today it's high summer. It's as if someone imagined the sun. We never see Orion in summer.'

Jack stared at Amanda. Her cheeks flushed. 'I wanted warm weather to wear my shorts.'

'You will need to ask the mayor about the cocoa plants,' the Emperor continued. 'I don't leave the palace grounds these days. There are yellow crocodiles in the rivers. Yellow crocodiles have more powerful bites than dragons. Most of our crocs have weak jaw muscles. They can't keep their mouths open for more than five seconds before they clamp shut. Perfect for killing things, but useless for conversation. That's not the case with the yellow blighters. They know how to have a good chinwag. Yellow crocodiles can do your head in, discussing the price of fish and the best schools for dolphins.'

'You know a great deal about the island crocodiles,' Jack said.

'I'm writing a book about them. There are fifty-seven species on the island, or there were at the last count.'

Amanda coughed, 'About the problem of the dying cocoa beans…'

'I don't see how that has anything to do with the crocodiles. None of the crocs like chocolate. The turquoise croc has a sweet tooth, but it prefers mints. It's easy to mistake a turquoise croc for a green croc. If it were turquoise crocs you saw in the harbour, they were looking for crumbs from your ship biscuits.'

'They were green,' Jack said.

'Would we be able to see inside the volcano?' Amanda asked, afraid of having to listen to descriptions of fifty-seven crocodile species.

'A splendid suggestion.' The Emperor stood up and the tea vanished.

'That's your imagination again,' Amanda said.

They followed the Emperor to the crystal lift that whizzed them down to the volcano rim. Jack looked over the edge to see a bubble of lava rising like a soufflé.

'Is this where you throw your cocoa bean every Saturday to appease the chocolate-giving gods?' he asked.

'Yes.'

'But the gods have failed to be appeased?' Amanda clarified.

'At first I thought a rogue turquoise croc had found its way into the volcano and was snaffling up the beans, but they are accounted for. According to the mayor, we need a sacrifice. He said he would organise it.' A smile edged across the Emperor's lips. 'Why, it was good of you to come up. It saves the trouble of sending guards to get you.'

'We haven't come to be sacrificed.' Amanda turned pale.

'There's no rush, we can wait until after supper,' the Emperor said. 'I'd like to show you my sketches for the book. I haven't mastered the snout of the purple-backed croc. It has a knob on the end, like a mushroom. I've got a bath full of them. They're only nine inches long, but there's seeing and there's seeing, you see.'

'It's that phrase again,' Amanda whispered to Jack. 'It must be important. What are we seeing that we're not seeing?'

'You're seeing the palace with your glasses. If I walk into another wall, I'll have more bumps than the pink-spiked crocodile.'

'You've seen a pink-spiked crocodile?' the Emperor overheard.

'No, he's made it up.'

'Are there any on this island?' The Emperor peered at Jack

'The place is alive with them, but you need special contact lenses to see them.'

'Don't be facetious,' Amanda said. 'Now move out my way. I need to speak with the lions.'

'I wouldn't advise that, my dear,' the Emperor said, but Amanda strolled across the lawn towards the colourful beasts. The conversation involved double-jointed hand movements, and a wiggle of Amanda's bottom, before she returned.

'As I thought,' she said.

'You speak "lion",' the Emperor was impressed.

'It is similar to "cat", and at home I talk to my cats every day. Both languages can be traced back to the sabre-toothed tigers, but whereas "lion" was influenced by cheetahs and leopards, cat language merged with that of Northern lynxes, which is where the "meow" sound comes from. The lions adopted a harsher vowel sound from copying elephants, although the rainbow heads have a singsong accent that comes from eating pomegranates.'

'Show-off,' Jack grumbled.

'Only insecure people need to show off,' Amanda informed him.

'Look, isn't that a pink-spiked crocodile snapping at your ankles?' Jack said.

Amanda jumped. She scowled at Jack before continuing. 'In the town hall I saw the mayor counting cocoa beans. He had thirteen healthy beans.' There was silence while the Emperor and Jack worked out what Amanda was saying.

'Thirteen beans would be thirteen Saturdays, which is… three months.' Jack counted on his fingers, then borrowed three of Amanda's.

'Exactly,' Amanda agreed.

'That is how long the gods have been angry for,' the Emperor said. 'That's when our beans rotted. I have only one healthy bean left, but if you say the mayor has more, that is wonderful news.'

'Is it?' Amanda asked.

'What do you two know that I don't?' the Emperor said. 'It is my island, I should be kept informed.'

'It's a matter of seeing and seeing,' Amanda said. 'The mayor has been stealing the sacrificial beans before they reach the gods.'

'Impossible,' the Emperor declared.

'The lions have seen the mayor creeping up the volcano every Saturday morning carrying a fishing net.'

'I'll have him boiled in a vat of molten chocolate,' the Emperor spluttered. 'No, I won't waste the chocolate. I'll feed him to the green crocodiles.'

'It's circumstantial evidence,' Amanda said. 'He could say he was capturing butterflies with his net.'

'The tiger-striped gharials wouldn't permit anyone to chase butterflies,' the Emperor insisted.

'Nevertheless, it won't stand up in court.'

'That would depend who chose the card from the hat,' the Emperor said.

Jack had been shuffling from foot to foot with a hand in the air while the others spoke. 'We could set a trap for him,' he broke in.

'Is this another of your daft ideas?' Amanda furrowed her delicately clipped eyebrows.

'The townsfolk saw the police arrest Amanda. If a message is sent to the town to say she is here, they will expect her to be sacrificed tomorrow and are bound to come to watch.'

'As I said, it's a daft idea.'

'You won't actually be thrown into the volcano, ma'am.'

'I should think not.'

'Once a crowd has gathered, the Emperor – may he, you sir, dine on chocolate for ever – will change his mind. Since tomorrow is a Saturday he will throw his last healthy bean into the volcano instead. The mayor will panic. A healthy bean will appease the gods and he doesn't want that, not with control of the island within his grasp. He'll be desperate to stop him.'

'How does that help?' the Emperor said.

Amanda snapped her fingers. 'If you delay throwing in the bean, Your Excellency, it will give the mayor time to scramble onto the ledge below the rim of the volcano, ready to catch it as it falls. You can have guards stationed to arrest him when he does. Half the town will witness it.'

The Emperor rubbed his head. 'It seems complicated to me.'

'It will work, sir,' Jack asserted.

'Then there is time for supper,' the Emperor said. 'I want to hear from you, young man, about these pink-spiked crocodiles.'

The butler found a pair of guest specs for Jack, which Amanda swapped for the inferior pair she had. Afterwards the Emperor made them welcome for the night. A message announcing the upcoming sacrifice was attached to an eagle-beaked carrier pigeon and sent down to the town.

'None of the crocodiles dare mess with an eagle-beaked pigeon,' the Emperor explained. 'Although we'll have to hope there are no dragons about today.' Amanda's face dropped. 'Joking,' he laughed.

'Oooh, I'm tired.' Amanda stretched her arms and gave a massive yawn when the Emperor brought out his crocodile scrapbook. She was able to retire to her room, but Jack was forced to look at pictures of imaginary reptiles for several hours.

Sleeping on glass beds was tricky, as the sheets slipped off, but it was warm enough to sleep without bedclothes. When Amanda looked out her window the following morning there was a spectacle-wearing crowd gathered at the top of the volcano. Families had brought breakfast muffins and photographers were setting up lights and tripods.

'Bloodthirsty bunch,' she told her reflection, then kissed the glass. 'You are so beautiful, Amanda. They don't deserve you.'

There was time for a hearty bowl of salty porridge and a look at five albums of crocodile pictures before it was time to approach the volcano. Jack and the Emperor got involved in a debate about the shape of the horseshoe alligator's toenails. Magnifying glasses and high-powered microscopes were called for, but the problem was unresolved by the time the Emperor's personal assistant grew impatient of making excuses and ordered the guards to escort everyone outside. The imperial party arrived at the same time as the mayor's sedan chair. The mayor waited until a red rug was placed on the ground before climbing out.

'Emperor – may you dine on chocolate for ever.' The mayor feigned a bow. 'If I can be of assistance in the preparations, please allow me the honour.'

'I believe we are ready,' the Emperor said. He and Amanda positioned themselves in front of the volcano. A guard shoved the mayor back. The Emperor raised his arms to address his subjects. 'The sacrifice is prepared…' There was a roar from the crowd. The Emperor quietened them with a twitch of his little finger.

'Before I toss her over, I shall throw my final bean to the gods.'
The audience gave a communal groan.

'It needs to be a healthy bean,' the mayor said. 'The gods will not be appeased by a rotten one.'

'I have a wholesome bean.' The Emperor rolled it between his fingers.

The mayor frowned. 'It would be wonderful news if there was no need for a human sacrifice.'

'Indeed,' the Emperor answered.

'But wait,' the mayor raised his voice. 'Isn't it customary to perform the sacred rite of the cocoa toss first?'

'The sacred what? I have never done that before.'

'I read about it in a library book.' The mayor gave a nervous titter and raised a hand to cover his mouth.

'It is time the library was scheduled for closure,' the Emperor said. 'The island needs a new reptile house. It can do without a library.'

'A short poem will suffice,' the mayor said.

Jack placed his palms over his ears. The townspeople hushed to allow the Emperor to recite.

'The mayor is heading off,' Jack whispered to Amanda as the Emperor launched into a second verse.

'The guards are in place,' Amanda answered. 'Let's hope our assumptions are correct.'

The Emperor balanced on one leg and shook the other in the air. 'I am standing on my right leg...' He looked down and changed legs, '...holding the bean aloft. I am about to throw it in, after I have coughed.'

'Is that a foreign, five-fanged fork-tail behind him?' someone called from the crowd. The Emperor started and dropped the bean over the edge. He would have dropped himself had Amanda not grabbed hold of his coat. The crowd made an 'ooh' as the bean fell in slow motion.

'I call to the chocolate-giving gods – are you appeased?' the Emperor shouted down the volcano, holding a hand to his ear.

The people raised their hands to copy him. Those at the back of the crowd, nearest to the cocoa plants, shook their heads and stamped their feet. 'We need a sacrifice, we need a sacrifice. Toss the tosser over.'

Amanda felt a hand on her shoulder and she was jostled towards the rim.

'There hasn't been time for the bean to reach the bottom of the volcano. I haven't heard a plop,' she protested.

'You won't.' A deep voice silenced the crowd. Two guards marched forwards, swinging the mayor between them. 'We apprehended this man with this net.' The man who had spoken demonstrated a child's fishing net. The cocoa bean that the Emperor had thrown into the volcano was resting in the mesh.

'There has been a mistake. That is my own, personal bean.' The mayor assumed an affronted air.

Jack freed the bean from the netting and held it up to show the letter "E" painted on the surface in imperial purple. The guards thrust the mayor to the ground at the Emperor's feet. He remained on his knees, grovelling.

'We have our sacrificial offering.' The Emperor raised his arms and the crowd responded with a cheer. The mayor tugged the hem of the Emperor's coat. 'Unhand me, you rogue, or I shall need a suit of new clothes,' the Emperor said.

'You can't throw me into the volcano. I have a wife and five young children to support,' the mayor cried.

'No you don't,' the Emperor said. 'What's wrong? You were happy for others to be sacrificed – including me.'

'We can let the hat decide,' Amanda declared.

'Good idea.' The Emperor gave her a jaunty slap on the back.

She had requested that the hat be brought up and it was set in front of them. 'Should the mayor...' Amanda began.

'The ex-mayor,' the Emperor interrupted. 'He is sacked forthwith.'

'Should the ex-mayor be thrown into the volcano?' Amanda asked. She peeked into the hat. There were two cards lying at the bottom. Both of them said 'yes' in red lettering. The crowd chanted 'yes, yes, yes'. Amanda reached in and picked a card. She looked at the ex-mayor, cowering like beaten eggs and whipped cream, and hesitated to read it.

'What does it say?' the Emperor asked.

'Yes, yes, yes.' The chanting rose.

'It says "no",' Jack said, reading the card over Amanda's shoulder. The mayor collapsed with a sigh and the crowd booed. Before anyone could query the answer, Jack seized the card and tore it into four pieces. He threw it, and the cocoa bean, into the volcano. A puff of blue smoke blew up.

'Look, the gods are happy,' the Emperor declared. 'They are appeased.'

'Will they heal our cocoa plants?' a woman asked.

'Indeed,' the jailor answered. 'Look.'

The cocoa plants were bursting into flower before their eyes. The crowd gave a cry and the Emperor was hoisted aloft in the strong arms of a dozen islanders.

'Three cheers for the Emperor – may he dine on chocolate for ever. Hip, hip hooray.'

'Take this fellow to the dungeons, my good man,' the Emperor said to the jailor. The ex-mayor with the bald, wrinkly head was hauled to his feet and handcuffed.

'You haven't heard the last of me.' He shook his manacled fists at Amanda and Jack before the jailor marched him off.

'Ungrateful man,' Jack said. 'We should have let him be thrown into the volcano.'

'Don't worry,' Amanda said, putting a hand on Jack's shoulder. 'That's what baddies are supposed to say. We won't see him again, at least not in this story. I thought you were magnificent. Your quick thinking got me out of a tight spot. That fast track promotion won't be far off.'

'I think it's time we finished this adventure first, ma'am.'

'After we've stocked up on chocolate,' Amanda agreed.

The Emperor promised Amanda and the Tantalising Chocolate Company™ enough cocoa to fill the ship's hold. Amanda returned her spectacles to the butler and they made their way back to the pier. Jack thought it best not to mention the pink-spiked crocodile snapping at her heels on the way down the mountain.

And that, my friends, is the secret behind the unique taste of Tantalising Chocolate™.

The One-Armed Bandit

The king stood at the top of the stairway, running his fingers along the alabaster bannister. The smoothness pleased him. He put a slippered foot on the intricately patterned Persian carpet and felt rich. He descended the stairs to the grand hall, allowing his footsteps to echo around the marble walls and felt powerful. He stood alone in the chamber and knew he was perfect.

Outside the palace, his subjects gathered in the market square, as they did every month, to await his decrees. His ministers huddled in their ermines on the balcony, slate tablets in hand, ready to implement his commands. The king counted to ten as he admired the Doric pillars, hand painted frescoes and carved ceiling. Satisfied, he tip-toed to the centre of the hall, where a jaded one-armed bandit was propped up with a wooden block. The slot for pennies was sealed over with duct tape, and a sign declaring "NOT IN USE" was pasted on the side, with the final "E" scratched out. The king reached for the lever, tightened his fingers round the metal, then jerked it down. The mechanism creaked and the symbols in the little windows spun round; not as fast as in previous years, but fast enough to allow the king to anticipate what would appear when they finished their revolutions.

Click, click, click.

Three new symbols, three new decrees.

As the king marched towards the balcony, he noticed a tiny gold thread hanging loose from the sleeve of his jacket. That didn't please him.

The crowd nudged one another and hushed as their king appeared. He cleared his throat and announced the salutation: 'Greetings nonentities.' The audience applauded. 'Here are this month's decrees.' An expectant hush cut the air. 'One: the tax on citrus fruits will increase by ten percent.'

There were groans from parts of the square, changing to cheers when the royal guard made their presence known.

'Two: Tuesdays shall be public holidays.'

This time the celebration was genuine, especially among the schoolchildren. They were brought into line by a sharp blast of the headmistress' whistle.

'And finally, on the last day of the month, a tailor shall be led blindfolded to the market square and shot by firing squad.'

The sun darkened, and the birds stopped singing. A decree of such a nature had never been heard before, not even in the king's grandmother's day, and she had been an evil witch.

'The one-armed bandit has spoken,' the king finished. He looked around at his ministers and smiled. 'I think I'll have duck for dinner today.'

Claudius stood still as the townsfolk around him dispersed. The colour drained not only from his cheeks, but also from his suit. He felt under-dressed, naked. It took him a moment to realise someone was waving at him from across the square. Feebly, he lifted a hand to wave back. The other man approached him.

'What do you make of that, then?' Stanley asked.

'It's preposterous!' Claudius thrust the words out like a needle through leather.

'Which one of us will it be?' Stanley's voice implied it wasn't going to be him.

'We need to call an extraordinary general meeting of the guild. This situation must be thoroughly thought through before a decision can be made.'

'Aye.' Stanley ran his tongue round the inside of his mouth.

'Thoroughly thought through.'

Claudius took a pocket diary, bound in kid-leather and edged in gold, from his inside pocket. He tweezed out the pencil lodged in the spine and chewed the end. 'Where and when should we meet?'

'We're here now.'

'But it isn't in my diary. We need time to come up with a solution to our dilemma.'

'I've come up with one already,' Stanley said with a grin, that was nipped by Claudius' frown.

'I am the king's personal tailor,' Claudius reminded him. 'I create bespoke clothing for lords and ladies. My shirts dance into shape on the chest. My jackets are sewn with...'

'Stardust; aye, I know. Meanwhile, I employ half the town to churn out shirts and trousers for the rest of the population. Who do you think would be more missed?'

'I see you don't wear your factory suits, but we needn't argue about it. I suggest we meet this evening, in the Hat and Rabbit at half past seven.'

'Eight o'clock,' Stanley replied. 'And it's your round.'

The inn was crammed to bursting, thanks to a live screening of the lettuce growing championship final. Lettuces brought Claudius out in suppurative boils. His skin tingled at the mention of the word and he feared sitting would be a delicate manoeuvre. Stanley relieved two tourists of their seats while Claudius bought the drinks. He shifted his way past the revellers, carrying the glasses close to his chest. On screen, the kingdom champion produced his lilac cos and the spectators rose to cheer. The pumping fist of a local farmer nudged Claudius' elbow, sending his Advocaat and lime dribbling down his silk shirt.

'You clot! I'll see you dunked in the frog pond for that.'

The farmer stammered an apology, wiping at Claudius' shirt

with his stained neckerchief. Claudius pushed him aside. The rest of the lettuce fans in the room parted to allow him to pass.

'You shouldn't get uptight,' Stanley advised, as Claudius set his beer on the table. 'You only have thirty days to live. Enjoy them.'

'What makes you think I will be the one to be shot?'

'I have a wife and five children. Nobody cares about you.'

'That isn't true, there's ... and ... perhaps ...' Claudius counted on his fingers, gave up and sulked.

'When the time comes, can I have your sewing machine?' Stanley asked.

'Certainly not.'

'There you go, being peevish again.'

Claudius sat in silence, sipping the remains of his drink. Stanley gulped his down and waited for Claudius to fetch another. 'If you've nothing further to offer, I'll be on my way,' he said, when the refill didn't materialise.

'Wait!' Claudius jumped in his chair. 'I have an idea. I believe it is time we allowed a new member into our sacred guild of tailors.'

'Oh? You have always argued for a closed shop, to safe-guard our stitching.'

'In the past, yes, that has served us well; but the town has grown, and we are getting older. There is work for another tailor.'

'Do you have somebody in mind?' Stanley probed.

'No-one in particular, but there would be certain requirements.'

'Such as?'

'Someone from outside the kingdom.'

'Unfamiliar with the king's decree,' Stanley qualified.

'Someone whose language skills aren't sharp.'

'So they won't understand.'

'Someone with little money, and a family that need providing for,' Claudius continued.

'A desperate man, who will agree to anything to help his family.'

'Exactly.'

'You are inviting someone into our guild to be shot,' Stanley clarified.

'I didn't make the decree. Besides, can you be sure the king will choose *me*?'

Stanley ran his tongue round his mouth. It was an annoying habit that Claudius deplored, but he kept this opinion to himself. Stanley gave a nod and clicked his empty glass against Claudius'. 'Proposal seconded.'

'Good.' Claudius smiled. 'I suggest we take a trip to the refugee camp tomorrow to select a suitable candidate.'

'You can go on your own. I'll be busy in my vegetable plot, laying a long-acting nerve poison to eliminate snails.'

The train line terminated a mile from the refugee camp. There were no buses or cabs. There was no need for them. The unmanned railway station was the only building in sight.

'The camp is that way, sir,' the guard informed Claudius, before blowing his whistle and jumping back on the train.

The engine wheeled out of sight, leaving an eerie silence. Claudius felt like he was in a vacuum on a distant star. He stumbled along a dust track towards the camp, with vultures circling overhead. He thought he could make out the silhouettes of coyotes. Red signs warned him he was approaching a restricted zone and he was stopped by armed soldiers who demanded to see his papers. Ahead of him, Claudius could see a twenty foot high stone wall, trimmed with barbed wire. When he reached the gate, a notice informed him the wire was electrified.

'What business have you here?' the sergeant at the entrance demanded.

Claudius pulled himself up and puffed out his chest. 'I am the king's tailor. I have come to find an apprentice.'

The sergeant and his junior officer burst out laughing. Even the Rottweiler on its flimsy lead rolled on the ground, kicking its legs. Claudius guessed that news of the king's decree had reached their barren outpost.

'Do you have the king's permission?' the sergeant asked.

'I have a proclamation from the President of the Sacred Guild of Tailors, ratified by the Vice-president, Secretary and Treasurer of the aforementioned guild.' Claudius produced a scroll from his travelling bag.

The sergeant scrutinised the writing.

'This is signed by yourself and someone called ... Hanley? Manley?'

'Stanley. Stanley Sewman: the Vice-president and Secretary.'

The sergeant flicked his eyes back and forth across the paper, then examined Claudius, before relenting. 'Very well. Wait here while we find suitable candidates.'

Claudius wobbled on a rickety stool in the guardhouse and smiled at the junior officer, as the man oiled his rifle. 'Is there much call for that?' he asked, nodding towards the gun.

The man ignored his question. In the yard, Claudius could hear shouting. A whip was cracked, and he lost his balance and fell off the stool. He got to his feet and was arranging the folds of his tweed jacket when the sergeant returned, pulling a chain. Three men in filthy yellow tunics were attached to it by ropes, the ends tied round their wrists. The sergeant stopped and gave the chain a tug, knocking the three weak-legged men to their knees.

'These are refugees, not criminals, yes?' Claudius said. 'I wouldn't want to enrol anyone of a dubious character into our sacred guild.'

'Introduce yourselves to the King's Master Tailor,' the sergeant growled.

Two of the men cowered and were silent, but the third tutted and reached over with his bound hands to brush a flake of dust from the sleeve of Claudius' jacket. 'Much better,' he said.

'Who are you?' Claudius asked.

'I am not a criminal, sir. I too am a master tailor, forced to leave my home and position, because of war. I once made gowns for my Empress and dancing suits for her consort that could waltz on their own. I was a rich man, an important man, but I spent my money getting here. I am no longer honoured.' He raised his roughened hands to inspect them. 'My fingers are swollen and my palms are cracked, but I can still sew.'

'I imagine you will find standards in this kingdom much higher than in your own,' Claudius replied, 'but you will do. Do you have a family?'

'A wife and three children. They are the reason I left my homeland.'

'Excellent,' Claudius smiled. 'Do you have a name?'

Claudius marked another day off his calendar as he prepared for bed. There were only twenty days left in the month. The new tailor, Aslo, was settling in well. So well, he had been asked to make a shirt for the king. His children were invited to play with those at the royal court. Claudius couldn't sleep. His plan wasn't working. He was being usurped. There was only one thing left to do: a drastic measure, but a necessary one. That night, Claudius broke open his piggy bank, packed his valuables in a travelling case, and fled the kingdom.

'We don't need tailors here,' he was told, when he applied for a work permit in the next country. 'In fact, we're overrun by them. Citizens from your kingdom who can't get into your guild; funny that.'

'I have money,' Claudius offered.

'Give me a thousand and I'll see what I can do.'

Claudius counted out the notes, but a permit didn't arrive. He waited in a five-star hotel, then a bed and breakfast establishment, and finally a hostel, before realising he should move on. In the next kingdom, he was requested to attend an interview with the employment official's trainee assistant. The meeting was in a dimly lit basement. Claudius took a seat opposite a puffy-faced woman wearing a plain, cotton tunic. His gaze was drawn to her elaborate headwear. To call it a hat would have been a criminal injustice. The brim accommodated a model train that whirled round a miniature domed city, constructed from chocolate and candies. At every puff of steam, the delicious fragrance of spring rosebuds wafted across the desk.

'It's a grade three,' the woman explained. 'When I finish my training, I'll earn a grade five: an ocean liner with the aroma of sandalwood.'

'Delightful.' Claudius clasped his knees. 'About my work permit ...'

The woman shuffled a pile of papers. 'Occupation?'

'I'm a tailor.'

'You make tails?' The woman rubbed her chin. 'A new fashion for us, but I can see it catching on. Wagging tails when we're happy, swishing tails when we're cross. Luxury furs or rat tails for the unemployed.' She stared at Claudius.

'I make clothes,' Claudius corrected her.

'Not tails?' The train on the hat screeched to a halt. Sparks flew from the rails.

'Tailcoats, perhaps,' Claudius offered. If the woman had had a tail, it would have been swishing. 'But mainly shirts, jackets and trousers.'

'We have no need of those.'

'Tunics?'

'Good afternoon,' she said, dismissing him with a puff of steam from the train.

It was still morning. Claudius was tempted to break off the ginger snap, model clock tower on her hat to show her. Although he was partial to these biscuits, he didn't feel that would help his case.

He paid two hundred coins to enter the neighbouring state, but no-one required a tailor there either. When his money ran out, he sold his fine clothes. He walked the streets dressed in rags and bit his nails to temper the pangs of hunger. Children threw mud at him and shouted names. He wasn't familiar with the language, but he knew what they were calling him. It came as a relief when he was arrested as a vagabond and thrown in the dungeons.

'We don't want parasites here,' the jailer chaffed. 'You will be deported back to your own country.'

A number was painted on a board and hung round Claudius' neck. His head was shaved and he was hustled into a cattle truck that bumped its way back to his homeland, passing the refugee camp with its wailing inmates.

'Hurry up, or you'll miss supper.' The prison guard jabbed Claudius in the backside with his bayonet, to speed him into an overcrowded cell that smelt of urine. 'It's leftover lettuce from the championship final. A tad soggy, but the slime can be wiped off. If you're lucky, you'll find a snail.'

Claudius scratched his itchy scalp. 'Thank you, but I'm not hungry.' His stomach gurgled. 'What day is it?'

'It's the last day of the month.' The guard clicked his tongue to make a noise like bullets popping from a gun. 'I'm to be part of the firing squad in the market square this evening. I've polished my rifle already.'

'Congratulations.' Claudius swallowed. 'And has a tailor been selected?'

'Certainly,' the man answered. 'The Sacred Guild of Tailors has nominated ... you.'

'But I'm the President of the Guild.'

'Then you have made a noble gesture, sir.'

Claudius' legs were shaking, but he pictured himself shoving Stanley's head down into a tub of tacking pins and managed to stand his ground. 'Would I be allowed a last request?'

'Why, of course.'

'I would like to speak with the king, before my execution.'

'It would be difficult speaking to him afterward,' the guard joked. Claudius didn't laugh.

The king agreed to this request and Claudius was brought before him in his mouldy rags, stinking of the rat-ridden dungeon. He couldn't help noticing how sharp the king's suit was, exquisitely tailored with not a stitch visible. It wasn't one of his suits. He fell on his knees before the king.

'Majesty, please, I have done nothing wrong. I haven't stolen or killed. I have always paid my taxes.'

'It's nothing personal, Claudius, although the last suit you made for me did have a loose thread.'

'If you are unhappy with my work, allow me to make you a wonderful new suit, better than anything you have worn before. Sumptuous silk, hand-dyed by the craftswomen in the mountains, with the threads spun by silver spiders. The buttons will be crafted from pink topaz, set in white gold.'

'Hmm.' The king pondered the suggestion.

'And a hat,' Claudius added.

'I'm afraid the one-armed bandit has spoken.'

'It is a mere gaming machine.'

'And what is life, but a game. Sometimes you win, sometimes you lose. Start changing the rules and it leads to anarchy. Take him away, guards.'

'Nobody wins against the one-armed bandit,' Claudius muttered, and was biffed on the head by the butt of the guard's gun.

A crowd gathered in the market square. Claudius could hear their excited murmuring, as he was led blindfolded to the execution spot. His bladder was weak and he feared making a fool of himself, even in death.

'Halt.'

Claudius stopped. He felt strong arms on his shoulder and he was twirled round. He heard the shuffling of footsteps as the soldiers took their positions. The crowd was quiet. Claudius' teeth chattered.

'Ready. Aim. Fire.'

Claudius heard the blast of the guns discharging and fell to the ground. Apart from skinning his knees on the stone, there wasn't the expected pain. He was alive. He felt his chest for gunshot wounds and blood. The blindfold was whipped from his head, and the king was standing before him.

'Stop sniveling, nincompoop; they fired blanks.'

'Blanks? I see. Can I go home now, please?' Claudius' bottom lip quivered as he spoke.

'Go home and get to work. I want that suit you promised me ready by Friday, or you'll be dunked in the frog pond.'

'Th ... this Friday? I may need help.'

The king was walking off. Claudius took his lack of a refusal to mean he was in agreement. A picture of the fortress and its desperate inhabitants flashed into his head. He would need lots of help, he decided. It really was time the guild opened its door to new members.

The king returned to his palace, and the next day descended to the great hall to pull the lever of the one-armed bandit. The symbols wheeled round and stopped where fate intended. The king strode to the balcony to address his subjects.

'Greetings, my loyal servants. Here are this month's decrees. One: bars will be closed on Mondays until further notice. Two: church bells will be rung at four o'clock every morning. Three: all snails shall have their shells painted gold, and will be given the freedom of the kingdom. Anyone hurting them, even unwittingly, will be thrown in the dungeons for a month.'

In the crowd, Claudius looked over to Stanley and gave a wry smile.

Zuri Mtu

Kofi closed the door, balancing his fingertips in the joint to prevent a draught slamming it shut. He bowed so that his bony forehead touched his bony knees. His spine cracked as he stood up. His first task was to check the thermostat. He tapped it with his knuckle. On occasions the indicator had been known to jam. He checked the sprinkler timer was set correctly. When any adjustments had been made, he toured the room to make sure no jungle rats had burrowed their way in overnight to gnaw on the bark with their yellow fangs. Then it was time for the methodical study of the trunk, using a magnifying glass to spot the first powdery signs of fungus. Only when the leaf by leaf inspection of the sacred tree was complete, could Kofi sit down and unwrap his butter sandwich.

Once a week, every Monday afternoon, there was the detailed measuring of the fertiliser – two scoops, flattened with a metal bar, mixed with water to reach the red line and heated to body temperature. Kofi had to drip the liquid over the base of the tree, not too fast or the mixture would scald the roots. He marked everything down in a battered jotter with the stub end of a pencil. The height and width, the number of new leaves and the number of leaves lost. The presence of buds he marked with a special symbol, like that of a heart. Zuri Mtu, the ancient tree of their people, hadn't flowered for 2,597 days. It hadn't produced fruit for 4,842 days. It was over six hundred years old.

People said it was dying.

The forest surrounding the tree was cut down centuries before to build the city. Trees across the country were chopped down.

Zuri Mtu was the last of its kind. Kofi had tended it for thirty three years. His father, grandfather and great grand uncle tended it before him. The burden on him was heavy. He did not have a son and Zuri Mtu did not produce seeds. In the days before the protective tent was erected, before the heating system, controlled feeding tubes and daily watering regime were started, Zuri Mtu was at the mercy of the sun, droughts and sand storms. In those days it produced good fruit. Birds rested in its branches, taking twigs for their nests. Insects gobbled into the bark, leaving behind a green, flaky dust. Zuri Mtu embraced it all and flourished. It was happy. Now, to Kofi, the tree looked sad.

Could it feel it was dying?

At eight in the evening, as the sun went down, Kofi once more bowed to the tree and silently closed the door before heading home. He lived alone, since his mother died, in a one-roomed apartment in a block of flats with no foundations - ready to crumble when the land shifted. In the morning when he stepped outside to cross the street and walk the three miles to the nearest water pump he was met by goats and chickens. His nostrils were assailed by the aromas of pigswill and untended garbage left to rot in the sun. Refuse that even the beggars rejected. Babies wailed, growing thinner and fouler. Kofi washed at the pump then continued a further two miles to the tree. His sandals had holes in the soles and the thorns on the path scratched his feet. He was saving his wages to buy a new pair. He supped on boiled rice and vegetables grown in a window box, heated on a camp stove fuelled by goats' dung. He coughed his way through prayers before bed.

On Tuesdays, visitors came from the richer parts of the country and from foreign lands to pay their penny and admire the six hundred year old history lesson.

Look, don't touch.

Kofi took their money and tore off receipts from his book. He was happy to recount stories from past generations.

'Six hundred years old, you say?'

'Nearer seven.' Kofi would swell, choking with pride.

'The only tree of its kind in the country?'

'In the world.'

The tourists were impressed. They gave Kofi an extra penny. Today the group was smaller, but the lingering whiff of aftershave and body perfumes promised hefty tips. Kofi smiled at them.

'All this must cost a fortune to maintain.'

The voice was nasal. Kofi wasn't sure whether to agree or deny it. He rubbed his fingers together.

'Zuri Mtu is a gift beyond cost.' He had heard his father say that and rub his hands together. It sounded clever.

'What does it do?'

'It is a tree.'

'All this heating, lighting and goodness knows how much water for a half dead lump of wood. Outside this tent people are starving and dying of thirst. They are forced to walk miles for a few bucket of untreated water.' The female voice was loud and high pitched.

Kofi cowered, listening to the growing mumbles of discontent.

'It is immoral.'

'Something should be done.'

'They could build hospitals with the money. Get decent plumbing in the schools. Provide meals for the elderly.'

'Zuri Mtu is a national treasure.' Kofi wiped his neck with his handkerchief. He would give these people their pennies back if they weren't happy.

The group wouldn't hear of this, but they left disgruntled. Some people were only happy when they were moaning, Kofi thought.

'Don't listen to them.' He wiped the lower leaves with his stained handkerchief. 'You are Zuri Mtu grown from the seed of the great tree of wisdom and knowledge, where birds of paradise frolic in the branches.'

The following Monday a group gathered outside the tent. Men with too much money to work and women who liked excitement. They carried banners. Kofi had never learned
  to read.

'Visiting is on a Tuesday,' Kofi said.

'We are not here to pay our pennies and stare at a tree.'

They told Kofi what their banners said.

Water for people, not trees.

Money for wards, not wood.

Kofi recognised one of the men from the previous week, but not the others. They didn't belong to the neighbourhood. Their clothes weren't the hand-me-down shreds of generations and they could write the words on their placards. Kofi squeezed past them with a toothless smile, ruffled by the elbows of two women as he opened the door.

'Blackleg. Scab.'

Kofi shut the door with less care than was due. He locked it behind him, bending over to regain his breath. 'Do not worry, Zuri Mtu. All this will be forgotten in a few days. You must have seen much of this in your long life.'

By the time Kofi left for home the protestors were gone, but their banners were left at the side of the road. They provided a surprise supper for a goat that was munching its way through 'books not bark'.

The next day the protestors were back, angrier, and complaining about their chewed up banners. They blamed Kofi for the damage.

'It is not my goat,' Kofi said.

They were joined by people from the shanty huts on the outskirts of the city - people with no jobs, no legs, missing eyes, pox scars and time on their missing hands. The group had a leader, a man no older than Kofi's cousin's son, with golden hair bleached by the sun. An Adonis in jeans and a well-ironed polo shirt.

'It is time, friends, to be free of meaningless traditions. It is time to put people first. What use is a barren tree? Step into that tent and you will be charged a penny to see water sprinkled into the air to keep a tree moist. There is enough water inside that tent to quench the city's thirst, but ask the old lady by the roadside why she falters. She has not drunk for two days. She is too weak to walk to the well. Ask the infant dying of diarrhoea why. The water is unclean. The money spent mollycoddling a piece of wood as if it were a premature baby should be spent on real children.'

The girl at the front cheered and the others joined in. They moved to block the door of the tent.

'Excuse me please,' Kofi tried to get through. He had listened to what the young man said. He spoke well. Kofi didn't disagree that more should be done for the needy. More money should be spent on schools and hospitals, but why pick on Zuri Mtu? The tree was the last of its kind. Once it was gone, it would be no more.

'Forget the tree, old man. Get a proper job.'

The crowd surged round him, hands waving in the air, fingers prodding towards his face. He wanted to vanish into the air. For the first time in thirty three years Kofi didn't go to work. He turned round and trudged home wondering what he would do with the day. The following morning he set off early, hoping to avoid the demonstrators. The area was clear, but thick red tape was stuck across the door to the tent, barring his way.

No Entry.

'We've won.'

Kofi recognised the ringleader, standing alone with a whitened smile. 'No more money is to be wasted on a tree.'

'What about my job?' Kofi's knees shook.

'There are plenty of other jobs.'

Other jobs maybe, but nobody wanted a fifty year old, unskilled labourer. The jobs were taken by sober faced teenagers and family men in smart suits. Kofi walked the streets, waiting for the new schools and hospitals to be built with the money, hoping to apply for a job as a janitor. Nothing came. Three months after the tent surrounding Zuri Mtu was pulled down, the top branches snapped and fell to the ground with a crack like dry firewood. Another month and the leaves turned black and dropped onto the arid earth. In December the tree was declared a danger to the public and the chain saws moved in to demolish all that was left of the six hundred year old tree. The city was no better off. In fact it was poorer, because the visitors with their foreign accents and shiny pennies no longer came. The demonstrators moved on to another city, another cause, freeing thousands from the shackles of ancient traditions.

Kofi stood in the sun, shielding his eyes, on the spot where Zuri Mtu had viewed the world. He was a simple man and his simple thought was that there should be room in the world for simple people with simple ideas. Perhaps Zuri Mtu wasn't a descendent of the tree of wisdom and knowledge, carried from paradise on a cherry blossom breeze. Perhaps the great tree of wisdom and knowledge did not exist. Zuri Mtu was six hundred years old. It was the last of its kind. It had a spirit and that spirit had a voice. Kofi removed his hat to run his hands through what was left of his hair. Before putting it back on he paused to wipe the red sand that had gathered on the rim. He'd worn the hat to work every day for the past thirty three years. His father gave it to him the day he took over the role of keeper. A rite of passage. A simple gift. As Kofi rubbed the worn fabric he spotted something stuck in the fold. His knotted fingers freed the small, brown oval. Crinkled, but solid, it was a seed. A seed from Zuri Mtu. A gift to its loyal servant. Kofi held the seed between his forefinger and thumb, felt the life pulse within it and smiled.

By the Light of the Moon

I

'Sorry, you can't go through there miss.'

Eyes to the ground, searching for thoughts, Dawn hadn't seen the barrier or the police officers. She dropped her shopping bag.

'That's my house. What's happened to dad?'

'Don't worry, nothing has happened to your father. Do you know that man?' One of the officers pointed at the roof of Dawn's red brick, mid-terrace cottage.

She looked up to see a young man in the lotus position, with the sun casting an aura round him that lifted the grey slates he sat on to the level of an altar. He was wearing blue jeans and a white T-shirt with a logo. She took him for a student with time on his hands to delve into the mysteries of the universe. Even so, a sit-in on her roof was weird.

'No, never seen him before,' she said. 'What's he doing?'

The policeman didn't answer. His attention was taken by a black Rolls gliding to a halt. The driver opened the door for his passenger. Cameras flashed. The man raised an arm to cover his face and the driver moved towards the photographers. Dawn thought she knew the passenger, but with a fancy car, a chauffeur and a hand-tailored suit, it could be anyone from a magazine or one of her books. The police sergeant fussed around Mr Bigwig, convincing him that matters were in hand.

'Is there any change in the situation?' the man demanded.

'Not as yet, sir.'

'Well that's good,' Dawn said, forgetting the conversation

didn't involve her. The corner of the great man's mouth turned down. He flicked a misplaced silver hair from his eye and reached for the megaphone the sergeant offered. Shoulders taut, he was confident of getting what he wanted. His clean-shaven chin was baptised in Oriental amber, vetiver, heliotrope and ylang ylang with a top note of citrus and lily of the valley. The regimental tie and cufflinks shouted "old school", but wasn't that a cartoon mouse pin badge on his lapel?

It was.

The man strode forwards and spoke into the funnel. 'Sholto, this is your father speaking.'

Dawn picked up her shopping and edged towards him. 'That's my house,' she said. 'My dad is waiting for his tea.' He showed no sign of hearing her. A name popped into her head. 'You're Abelard du Niaull, aren't you?' There was no response. No doubt he was used to people telling him who he was.

'Sholto, I am ordering you to stop this childish nonsense and come down,' he called.

He was used to being obeyed. The notion left a gritty feel in Dawn's mouth. 'I think you are the childish …the childish…' She couldn't think of a fitting insult. '…Hobgoblin.'

Abelard looked down. The edge of his lower lip twitched. 'And who are you, miss?' He spoke through the megaphone. Dawn jumped.

Was it so obvious she was unmarried? The flat-soled shoes with her bunions pushing out, the own-brand eau de Cologne or the cat fur on her knitted sweater, but why should that matter?

'Dawn. Dawn Adamson. I work in the library.'

He lowered the megaphone. 'The library?' Dawn could taste the disdain. The library was a blot on the townscape earmarked for redevelopment. He looked her up and down. She guessed he wasn't undressing her in his mind. 'Are you a friend of my son's?' It sounded like an accusation.

'Him?' She tried to point, but in doing so she tipped her bag and a book fell out. It bounced on the pavement and landed on Abelard du Niaull's brogues. He leant down and picked it up by the edge of the cover. Dawn grimaced at the damage to the spine.

He held the book at arm's length and she snatched it from him. Her hand touched his and her fingertips tingled. A girlish giggle arose from deep in her chest. It took her a moment to realise what it was. She smothered it before it surfaced.

Abelard du Niaull pouted. 'That house isn't yours. It belongs to the land lieutenant. It belongs to me.' He dismissed her and glanced at his Swiss watch before handing the megaphone to the nearest police officer.

The boy on the roof hadn't moved and Abelard du Niaull stood fidgeting with his ring. He wore it on the little finger of his left hand, but it was a wedding band.

Of course.

"Maverick" Mauritia du Niaull was what was happening in the art world. She had an exhibition in London: *Life beyond time and place*. The title had intrigued Dawn. The wide-eyed, haunted stare of the artist told its own story, although the tabloids pretended to be shocked by her premature death. She was found by her son fully clothed in a running bath. It reeked of heroin, but the story fizzled out – a cover-up. Now his son was going off the rails. Dawn could feel sympathy for du Niaull with his cartoon badge, but he shouldn't treat his son like a kid, and it *was* her house.

The sergeant and a female colleague caught hold of Dawn's arms and dragged her towards the cordon – a line of tape strung between a litter bin and a lamppost. The boy on the roof stood up, dislodging a tile that shimmied down the side. The onlookers moved back as it hit the pavement and shattered. The police officers let go of Dawn.

'He's on the move. Quick, after him.'

Sholto took a run and leapt from the last house on her row to the first house on the next, a gap of ten feet – that was class.

'Out of the way, miss.' The police tried to keep up with him on the ground. Within minutes they, the local journalists and the spectators were gone.

Dawn didn't follow the parade. Neither did Abelard du Niaull. He stood gazing at the weather-beaten roof with its slates missing.

'Who'd have kids?' Dawn said.

Du Niaull twisted sharply. 'Jenkins, get the car.'

The chauffeur opened the door of the Rolls and Abelard du Niaull stooped to enter. He slid his window down.

'You can go in now.' He flicked a hand to indicate Dawn could enter her house then gave a wry smile. 'Your father is waiting for his… tea.'

'Who do you think you are, His Majesty?'

The window was raised and the car drove off.

Dawn pulled the police cordon free of the lamppost, but a smile surmounted her indignation. He had heard what she said. He had listened. She marched to the door with her head up and took the key from her pocket. Dad was in; she saw his nose peek round the curtains, but he wouldn't answer the door.

'It's me, dad,' she called.

'Get the kettle on, I'm parched,' the voice answered from the living room. 'What was that rumpus outside?'

Dawn carried her shopping to the kitchen. She heaved the bag onto the table then filled the kettle. As the water bubbled, she unpacked. The bread and scones she put in the fridge, the cat food and tins of peaches in the bread bin and the yoghurt in the cupboard below the sink with the drain cleaner. She was about to stuff the biscuits in the cutlery drawer when her father unbuttoned himself from the television and hobbled into the kitchen. He leaned against the cupboard Dawn wanted to get the mugs from. She knew he wouldn't shift until he got the answers he wanted.

'There were police outside. Are you in trouble?' His eyes danced.

'It was nothing, a boy fooling around,' Dawn said. 'I forgot the milk.'

'No milk.' Her father thumped his bony knuckle on the worktop. 'I fought for king and country and I don't get a spit of milk for my tea. A little milk and one sugar, that's all I ask.'

'Dad, you weren't in the War. You were at primary school when it ended.'

'I'd have fought if they'd let me. Wilma doesn't forget the milk.'

'Wilma is dead. She has been for seven years.'

Her father grunted. 'What's that damn squirrel doing in the

garden? Wait 'til I get my gun.'

'You don't have a gun.' Dawn looked out the window. A fat, grey squirrel was perched on the dividing wall between the properties. 'It must be from the park.'

'I don't see that useless cat of yours doing anything.'

Billy was weaving between her legs. Dawn bent to stroke him. The squirrel ran along the wall. It stopped to peer in the window and winked at her.

'Did you see that?'

'What?'

'Nothing.'

Her father stumbled to his armchair and Dawn poured the tea. She spooned a teaspoonful of sugar in her father's football mug, balanced a digestive on top then carried it to the living room and placed it on the coffee table.

'Out the way, I can't see the screen.'

She returned to the kitchen for her book. The cover showed a faded picture of a World War II plane with fire pluming from its engine. In the foreground, a broken China doll lay beside a large, grey dog. It was the dog that drew her to the book. The title was uninspiring. "Thirty Seconds to Impact" would have had more of an… impact, Dawn imagined, but the author had chosen *Nobody Loves Rose?*. There was no mention of the author's name, which was odd.

She took her tea and the library book to her bedroom and began to read. Although she was a patient reader, four chapters to draw out the drab, day-to-day lives of the Morton family members seemed excessive. She skipped three pages, but couldn't concentrate on the story.

What had the Buddha of Suburbia been doing on her rooftop? And why did Abelard du Niaull's touch still give her a delightful shiver?

II

'See you on Monday,' Eliza said.

'Yes, don't stay too late,' Corine added.

Dawn smiled, feigning ignorance of the message lurking below the surface of her colleagues' remarks.

It's time you got life – and a man.

She restocked the shelves, removed the damaged books and flicked through pages of unsolved murders, historical adventures and fantasy battles, before catching the seven o'clock bus home. It was empty. She popped a peppermint in her mouth, took her library book from her bag and opened it at her marker. Rose Morton, a nursery teacher, was in London visiting a sick aunt. It took her two pages to select a bunch of daffodils. Dawn was about to give up on the four hundred page saga when Gideon Davenport stepped off the train at Paddington station, trench coat over his arms, trilby cocked at a roguish angle and a lopsided smile on his chiselled face. By the time he bumped into Rose in the queue for a cab, he had snared Dawn in his trap.

She was the one hustled among the crowd at Paddington station in 1948, hearing the whistling of the trains, the shouting of the porters and the rush of the commuters. She could taste the smoke, smell the chicory coffee and feel the urgency in the air.

The unnamed author drew Gideon down to the last mole on his crushed left palm. He was a veteran of Dunkirk, scarred, mistrustful and bald.

Bald.

Dawn didn't like that. She blotted out the writer's detail, cut ten years from him and painted sharp eyes, greying hair and a strong chin – a bit like Abelard du Niaull. A lot like him, in fact. Dawn laughed. The driver had stopped at lights and he looked round.

'Good book?'

'Rubbish,' Dawn said.

To hell with Dunkirk, the spitfire on the cover made her see Gideon as an ex-fighter pilot. She gave him a regiment tie and a limp that the writer forgot to mention in the four hundred pages.

The bus passed the fire station. When a splatter of pigeon poop plopped against the window, Dawn was brought to her senses. They were at the park, three stops on from her house. Bustling Gideon and Rose into her bag, she pressed the button, dislodging an age-old gobbet of chewing gum.

'Are you sure, love?' The driver signalled and pulled in, moving off as soon as Dawn alighted.

It was a no man's land. The breeze blew fast food wrappers along the pavement and garden fences were scarred with crude graffiti. A boy kicked a football against the side of a house.

'Wot you gawking at?' He stepped towards Dawn. She hurried on and peeked through the bars into the park. Spray-painted boards hid the Victorian statues on the fountain and in the children's playground the swings, swung over the top bar by show-off hooligans, were roped off as a health hazard. Dawn felt a weight in her stomach, but a couple walking their Alsatian persuaded her it would be safe to take the shortcut.

She made her way along the nettle-choked avenue of flowerbeds, recalling their prize-winning days in the glam rock seventies when her father took Wilma and her there. She convinced herself she could still pick up the delicate scents.

Her father – she should phone him to let him know she would be late.

She rummaged in her bag then pictured her mobile lying beside her work computer. It didn't matter. The football programme would have started and dad wouldn't hear the phone.

'Salve domina.' A man dressed in a Roman toga saluted.

'Salve,' Dawn answered. Funny, the library hadn't been asked to hand out flyers for a "Bard in the Park" festival.

The bowling green was derelict, with only ghostly memories marking their ends. That couldn't be green smoke coming from the clubhouse roof. A rocket whizzed out the chimney. When she rubbed her eyes the building was dead. There was no lingering sulphurous smell. She carried on towards the gate. Someone was close behind her, invading her personal space. She quickened her step. The footsteps quickened. She stopped. The footsteps stopped a millisecond after her. She felt a tug on her shoulder and twisted round. The musky smell of male deodorant hung in the air as her bag was yanked from her. Before she could grab the strap, the youth ran off.

'Stop,' Dawn called. 'Come back.'

She set off after him – a flash of blue denim with a baseball cap low over his head. He wore it backwards, displaying the cartoon mouse logo. Pushing out the gate, Dawn kept going. She had a stitch in her side and her running was a walk-jog-walk. What would she do if she caught him? Shake him stupid, unless someone stopped her. Reaching a row of late opening shops, she lost him and halted to get her breath.

What now?

She was unharmed and her purse was safe in her jacket pocket. There was nothing of worth in the bag, only a handkerchief and the library book. Rose was bound to fall for Gideon's charm and hand over her inheritance, it was that kind of story, but it was library property. It was her duty to report it stolen.

'Oi, what are you up to?'

The voice came from the grocer's. The shop door was open and a youth darted out. He barged into Dawn, shoving her off the pavement. Without speaking, he pushed a leather bag into her hands.

It was her bag.

Bulging from the open compartment was a medley of apples, bananas and pears. The boy was halfway down the street, but turned to wave. It was Sholto, the boy on her roof, Abelard du Niaull's cartoon mouse son.

The grocer stomped out of his shop, mobile phone in one hand and a cricket bat in the other. Dawn looked from the missing end of his right thumb clasped round the bat to her bag. She opened her mouth to explain, but nothing came out. Her feet stuck to the pavement.

'Someone your age should know better. Don't give me sob stories. I'm calling the police.'

The grocer waved his bat. Dawn grabbed an apple from the bag and threw it.

Her aim was wide of stump and the apple missed the man and the bat, but the grocer staggered back holding his chest. Dawn ran, expecting a hand to grab her. She rounded the corner and knocked into Sholto outside a newsagent's. He was crushing his baseball cap into his back pocket. She took hold of his arm and dragged him into the shop until the grocer puffed past.

'What do you think you're doing?' she demanded. 'Does your father know?'

Sholto walked to the shop door, jerked his head at her and hopped out. She looked down the street, checking it was clear before stepping out after him.

'I was speaking to you,' she said.

The boy didn't respond.

'Beans not cold yet?' Dawn asked. It was an old joke; the twenty year old who didn't speak until his beans were cold. Life had been fine until then. She was about to explain, until it hit her. The papers had reported his inability to talk – a medical condition brought about by the shock of finding his mother. She reddened. 'Sorry.'

Sholto snatched a pear from her bag. He crunched into the fruit and the juice dribbled down his chin

'How do we communicate? How do you communicate with your dad? I don't do sign language.' Dawn fiddled with her fingers.

The boy pointed into the distance.

Dawn shook her head. 'You need to go home.' She was talking to him like he was a child, but he looked sixteen or seventeen, a full head taller than she was.

Sholto poked Dawn lightly in the abdomen, then pointed again to the spot past the new housing estate and out of town. Far, far away.

For a second the hazy image twinkled like in animated films and Dawn felt the warm glow she got when she drank mulled wine. 'What about your father?' she asked. 'Won't he mind?'

Sholto dropped the remains of the pear on the pavement and stamped his foot down to crush the pulp into the slabs. Dawn didn't react. He took an apple from her bag and offered it to her.

'It's stolen,' she said. 'I can't eat it.'

He tossed the apple in the air and watched it fall. Before it landed, he booted it across the road. The apple thumped against the windscreen of a parked car. He looked at Dawn, daring her to scold him.

'Very clever,' she said. 'If you're going to be childish, I'm going home.'

Sholto turned and strode off.

He had chosen her roof. Did that make her responsible for him?

Swinging the handles of her bag over her shoulder, she walked after him. He led the way through unknown alleys, out into the suburbs. A playground with a freshly painted climbing frame and shining swings edged onto a row of fields, marking the town's green belt boundary. Dawn's shoes pinched her toes and her feet hurt.

The match would be over and the pundits would have run out of clichés and superlatives. Her father would be shouting at Billy. He would want his dinner. She saw his unshaven face with its thin nose and lips.

'Wilma never left me alone in the evenings.'

'We've gone far enough,' she told Sholto.

He stopped and hunched in front of her like a garden gnome, smiling away their problems. He put his palms together and laid them like a pillow against his head. Dawn couldn't help laughing.

'You haven't a clue, have you? I'm going home.'

She took five steps towards the town. Sholto walked in the opposite direction, into the wild unknown.

She hesitated, then made her choice. 'Wait for me.'

On the right was a field of cows, ghostly shadows in the dusk that flickered between reality and secret realms. On the left was a harvested field with the sheared grass spikes protruding from the earth like spearheads. Despite the hostile imagery, Dawn could smell the homely silage. There was hope of finding a jolly farmer's wife who force-fed guests tea and scones. Her mouth watered.

When they reached the track to the farm, Sholto increased his pace to pass it. Dawn stopped, kicked off her shoes and planted herself on the verge to wriggle her toes. It hadn't been raining, but the grass was damp. She reached to pick a handful of daisies and laced the stems together in a chain. From the corner of her eye, she saw Sholto walk back. When he reached her he held out a hand.

'Thank you, kind sir.' She took his hand and he pulled her up. She rewarded him by placing the daisy chain round his neck, then leant on his shoulder to put on her moccasins. 'I'm not walking any further.' She put her hands together on the side of her head the way he had.

He stood for a moment, then shuffled in an exaggerated manner along the path to the farm. Dawn followed. The farms she knew were in library picture books, where the animals had alliterative names and spoke in rhyme.

Clarissa the crazy cow chewed cud
While Peter Pig enjoyed the mud.

The house was grand, old sandstone, built in a baronial style with a turret and arched entrance, but slates were missing from the roof and the guttering was damaged, leaving a stain where rainwater had dripped down the building. Dawn was drawn to the vintage car in the courtyard. Before she could run her fingers along the bonnet Sholto grabbed her sleeve and pulled her into the barn.

'Hey.'

The mould from the stored hay caught in her throat, although she found it wasn't unpleasant.

'I'll make myself at home,' she said, plonking her backside on the nearest hay bale, only to jump up with a screech.

Fred the farm cat gave a hiss
And warily eyed the little miss.

The cat darted out the barn door, tail up like a toilet brush. Sholto grabbed her and manhandled her to the back of the barn, behind a stack of bales. Before she could protest, she heard voices. Two men she couldn't see were talking in the doorway. A gruff voice spoke first.

'If they are in here the dog will sniff them out.'

III

Dawn held her breath. She edged along to see a shaggy dog the size of an exercise bike standing at the door. It had a nose to make an anteater proud and its mouth hung open, showing teeth stained by dribbles of saliva. The lines on his face smoothened. She glanced at Sholto. He lay back and chewed on a sprig of straw. He smiled at the dog and raised a finger to his lips. The dog padded out.

'Naw, he's no here,' the farmer said. 'Morpheus can sniff a penny in a petrol butt.'

'Very useful,' the second man said.

Dawn gasped. She remembered the car. It belonged to Abelard du Niaull. He was looking for his son and the tracks led here. She didn't move. The farmer had said "them". How did he know she was with Sholto? She squeezed her fingers to stop them fidgeting. The tension held for a moment, but the voices faded as the men left.

'I know where he will take her…'

There was the silence of mice scratching in the straw and birds testing the rafters for places to build nests. After a minute, Sholto got up and crept out. He returned holding the farm dog and beckoned her to stroke it. Dawn was a cat person. She had been bitten by the neighbour's spaniel when she was five, although it was Wilma, four years older and braver, who had pulled its ear and ran away. She tightened the knuckles of her hand and held it out. The dog nestled its head against her and she saw its name tag.

MORPHEUS MCGRAW – DO NOT FEED

Sholto pulled an apple from his pocket and offered it to the hound. Morpheus McGraw snatched the fruit, bit it in two and swallowed the pieces in one gulp. Dawn made a nest in the hay and settled. The hay was prickly but, warm and barring rats, it would do until morning.

'That apple better not give the dog wind,' she warned Sholto.

The shuffling of farmyard chickens, the smell of the hay and the itching of dust mites didn't prevent Sholto from enjoying the sleep of the just. Dawn was more sensitive to the environment. She rolled in a ball then stretched out, but couldn't get comfortable. She needed to empty her bladder, but it didn't seem right to do it in the barn. The dog was lying at the door with its head propped on its front paws.

Dusty the dog kept guard at night
The farm was safe 'til morning light.

The rhymes were getting silly. His name wasn't Dusty and she didn't feel safe. The hound watched as she tiptoed barefoot across the cold cobbles of the yard, turned behind the tractor shed and crouched against a convenient bush. As she searched in her pocket for a tissue, she heard a wolf whistle. She pulled up her clothes and stood up. Was that a shadow beside the fence? She caught the whiff of cigarette smoke.

'Is anyone there?'

Don't be stupid, who would wolf whistle at you?

The voice in her head was her sister's. When she returned to the barn the dog was on his feet, ready to search for her.

She settled into the imprint she'd made in the hay. At first light she reached in her bag for *Nobody Loves Rose*. Gideon, smoking American cigarettes, was taking Rose to a dance in the village hall. She was wearing her mother's chiffon dress. Dawn pictured herself with her best dress on as a teenager. It was a printed wrap that had belonged to Wilma and, although she had taken out the waist and pinned in the chest, it never hugged her figure the way it had her sister. Gideon was being eyed by a Chanel Vamp with pink champagne and Rose left early. Dawn knew the feeling. She read three more pages, but the party was over. She closed her eyes and dropped off with the book drooping from her hands. She woke to the sound of Sholto relieving himself in the corner of the barn.

'Can't you do that outside?' she complained.

Rubbing her neck, she looked round. Something was different. She couldn't say what exactly, but the colours were brighter, the outlines clearer. Her book was on the hay, an arm's width away. She put the bookmark between the pages and slipped it in her bag. Sholto brushed his teeth with a handful of straw and spat out a mouthful of dried grass. She shuffled into her shoes. Her tummy rumbled and she conjured up a plate of bacon, sausage and eggs, her imagination throwing in baked beans on toast for good measure. Sholto tugged at her sleeve.

'I haven't finished breakfast yet.'

They sneaked out the barn. Dawn splashed her face with water from a trough in the yard. The water got in her mouth and tasted foul. The farmer's voice came from the tractor shed. Sholto tiptoed past like a silent movie villain. Dawn wasn't in the mood to find it funny. When they reached the main road they turned away from the town. Lunch time came and went. By three o'clock, Dawn could feel blisters and her bunion was acting up. The road sign told them Dawn was as far from her home as she'd ventured in ten years.

'Where are we going?' she asked.

There was nothing there. There was *nothing* there, but as Sholto pointed the grass parted and a track emerged. She half expected it to be made of yellow bricks and run through a field of poppies. A dry stone wall ran alongside the path and she leant against it to rest. Put off by the smell in her bag, she had emptied out the mushy fruit the night before, but a green banana and five apples remained. She wiped one of the apples on her sleeve and took a bite. Stolen or not, it tasted delicious. Sholto stuck his hand in her bag.

'Manners!'

She jerked the bag away, but he nabbed the banana, peeling it and eating the flesh in three quick snaps. He threw the skin over the wall then snatched a couple of apples and shoved them in his pockets. With a deft swing of his limbs, he leapfrogged into the field behind. Dawn scrambled over, ripping the leg of her trousers below the knee. She trudged across the field behind Sholto; Catherine desperately clinging to Heathcliff's shadow on the Yorkshire moors.

The land sloped upwards and two dark dots marred the clean line of the horizon. Dead bushes, Dawn thought, wondering why she assumed they were dead. Sholto was communicating with them. He set off and the dots advanced towards him. Her poor feet would hardly make it beyond... the small cairn that had risen in front of her like Excalibur from the lake. Her eyes were deceiving her. She felt a panic attack coming on.

Breathe Dawn, deep breaths.

By the time her blood pressure was restored, Sholto was

walking towards her with two hairy moorland ponies keeping pace behind him. The larger animal had an evil look. Dawn checked herself. The horse had a walleye, the white showing more than was decent, but it was a dumb creature and not a demon. It stopped and pawed the ground. Dawn moved towards the other pony, a rough-coated grey mare. It let her stroke the white blaze on its nose and ruffle its ragged mane. She searched for an apple in her bag and offered it to the pony. Its floppy mouth sent pieces of fruit splattering over her jacket and blouse.

Sholto was sitting astride the larger horse. She didn't see or hear him mount. He was beside her then he was on the horse with no intermediate stage. She expected him to be wearing a suit of armour and carrying a sword. The ponies weren't used to being ridden and his mount circled, trying to knock him off. He held its mane with one hand and waved at her to mount the other pony.

'You are joking.'

The last thing with a mane and tail she had ridden was called Dobbin and had rockers. Sholto kicked his heels into his pony's flanks, sending the beast flying as if a swarm of bees was making honey in its ear. Dawn imagined wings unfolding around him. The second pony started to follow, but stopped to pull at the grass. She walked towards it, making soothing noises. When she reached it she stroked its neck. It gave a snort that sounded like a laugh and lifted its nose. 'Let's see. Maybe…'

The straps of her handbag reached over the animal's head. It drew back, neighing, but she succeeded in getting her bag round its neck and that gave her a feeling of control. She couldn't mount from the ground. The sunlight caught the cairn and she coaxed the pony across the field.

At first she tried climbing onto the pile of stones while holding the animal, but when its nose touched the stones it shied away, yanking Dawn's shoulder with it. She let go of her bag. The pony stood still, allowing her to scramble onto the cairn and wobble to a half-standing position. She thrust a leg into the pony's belly. It pranced sideways and Dawn waved her arms to keep her balance.

At the third attempt she got across its back and grabbed her bag to right herself. The pony smelt of wet grass and something unfamiliar – earthy, but nice. She pulled at her trousers to get comfortable

'Giddy up, Daisy.'

Daisy dropped her head to pull at a clump of clover and Dawn was catapulted forwards. She grabbed a handful of hair to stop from tumbling over the animal's ears and gave the pony a kick with her heels the way Sholto had. It plodded at a slow walk, but Dawn's insides bubbled with every bounce. Her buttocks felt like they were attending a step class and despite the fat covering them, they ached. Sholto was waiting across the field. He edged his pony on when she caught up and she was bumped and swivelled on Daisy's back for another two miles.

When they came to a stream, Daisy refused to budge. The sparkling water was tempting and Dawn slipped off her back to drink. Sholto sprang from his horse and gave it a slap on the rump, sending it cantering into the great blue yonder. Daisy looked up, snorted water over Dawn then trotted after her companion. Sholto knelt to scoop a palmful and drank the water. He flicked the remaining drops from his hand and strode off. Dawn followed him up the bank. The ground was muddy and she slipped back, dirtying her hands. She looked for her tissues.

'My handbag,' she groaned. 'Daisy, come back.'

The tail end of the horse was visible swaying in the distance. Dawn tried to jog after the pony, but waddled to a stop. She bent to gather air into her strangled lungs. When she recovered, she lifted her head.

Jumping jellyfish.

They had only covered a few miles on the ponies and before that her stop/start hobbling would never have got her to Kansas, so who had dumped the semicircle of snow-capped fairy-tale mountains ahead of her on what should have been acres of prime arable land? Dawn shivered. A wind blew round her blouse.

'I know where he will take her…'

'Sholto,' she cried. 'What sort of stupid game are you playing?'

She couldn't see him and she twisted round. The stream was there, bubbling from the mountains. She saw the patch in the mud where she fell, but something was different. She felt different. An ocean was trapped in her head, pounding her eyes and ears to be released.

'Sholto,' she called again.

The sun smiled on the snow, blinding her. She shielded her eyes and felt a blow on her forearm. She staggered, caught her foot and fell, landing beside a bruised apple. A blurry outline of arms appeared, urging her to take hold.

Six arms, four arms, two arms.

The six arms morphed to four and then two came into focus.

They came into focus and she grabbed them, pulling Sholto down before he could take her weight. He rose and heaved her up.

'Where are we?' Dawn stopped speaking when she saw her handbag. He had rescued it from the pony. She wanted to cry, or throw her arms around him. Instead she grabbed the bag.

Sholto set off towards a gap in the mountains. The sun was going down with the speed of time-lapse photography. Dawn glanced at her watch. It had stopped. She wasn't surprised, but she was annoyed. She increased her pace to catch up with Sholto. He was talking to himself, moving his lips, although no words came out. She didn't interrupt. It was dark when they reached the pass, a thin track of land lined by ranks of evergreen trees. Their trunks touched and branches intertwined as they wove up the slope. At the end of the track, she could see flickering, orange lights and the shadowy outlines of buildings.

'Is that a village?' she asked.

She could phone her father. Set his mind to rest – and her own. Wilma wouldn't have left him without preparing his meals and labelling them in the fridge.

Sholto was sniffing the air like a wild fox.

'What is it?' Dawn's nose was frozen in the chill wind and if they stood any longer she would sneeze icicles. She copied his exaggerated movement. The sharp air bit her sinuses, but the aroma of pine tinkled through. It wasn't unlike her bathroom cleaner. Then a musky animal scent was broken by the rawness of smoke. Above that there was a hint of moss, struggling to be recognised over the wild garlic. She gasped then smiled. At home her sense of smell was dulled by the overzealous spraying of air fresheners. This was an aromatic wonderland.

'It's fantastic,' she told Sholto.

He crouched behind a tree and gestured Dawn to do the same. She hunched beside him, balancing a hand on the ground. Her knuckles sank into the snow. The cold numbed her fingers, but she could feel something buried there. She edged her thumb under it and eased it to the surface. It was a ring. She wiped it against her trouser leg. The metal was dull, but heavy – a gold wedding band. On cue, church bells played in the air around her.

Always the bridesmaid, never the bride.

Wilma was in her head again. Dawn shoved the ring in her pocket.

Sholto crept to the next tree, but Dawn remained on her haunches. Her knees were stiff and she was in danger of tumbling into the snow. She felt a hot draught on her arm.

Beside her, red eyes at her chin, mouth open with fangs drooling saliva, was a timber wolf.

IV

The creature shook the snow from its coat over Dawn and she laughed. It was the shaggy dog from the farm.

'How did you get here?' she asked. It gave her cheek a rough lick.

Sholto looked across and raised a finger to his lips. There was no-one around and Dawn was tired of his dramatics. Nevertheless she pricked her ears.

Wow.

In the crisp air she could hear the insects gossiping, a twig bending, the sound of a snowflake landing on a pine, Sholto's cold breath – she could hear that it was cold. The crack of a snapped branch sounded like the announcement of an avalanche. Someone was approaching. Dawn moved closer to Sholto. When she looked back, Morpheus had disappeared. There were no pawprints in the snow, but she hadn't imagined him.

'There you are, Katter. I've been searching for you.'

Dawn heard a soft, male voice, but didn't see the speaker

until Sholto pointed through a diamond-shaped gap between the branches. She focussed on the dark blob until it formed into the figure of a man dressed in a brown robe. His head was uncovered, showing a tangle of silver hair reaching down his back. He was bending to lift something in the snow. Dawn smiled. Katter was, as his name implied, a chunky grey cat with long, silky fur. The man picked the cat up and wrapped it in the ample sleeve of his gown. Dawn could hear the animal purring as it clawed the wool. She could hear the wool cringe. The man started walking back to the village, unaware he was being watched.

Sholto stood up. He stretched his legs then stepped out from the trees to examine the man's tracks. He slid his foot back and forth over the prints to blur them.

Dawn joined him. 'What was that for?' she asked.

He started down the pass without answering, keeping close to the trees. Dawn hurried to catch up, slid across the snow and landed on her backside. She wanted to cry, then laugh, then do both. She got to her feet, brushed the snow from her clothes and walked on as if nothing had happened.

Sholto kept a distance behind the man.

'Does he know you're following him?' Dawn whispered once she was level with Sholto.

He shook his head. Dawn watched the man, his back stooped, trudge through the snow. She wanted to call out. Hiding was stupid – a game with no purpose or prizes. From his grey hair and demeanour, she notched the man down as at least seventy. Handbag at the ready, she felt more than capable of overpowering him, but, in Dawn's book, anyone who went searching for their cat among the mountains in eight inches of snow couldn't be bad.

The trees thinned and the snow thawed as they reached the outskirts of the village. The lights she had seen in the distance had gone out. Some false economy by the council if someone stumbled and twisted their ankle, she thought.

'Let there be light,' she muttered.

A beam shone in front of her. Sholto was carrying a torch – a kid's toy – but Dawn could make out the shadows of rickety houses bunched together like conniving, scheming hags. They had seen better centuries. She couldn't see billows from the chimneys, but smelt burning and feared for the thatched roofs.

A cobbled track wove between the houses, preventing the buildings from rubbing shoulders. Dawn's ample frame knocked against the side of a house. The wooden beams juddered and a stalk of straw dug into her palm. Clumps of daub crumbled into her hand. She tried to stick it back before an angry homeowner came out rattling a stick.

Sholto pulled her away.

'Where on earth are we?' she asked. Putting two and two together equalled an experimental commune or heritage-themed village. There would be someone in charge. The old man was out of sight. Sholto squashed against the side of a house, hidden by the overhang of the roof and switched off his torch. Dawn teetered across the mud. Smoke nipped her eyes as she squinted to focus. A cow gave a subdued moo from the building behind her and a chicken ran in front of her. She leapt in the air, upsetting whatever was in front of her. A jangle of wood and metal rolled down the track.

'Who's there?' a voice called. Footsteps hobbled towards her.

Dawn grasped the handles of her bag as she came face-to-face with the old man. *Nobody Loves Rose* gave the bag weight if she had to wield it.

'Ah, I thought we might meet,' the man said in the soothing voice he used for talking to the cat.

'You knew we were here?'

'You speak English. Even better.' The man spoke with a mid-European accent.

'I live in the next town,' Dawn explained.

He bent to release the cat. The animal rubbed round Dawn's legs before walking off. She watched it go to avoid the man's examining gaze.

'You are a stranger here?''Yes.' Dawn turned to look at him. His face was weathered with contour lines that could indicate Ben Nevis. His white beard was ragged but clean, and his moustache edged up from his lip towards his most prominent feature, a hooked nose. His eyes were studs set deep in his skull.

'You must be cold,' he said. 'You aren't dressed for the weather and winters in this part of the world are not kind.'

Despite the burning in her face, Dawn was shivering. She wanted to ask what part of the world he meant. Had he misheard when she told him she lived in the next town?

'My house is along the lane.' The man gestured in the direction the cat had gone. 'You are welcome to have supper and warmth at my fire.'

Dawn liked the man. She wanted to say 'yes' and link hands with him. She couldn't go through life being suspicious of every stranger. She glanced to where Sholto was hiding. She didn't see him, but the man saw her look.

'You have a friend?' he asked.

'No, yes. No.'

The man smiled. 'I understand. My house is past the well on the right, should you change your mind.'

Dawn could hear his neck cricking as he gave a small bow. He took a moment to swaddle his cloak around his shoulders then walked on. Light beamed on her face and she shielded her eyes as Sholto swaggered up. When he dimmed the torch she put her hands on her hips. Sholto copied her. 'I'm going to find a phone,' she said.

Dawn found herself playing hopscotch as she avoided puddles of melting snow. She sensed Sholto was following her, making the same hopping movements. If she could find the village inn… she pictured a roaring fire and a waiter setting a dish of mince pie and potatoes in front of her. When she reached the edge of the village, the food and warmth disappeared and she began to fret.

The buildings were domestic residencies; dark, smelly and uninviting. She stopped to work out what to do. Sholto walked past her without even a shoulder nudge. He stopped beside a circular structure that Dawn assumed was the well. She waited a moment before joining him. He was drinking from a wooden pail and offered her water. Two half-drowned flies attempted the breaststroke on the surface. Her throat was dry and she accepted.

'I'm tired, hungry and my fingers are about to drop off,' she said.

Sholto nodded.

'I'm glad you're listening.' A cold touch on her neck told Dawn it was starting to snow. In the cloudy moonlight her eyes followed the patterned flakes as they melted into the stone of the well. She sat beside Sholto on the rim. Her work trousers soaked up the snow and clung to her legs.

'That old man is right; we're not dressed for a winter in the mountains,' Dawn said.

Sholto took off his jacket. He waved it in the air and jumped down to circle on the spot, dancing weird steps from his weirder imagination. His mouth was open, catching and swallowing snowflakes.

'You'll catch your death,' Dawn said. 'Your father will blame me.'

At the mention of his father Sholto stopped his capering. Dawn scrambled down from the well.

'I've made my decision,' she said.

Sholto stared at her as if she had told him she was his new social worker.

'I'm going to knock on the old man's door.'

Sholto threw his jacket on the snow, jumped on it, then turned away. The man had said his house was on the right past the well. They had found the well, so where was the house? A gap opened up between the mull of village houses and a larger wooden dwelling standing proud in its own grounds. A turquoise light winked at her from one of the lower windows. The other houses were in darkness, thick shutters keeping their light from strangers.

'Are you coming?' she asked Sholto. He pretended not to hear. Picking up his jacket, he walked back the way they came.

'Suit yourself,' Dawn grumbled.

There was nothing to be afraid of, she convinced herself, but she felt a tingle of nerves as she reached the door. She paused to examine a disc nailed to the wood. Snow clung to the metal, half-covering the plaque, and she wiped it clear with her sleeve. The etching looked like a cartoon character – a mouse.

Dawn stepped back. The sole of her sensible working shoes slid on black ice and she grabbed at the nearest thing to stop herself falling bum first in the air. As she righted herself and gasped for air, she realised she was clinging onto the cloak of the old man. She let go, mumbling an apology.

'Are you all right? I heard you approach.' The man looked behind her. 'Are you on your own?'

'Looks like it,' Dawn said.

'Come in, come in.' He took hold of her hands, rubbed them between his and led her inside. The hallway was dark, lit by a single wall torch. There was a portrait on the opposite wall, a woman seated at a mirror. The light caught the woman's eyes.

'Why, she looks just like my sister Wilma,' Dawn said.

'Does she? You must think about your sister a lot,' the man replied.

'Not really… well perhaps… I suppose…'

'Moreso since she has passed on?'

'How did you know…? Yes, you're right. She was my father's favourite and he makes it hard for me not to compare myself to her.'

'You wish you were like her?'

'Wilma was popular, full of life. Everybody loved her. She knew how to get what she wanted.'

'Once you know what you want, finding a path to it isn't so difficult,' the old man mused. 'What is it you want?'

'I want my father to be safe. I want him to be happy.'

'And is that what your father wants?' He paused, but Dawn didn't answer. 'Allow him to have his own desires. I'll ask again; what do you want?'

'Me? Nothing really, I have everything I need. I find it in the books I read –

adventure, excitement, romance.'

'And a happy ending? I am sorry, but I do not believe you.' The old man moved closer to the portrait. 'Perhaps this will help.' He ran a finger lightly over the oils, wiping clean a layer of ash. The woman's face lengthened, her cheeks sank and her hair darkened.

'It's me.' Dawn clapped her hands.

'That pleases you?'

'I haven't been the subject of an oil painting before.' Dawn didn't blink, fearing the picture would revert to its original form. 'I could be Browning's "Last Duchess" or du Maurier's "Catherine de Winter".'

'So much for a happy ending.' The old man smiled. He put out his arm. 'Come, this way.'

She was reluctant to leave the portrait, but the torchlight flickered and the picture darkened. She followed the old man into the main room, where a fire blazed in the hearth. She edged towards it.

'Wow.'

It was no ordinary fire. It spat out green vapours that danced above the flames like the aurora borealis. The logs crackled with the sound of distant gunfire. The seventh cavalry were advancing down the chimney. The fire surround was carved from dark oak with strange conjoined animals dug into the wood and painted gold. A rat or squirrel was perched astride a wolf. The wolf was leaping on an elongated cat, which in turn sprouted wings and morphed into a bird of prey, its talons clinging to a horse's mane. The horse was running from a lion whose tail was being swallowed by a sea serpent. Dawn didn't like the images.

'What do you see?' the man asked.

'The serpent flicked its tongue at me.'

'The serpent?' The man reached into a pocket and brought out a monocle. He perched it on his left eye. 'Do you mean the dolphin?'

'I'm tired,' Dawn said. She forced her eyes from the figures towards the grey cat. It was curled in a contented ball with its nose touching the fire grate. It twitched a whisker as it dreamed feline thoughts.

'Take a chair. I'll bring hot soup,' the old man offered. He hobbled out the door and Dawn looked for somewhere to sit. The room was a curio shop. She had seen more organised skips. The walls were obscured by bookcases, wood beamed floor to wood beamed ceiling. The cabinets seemed to push the spines of their charges into the centre of the room like alpha parents. Bindings jostled bindings. Volumes hung by threads to the lopsided shelves. Dawn's librarian eyes widened as she recognised ancient parchment she had read about in fantasy worlds. Egyptian papyrus wafted aromas of the Red Sea, sphinxes and pyramids. Mediaeval manuscripts concealed calligraphic conspiracies behind their gold seals. Kidron bound tomes, first editions, only editions, were covered in layers of powdered time. She put out her fingers, breathing in the rare smells of sepia ink and weathered paper, but drew back. They were untouchable, even with the finest kid gloves. She feared upsetting the delicate balance of the library. One wrong move and the shelves and books would come toppling down faster than the Walls of Jericho.

She continued her quest to find a chair. On the far side of the room was an oak table, perched on rickety stiltlike legs. Dawn manoeuvred towards it. Flasks, held by crooked metal holders, contained coloured liquids bubbling merrily. A swan-necked jar held blood-red, oily fluid that erupted every thirty seconds. Droplets splattered across the table, burning orange holes into the wood. The contents of a half-full carboy shimmered from red to viridian then argent as her eyes tried to follow the movement of the molecules. The reaction didn't follow any rule Dawn had learned at school. She bent over the glass and the liquid burst into a small flame which evaporated, singeing her eyebrows. She stepped away. On the floor next to the table was a raised plank of wood that served as a shelf for more jars and bottles. The acrid odour of ammonia rose from open lids and Dawn didn't venture near.

'Slugs and snails and puppy dogs' tails,' she said to the cat. It didn't stir.

Further round the room, pushed against the book shelves on the other side of the fireplace, was a dark-wood desk, cluttered with yellowed paper, quills, nibs and ink. Doodles, runes and arcane symbols were drawn on the sheet closest to Dawn. She made out the same creatures etched on the fire surround, but this time they were dancing a reel. The serpent wasn't a snake, but a giant fish, the proud stallion was a mule and the lion was wearing dentures. She moved closer and knocked against a three-legged stool shoved under the desk.

Dawn pulled it out and sat down. Her chin reached the top

of the desk. She stood up and carried the stool to a spot in front of the fire next to the sleeping cat, making room for it between a statue of Zeus and a hat stand. The weird experiments were unnerving, but she made herself at home by sitting down and slipping off her shoes and socks. Her host would have a reasonable explanation for his fantastic chemistry set.

The fire crackled and, lulled by the swaying of the flames, Dawn was nodding off when the man entered the room carrying a tray. She jerked awake.

'I startled you?'

'Not at all.' Dawn repositioned herself on the stool. The man looked round for somewhere to put the tray. He moved aside sheets of parchment and placed it on the desk. 'I brought this for you.' He offered Dawn a rough blanket that had been slung over his right arm. She thanked him and gathered the wool round her shoulders. It smelt like Daisy the pony, in a nice way.

'Drink the soup before it gets cold,' the man urged.

After a day with Sholto, it was reassuring to hear a human voice. 'What do you do here?' She tried to sound interested rather than accusing.

'Defining and refining. Distilling and purifying.'

'Distilling what?'

'Happiness.'

Dawn laughed.

'You don't believe me?'

'No. I mean yes. I don't know. How do you refine happiness?' Dawn hugged the earthenware bowl before lifting it to her nose. The soup smelt of good old-fashioned vegetables simmered with a hint of herbs. She took a slurp. After a tummy full of apples, the soup tasted like nectar.

'You are tired,' the man said. 'The mountain air can take time to get used to. We can talk in the morning.' He walked to the door then paused. 'I'm afraid you will have to sleep here. I have no spare room.'

The man departed and Dawn finished her soup. Her tiredness was gone. She eyed the shelf of books then reached in her bag for *Nobody Loves Rose*. After skimming through three unexciting pages she came upon an argument Rose was having with her father.

'Father, I love Gideon. You can't stop me marrying him.'

She had brought a boy home once to meet her father. Duh – he wasn't a boy, he was a man. They were both in their thirties.

'The bins get put out on a Friday. That'll be your job.' Her father told him. 'I take sugar in my tea, none of that fancy sweetener rubbish.'

John hadn't returned, although emigrating to Canada had been extreme.

Rose's father won the argument and she dutifully returned to keeping house and visiting her aunt in the nursing home. Dawn expected more from a book than common sense. She returned it to her bag and pondered her mystery host.

What was he up to? Something not quite legal, she surmised.

Before her toes toasted, she made a space on the floor for her bed by shifting one of the benches. She removed the alcohol burner, tripod and beaker and set them on the floor before attempting to lift the plank. It was lighter than she anticipated and she jolted backwards, knocking the tripod and stepping on the burner. The liquid in the beaker didn't spill, but the burner flame fizzled out. She placed the bench under the window and set the tripod and unlit spirit burner on it. The blanket was large enough to be wound round her body like a mummy. It didn't cover her feet, but within a minute the grey cat snuggled round her tootsies.

'That tickles.'

Dawn hadn't brushed her teeth for two days. She ran her tongue behind the top row. Her mouth felt fuzzy. Her breath stank. She needed to visit the ladies. She crossed her legs and closed her eyes, but the increasing pressure on her bladder wall kept her from sleeping. It was no good; she would have to get up and find a bathroom.

The cat thought about following her, then licked its front paw and curled up on the blanket. The fire was glowing and Dawn found her way to the door without disturbing the furnishings. She levered it open like a schoolgirl on a field trip, forbidden to leave the hostel dorm after lights out. The hallway was gloomy and she couldn't make out the picture on the wall. She turned right. The door along the corridor was ajar and she peeped inside. It was dark, but the pervading odour and nasal whistling told her it was the old man's bedroom. She moved on and pulled open the door opposite to reveal a storeroom crammed with flasks and bottles.

The noise of mice had her scurrying towards a dingy room where she gagged on the stink of rotten mushrooms. A light burned and she saw the remains of the soup, which had formed a crust in a large, blackened pot on the table. A patched up cupboard leant against the side wall with a flat stone wedged under the corner to stop it toppling over. Skillets and ladles hung on wooden nails. The room was disappointingly domestic. Dawn gave a nervous laugh. She was expecting cauldrons of sticky potions, vanishing mirrors and a broomstick in the corner.

As she moved to the table she heard the door creak. Footsteps came towards her. She grabbed a ladle and turned to find herself standing nose to neck with Sholto.

'How did you get here?'

He slipped past her and sat down at the table, reaching for the remains of the soup. He lifted the pot to his mouth and drank, dribbling half the broth down his T-shirt.

'That is gross.' Dawn slammed the ladle on the table. It bounced on the wood and catapulted to the floor. Sholto picked it up and began eating with it. When he finished he burped, got up and rifled through the cupboard, tossing bags of seeds on the floor.

'Stop that.'

Sholto turned. His face was masked by a wolflike snarl. Dawn steadied herself. 'What's come into you? I'm not afraid of stupid little boys. I'm going back to sleep. You'd better tidy that up.' She left the room and retraced her steps. She still needed to relieve herself. The torch in the hall had been extinguished, but moonlight found its way through an upper window and she found her way to the front door. It was barred with a wooden plank.

Sholto must have been in the house before the old man shut up for the night. Or had Sholto barred them in? Why would he do that?

Her mind was too fuzzy for thoughts to make sense. The bar was awkward rather than heavy. It took both hands and her chest to wrestle it to the side and open the door. She shivered in the chill air. The stars were fading and the first shafts of daylight vied for space in the sky. Fresh snow covered the doorstep and blew onto the toes of her bare feet. The cold made them red and itchy. Her bladder was close to bursting. Any moment there would be an embarrassing accident in the hallway.

Taking a deep breath, she dashed round the side of the house and crouched down, hoping no beady eyes were snooping. Midflow, she heard her father's voice.

'I told you to go before you came out.'

It was always her father's voice. Her mother died when she was four and Wilma was eight.

'Wilma was a good girl – not like you. You drove your mother to her grave.'

To be fair, he didn't say the second part, but he meant it.

Her feet were stuck to the snow by the time she finished. She yelped as she freed them and ran to the house on tiptoe. The door was open and the plank was where she left it. She closed the door behind her, but her fingers were too numb to replace the plank. Out of curiosity she made her way to the kitchen. Sholto had gone, leaving the scattered seeds unswept. A scrawny-tailed rat was helping itself. He couldn't have left the house while she was out, because there were no new footprints in the snow. He would be enjoying the fire. She thought of something smart to say as she returned to the room.

'Does this happen at every full moon…?'

He wasn't there, but someone had been. The burner she'd knocked over was relit, giving off an orange light. It would be typical of Sholto to hide and jump out at her. She stood at the entrance, feeling stupid when nothing moved. The fire spluttered and released new folds of flames. Red smoke formed clouds that swarmed into shapes before drafting up the chimney. Dawn crept beside it and borrowed a corner of blanket from Katter and curled up. The hair on the blanket tickled her nose. She tried to hold in her sneeze, which made it worse when it came.

The room shook. The heaviest volume on the uppermost shelf of the nearest bookcase teetered close to the edge and the contents of various glass beakers trembled. Dawn pulled the blanket over her eyes, desperately willing the book to stay where it was.

The room quietened, but Dawn remained on edge. She dosed sporadically until nosing her head above the blanket; the light through the window told her it was a decent hour to rise. The grey cat was gone. No-one had fed the fire during the night, but it was as lively as a Mexican fiesta. Somehow she wasn't surprised. The flames formed sausage and egg shapes and she salivated. Her tummy rattled louder than her eighties spin dryer, but the fire was deceiving. There was no smell of breakfast frying or coffee brewing, only a rusty odour from the grate. She tucked her head back below the blanket.

There was a crash.

She felt a sharp pain in her right hand which had fallen free from the bedding. When she sat up, the floor was alive with bouncing slithers of glass.

V

Her middle finger was bleeding, pierced by a shard that was sticking in her flesh. She eased it out and sucked the wound before spotting a stone on the floor a foot from where her head had been.

'What the…? Hey.' There was a shadow at the window. Dawn scrambled to her feet and hurried over, stepping on more glass.

Where were her shoes?

She found them under the stool, toasting by the fire, but there was no sign of her socks. She squeezed her bare feet into the shoes.

She should find her host.

She picked up the stone before moving to the door. As she reached for the handle it was pushed open. Sholto barged into the room.

'Was that you?' Dawn pointed to the broken window. He puckered his lips. 'You could have killed me.'

He ignored her as he crushed broken glass into the cracks between the floorboards. He kicked the nearest bench, knocking it over. Dawn's feet tried to move in different directions, going nowhere, as Sholto grabbed the precious parchments.

'No. You can't…'

He held the papers at arms length and began ripping, tossing the fragments in the air. She reached out, but he slapped her hands away. He was working himself into a rage, lashing out at anything. When the wall got in his way he headbutted that until there was blood on his forehead. The shelves shook and books tumbled. He seized them, using his teeth to bite at pages he couldn't destroy by hand. Dawn trembled. She clenched and unclenched her fists.

'What is going on?' The noise drew the old man into the room, wearing a red and yellow nightcap. 'Oh no, please.' He shuffled towards Sholto.

Sholto pushed him to the floor and he dropped knees first onto the broken bottles. He put his hands out to cushion the fall. Blood spurted from his palms. Dawn felt a rush of fierce energy. She pushed Sholto aside and bent to examine the old man's wounds. Sholto leapt across to the desk. The old man fell forwards as he lurched on his knees to stop him. Papers flew in the air. Sholto snatched them, screwed them up in his fists and lobbed them towards the fire where green and gold flames engulfed them. He upended the desk with one hand and snapped off the rickety legs.

'Please stop.' The old man was weeping.

Dawn caught sight of her handbag and rescued it from Sholto's destruction. She found her handkerchief and offered it to the man. He struggled to his feet.

'What do you want?' he pleaded. Sholto reached to bring down another shelf.

'Watch out.' Dawn saw the danger. The man hobbled towards the shelf, hoping to save his treasures. The wooden panels cracked and crumbled on top of him. Sholto pushed the man aside before the crossbeam hit him. He staggered towards the fire and the bottom of his robe began to smoulder. His face was ashen as he twisted from the heat. Dawn grabbed the blanket and beat his back as the flames rose up the material.

'Sholto, stop this,' she yelled.

He stared at her wide-eyed, as if noticing her for the first time.

'Happy now?' She succeeded in smothering the flames, but a

sickening smell of charred flesh ebbed into the remnants of the old man's clothing. 'I need water. Now.'

Sholto moved towards the man, unfastened his belt and unzipped his jeans. He fumbled for a moment before Dawn realised what he was doing. He aimed his stream at the old man. The few drops of urine grew to a hefty flow that splattered and splashed Dawn.

'Get out of here.' Dawn punched Sholto in the belly. He stumbled then zipped his jeans. Dawn rubbed at her soiled clothing, but Sholto grabbed her elbow. She tried to shrug him off, but he strengthened his grip. 'Let go of me.'

He dragged her towards the window. Despite her struggles, he was able to lift her with ease and thrust her through the broken window, headfirst. She landed on a patch of soft snow. Before she recovered, Sholto was clambering over her. He pushed her to the back of the house, where he stuffed her handbag into her palm.

'You'd better have an extra special explanation,' Dawn said. She didn't expect him to speak, but he could at least look sorry. He put a finger to his lips. Dawn heard clanking and rustling that sounded like a brigade of armoured knights advancing on the house. Sholto had a grip on her shoulder, preventing her from standing up.

She heard shouts in a foreign language; not quite German, possibly an Austrian or Swiss variant. Sholto moved to a spot where he could watch what was happening. Dawn crept next to him and wrenched her neck to get a better view. Torches flickered closer and as they emerged from the trees she counted twelve men, three rows of four, dressed in leather tunics with chain mail breastplates and metal shin guards.

Their leader brought up the rear, riding a white horse and sporting a polished metal helmet with a purple plume, similar to the ones in the museum next to the library. He urged his horse to the front. Reining it outside the man's house, he spurred it to rear. When he raised his sword the men halted, standing to attention with torches in one hand and swords in the other.

'In the name of…' The leader shouted towards the door of the house. Dawn couldn't make out the final word, but it was in

English. She waited for the old man to appear, but he didn't. 'I order you to come out.' The leader dismounted and handed the reins to the nearest soldier, who sheathed his sword to take them. He marched forward and banged a gauntlet-clad fist on the door. The house remained still. The leader turned and thrust his sword into the frozen earth. It wobbled and was about to fall, but he caught the hilt in time and raised it above his head. This was a signal for the men to break ranks and charge. The four soldiers in the front row swung their torches as they ran forwards, screaming a war cry.

'We've got to do something,' Dawn whispered to Sholto.

He traced pictures in the snow with a finger – a man with a conical hat and wand surrounded by stars. Beside it he drew a smiling face. Dawn gave him a shove and he changed the smile to a downward frown. She wanted to rant at him, but her throat was under siege from smoke.

'They've set the house on fire,' she croaked.

The timber cracked and caught. Flames leapt from the ancient wood. Sholto pointed towards the shelter of a grove of fir trees behind the house and Dawn followed him over. Fire was devouring the house and the old man's possessions. The straw thatch on the roof was reduced to powdered ash that fell like putrid snow into the shell of the building. The soldiers stepped back and laughed.

'Where are the neighbours?' Dawn said. 'Why doesn't anyone come to watch, if not to help? It isn't natural.'

Sholto tugged at her bag, urging her to move further from the scene. She tapped his fingers and he let go, but continued to walk away.

'You can't leave,' Dawn said.

Sholto didn't stop, but Dawn didn't follow. Her chest was tight, as if a rocket was about to be launched inside her. She prepared to swing her handbag in an attack.

Another beam crumbled as a soldier staggered from the doorway carrying a jute sack. He raised it above his head like a trophy. The men jeered. The material jerked and splayed in the soldier's grasp.

Katter.

Three guards stumbled out the door dragging the semi-conscious body of the house's owner. The man dug his feet in to the snow, attempting some halfhearted resistance. The leader aimed a kick at the prisoner's midriff and the struggling stopped. Dawn winced.

'Put him in chains,' the leader ordered.

'Aye, captain.'

Dawn kept her eye on the captain as he remounted his stallion, pulled the reins to turn sharply and signalled his men to fall into line. They marched past the well, down the main street and out of sight. When they were gone she crept from her hiding place. The sun was rising. Glancing up the hill she could make out Sholto silhouetted against the orange glow.

It was time to go home.

She wanted to rush after him. She was a middle-aged spinster, a librarian, who looked after her elderly father. She wasn't a teenage heroine with ninja skills and a passion for putting fairy-tale-cum-Gothic nightmare worlds to rights, but some things couldn't be ignored.

The snow was melting and it didn't take Davy Crockett to follow the footprints in the slush, but they vanished at the edge of the village where the track met a crossroads. Dawn scratched her head. She gave up and headed back to the well. The remains of the old man's house were smouldering. At odd moments the burnt timbers spurted out firework sparks of scarlet and magenta, as if they were bleeding.

At the well Dawn helped herself to water, freshening her face and tired eyes before drinking.

'Are you a witch?'

She twisted to see where the sharp voice came from.

'I don't mind if you are,' the girl said. 'I haven't seen a witch before.'

'I'm not a witch.'

'Oh.' The girl's face fell.

'My name is Dawn.'

The girl walked to the well without answering. Dawn supposed she had been warned not to talk to strangers. She looked about nine, dressed in a brown dress with a grey shawl. Her feet were bare and dirty and she held tightly to the bunch of wild plants she'd been gathering. Rowan berries and flax flowers to ward off evil.

'Does your mother know you're here?' Dawn asked.

'She's dead.'

'I'm sorry.' Dawn knelt to the child's level.

'Dad's gone to the fayre,' the girl said, levering her bottom onto the rim of the well. 'I've to wait for my silly little sister.'

'Where is the fayre?' Dawn asked.

'In St. Dunell's.'

'Where's that?' The girl giggled at her ignorance. 'I'm a stranger,' Dawn explained.

'A morning's walk that way,' the girl answered, studying Dawn's worn shoes. 'Can you spare a groat?'

Dawn found a fifty pence coin in her purse and gave it to the girl. She frowned, bit it then threw the coin into the well.

'That's good money,' Dawn complained. As well as feeling miffed, she wondered what she would use at the fayre.

'You're stupid,' the girl said. 'Stupid and ugly.'

Stupid and ugly. Ugly and Stupid. Ugly-pugly, stupid-wupid.

The playground chant Wilma used whenever other children were paying her attention rang in Dawn's ears. She turned away and walked down the street. When she reached the far end and looked round, the girl was gone.

At the crossroads she turned in the direction the girl had indicated and walked for over an hour with no sign of a village or a fayre. She stopped to remove a pebble from her shoe and heard the crunching of a wagon behind her.

'Out the way, wench.'

Dawn lurched into the ditch as a hay cart splattered melted ice over her legs. The cart was too large for the two ponies drawing it, but they pulled at speed. The bales of hay rocked and threatened to roll. Dawn recognised the smaller pony.

'Daisy.'

The mare let out a gentle neigh. The driver cracked his whip and the cart trundled on. Dawn stared at him. The end of his thumb was missing.

Wasn't he the man from the grocer's shop?

It was likely he was heading to the fayre. Heartened, Dawn lengthened her stride and soon met up with fellow travellers. They were dressed for a mediaeval-themed banquet and she felt underdressed. A young couple holding hands looked at her and laughed. The woman carrying the chicken spat on the ground and crossed herself. Coloured flags and buntings strung from the fir trees, directing visitors into town.

'Mind where you're going, wife,' a young man warned as he barged into Dawn. She found herself jostled towards the village green, at one point being lifted off the ground and in danger of losing a shoe in the mud. A wild boar was being roasted on a spit turned by two hefty, bare-chested men with lion tattoos. Dawn licked her lips. An acrobat cartwheeled in front of her. Jugglers in piebald tights and three-cornered hats tossed odd shaped objects round the heads and feet of the onlookers. Musicians mingled with the crowd playing lutes, pipes and handheld harps. Pastry sellers shoved their wares under noses and coins changed hands. A small terrier was standing on its hind legs balancing a ball while young men lifted heavy barrels of burning straw above their heads, egged on by the girls. Serving maids carried trays with mugs of dark beer. Flies floated on the flat heads. The girls elbowed their way through the crowd without spilling a drop. The aromas of ale, roast pig, smoke and pie tangled with one another.

Dawn felt giddy. She staggered towards the centre of the green, where a group of folk were lighting a bonfire. The flames struggled to catch and the attendants took turns to billow air over the broken chairs and dried moss. With a gust of air, the fire leapt into life. Dawn shivered. A drum beat in the background – a distant hum, no more – but it got closer and louder. The crowd parted. Dawn was slow to move and a hand grabbed her and shoved her to the side. The drummer, a smooth-faced lad dressed in blue velvet with a white lace ruff, walked in front of an elaborate parade. His polished shoes and shining buckle caught the sun.

Behind him marched two lines of guards dressed in red velvet livery. There was a gap, then came four bald-headed servants carrying a sedan chair with the curtains drawn. The design on the side of the carriage was etched in gold. Striding behind the litter was a troupe of bodyguards decked in the same uniform as the soldiers at the house. The last guard carried a jute bag. The thing inside was struggling to escape and the guard was forced to avoid claws and teeth jabbing at him from the sack.

Bringing up the rear was the old man. A wooden yoke was strung across his neck and shoulders. His feet were hobbled and a chain round his neck was attached to the saddle of the captain's horse. At intervals the captain would spur his mount on to keep pace with the rest of the procession, sending the old man sprawling on his face in the mud.

'Stop that, you bully,' Dawn cried.

The drummer halted and marched on the spot, rapping out a complicated rhythm. The litter bearers set their carriage down and rubbed their backs. The soldiers stood to attention, except for the man shielding his face from the fiend in the bag. The old man collapsed. Dawn wanted to rush to him, but she was squashed between a pheasant-eating man-mountain and a round-busted peasant woman carrying a wicker basket of eggs. She looked towards the litter. It was tempting to grab an egg and throw it at the carriage. The boy finished with a drumroll. A box was produced from somewhere and handed to one of the litter bearers. He laid it beside the door of the carriage for the passenger to step onto without dirtying his shoes.

The curtain moved and Dawn saw a jewelled hand. Before the rest of the important person could emerge, Katter hooked a talon into the wrist of the soldier who was carrying him. The man screamed and dropped the bag. It was knotted at the top and the shocked animal inside writhed around, but couldn't escape.

'Throw the demon on the fire,' a voice snarled.

It was a voice Dawn knew. Her attention had been on the bag, willing Katter to make it out, and she hadn't noticed the important person step down from his sedan. The red velvet robe, hemmed with ermine and embroidered with gold braid, made him appear ridiculous, which was possibly why Abelard du Niaull was frowning.

No wonder Sholto had skedaddled. Any boy would be embarrassed if that's what his father got up to in his spare time.

The crowd muttered. Abelard nodded to the drummer to silence them with a bang. The guard picked the bag up with a shaking hand and moved towards the bonfire. The flames were sprouting from the wood and, although it was no larger than a scout's camp fire, it was enough to smother a cat in a bag. The mob cheered.

'Burn the devil. Send it to hell.'

Dawn pushed past the egg woman, but found herself pressed against three sweaty pig farmers. The crowd wanted blood. It was only a cat, but Dawn had shared her blanket with it. Feeling helpless and afraid, she began to cry.

Katter let out a wild screech that sounded like a banshee rather than a cat. With a lunge and a tear, he ripped the jute sack and leapt out, landing on the man's face. The soldier let out a cry as he tried to disengage the cat from his nose. Katter was a mess of grey fur and pricked ears, with teeth and claws primed. The guard dropped to his knees. Someone threw a bucket of water. It hit the fire and the snapping of water on the hot wood startled Katter. He let go his grip. Three boys gave a whoop.

'Follow the cat. Catch the demon.'

They gave chase, rushing between the stalls and knocking over a peddler on crutches as Katter disappeared between legs. An apple wagon was turned over and the mob rushed to secure the windfall. Dawn lost sight of the cat in the melee. Abelard was standing with his arms folded, a wry grin on his lips. He waited for a minute before nodding to the drummer. Another rattle of drumming settled the mob.

'The demon animal has escaped,' a man called from the back.

'No matter.' Abelard held up a ring-smothered hand. 'We have its master.'

The soldiers parted ranks and the captain trotted forwards, dragging the old man behind him. This was going too far, Dawn thought. Much too far.

VI

'Stop this at once or I shall call the police.' Dawn pushed her way to the front, her feet wobbling like her first time on roller skates. Abelard's eyes peered down his noble nose and her courage drained. She didn't dare look at him, but fixed her gaze five feet behind him, where a large grey owl was judging proceedings from an oak tree.

There hadn't been a tree on the green when she arrived, and wasn't it early for owls to be about?

The bird turned its head three hundred degrees and winked.

'I'm calling the police,' she repeated, her voice faltering.

'The police?' Abelard appealed to his soldiers then to the crowd. The captain laughed and the others joined in. 'Do you know who I am, wench?'

'Abelard du Niaull,' Dawn answered. 'I know your son.'

The captain's laugh faded. Abelard stared at him. 'That's a lie. I have never set eyes on her before,' the captain answered.

'It wasn't your eyes I was worried about,' Abelard sneered.

'This is the Lord High Marshall, Sheriff of St. Dunell, Protector of the surrounding lands and cousin to the Grand Duke,' one of the soldiers piped up. 'On your knees or you will be thrown in the dungeons.'

Dawn stood her ground. Abelard walked towards her and stroked her hair. She tilted her head away from him. He touched her cheek and she felt a burning sensation, which wasn't unpleasant. In fact… her lips puckered.

'There has been a misunderstanding,' Abelard said, retracting his hand. 'The maid is a stranger here. Mark her odd clothes and foreign accent. St. Dunell welcomes visitors, does it not?'

'Even witches?' a small voice called.

'Witches? What do you mean?'

'She's a witch – a friend of the warlock.' It was the girl Dawn met at the well. She was smirking.

The crowd moved to form a semicircle round Dawn. A greasy hand reached for her shoulder.

'Let go of me. I'm not a witch. Witches don't exist.'

A flame leapt from the fire and took the form of a huge dog before subsiding. The crowd gasped. Abelard's face turned pale, but he kept his composure.

'The maid shall join me at the feast this evening,' he said. 'We will test her mettle there.' He raised his arm to deflect objections and turned to enter his litter. Three guards surrounded Dawn.

'What about the fayre?' The Burgher master asked. Laden down by his chain of office and suffocating in his oversized velvet cloak, he wanted the ceremonies over with.

'I declare it open,' the High Lord said without looking round.

'What about the prisoner?' the captain asked.

Abelard glanced towards the old man and their eyes met. Dawn sensed there was something between the two men before the High Lord looked away. 'Put him in the stocks. I'll decide his punishment later.'

Abelard disappeared into his litter and Dawn watched as the carriage was raised. The servant holding the back left pole tripped on the discarded jute sack, jolting the carriage and its important occupant. Dawn heard an oath from inside and laughed, but felt a grip on her shoulder.

'What do you think you are doing?' she said, rounding on the man holding her. It was the captain. His face reminded her of a more grown up Sholto.

'The Lord High Marshall wants you at his banquet. You will come with me.'

'A "please" wouldn't go amiss, young man,' Dawn retorted. 'Take your smelly hands off my jacket or I'll tell the Lord High Mr. La-de-da that you molested me.'

The captain chewed his bottom lip. He removed his hand. 'If it would please my lady.' He bowed.

Dawn wasn't delighted with the idea of dinner with Abelard and his fancy-dressed, weirdo chums. She didn't like the thought of her mettle being tested either, but she had no choice. The captain mounted his horse and leant down to offer her a hand up.

'Not on your nelly.' Dawn started walking.

'Nelly? Who is Nelly?' The captain kept his horse at a slow pace behind her. Dawn could feel its hay breath against her neck.

'The Lord High Marshall's house is three miles out of town,' the captain said.

'I like walking.'

They had gone half a mile, away from the bustle of the fayre, when Dawn stopped to remove her shoe. A blister had formed on her right ankle where the leather had rubbed against her naked skin. 'I don't suppose you've got a first aid kit?' she asked. The captain dismounted, peered at her foot and screwed up his face. 'That's a "no" then. How far have we still to go?'

'Over yonder hill, past the lake and by the wood,' the captain answered.

'Yonder hill?' Dawn laughed.

'Then past the lake. The banquet begins at sundown.'

Dawn heard the concern in his voice. She delicately replaced her shoe then gave him a light punch on the shoulders. 'We can't be late for the Lord High Drama Queen's party. Give me a leg up.'

Dawn felt a thrill as she held the young officer's waist. He spurred the horse to a canter then a gallop. She wanted to scream, remembering the time on the roller coaster with Marty Wilson. Marty was married, bald and a father of five now. Over the hill and down, her hair flying, Dawn watched the lake gush past, a streak of teal blue reflecting a reddening sun. The captain reined his steed in and slowed to a trot. The Lord High Marshall's house was before them.

Dawn caught her breathe. 'House' wasn't the word. She didn't know what she had expected. Something grimmer, grimier, greyer – a hall in a castle, hired for the day from the heritage society. It certainly wasn't that. Rose coloured marble, buffed and glistening in the setting sun, stretched beyond Dawn's imagination. Abelard du Niaull was rich, but he wasn't a king. Ornamental towers were topped with gilded turrets; campaniles housed bells for Quasimodo to drool over. There were balconies with glass balustrades from which heartsick lovers could toss roses and mock battlements that contested with flying buttresses.

The more she gaped, the less the parts seemed to join together. Magical walkways in the sky connected the pieces. When she turned her head, more walls, wings and spires appeared. Circling the palace was a moat with coloured fish louping from the water. It wasn't a palace, but an enormous bag brimming over with sweets. She could smell the candied sugar in the air.

'Where are we?' she croaked.

'Home. Don't you like it?'

'It's what I've always imagined.'

The captain drew his horse to a walk as they approached the drawbridge. The portcullis was down – an out-of-place grid of iron protecting the marble, decorated with what Dawn assumed was the family coat of arms. The captain shouted the password and Dawn heard the crank of chains.

'It won't fall on our heads, will it?' She kept an eye on the raised gate as they trotted below it to enter a hectic courtyard. Sentries saluted them and soldiers rushed to take the captain's horse. He leapt from his mount and held out his arms to help Dawn. She smiled and slipped a lock of hair behind her ear, feeling like a real lady, although a true blue-blood would know how to dismount from a horse without kicking her escort's nose, toppling him over and landing with her backside on his chest.

'Careful with that sword.' She tried to make a joke as she got up. The captain struggled to his feet. His nose was bleeding.

'What are you laughing at, sergeant?' he barked.

Dawn handed the captain her handkerchief. It was stained and he refused.

'Suit yourself.' Dawn looked around. Servants scurried across the yard carrying crates and rolling barrels. Geese were rounded up and shooed into pens. Men in leather tunics, jerkins and coloured hose shouted with raised fingers at women in hand-spun dresses and shawls. Her nose and ears couldn't identify the new smells and sounds, not all of which were pleasant. For a second she feared she would get lost in the hullabaloo. She felt a tickle on her palm and yelped. A large, grey hunting hound was licking her fingers. 'Morpheus.'

The captain stood beside her. He ruffled the dog's coat.

'Is he yours?' Dawn asked.

'Of course. He's the best hunting dog in the palace – in the county.'

Dawn stroked the dog's ear and Morpheus gave a delighted moan.

'He likes you,' the captain said.

Maybe the lad wasn't so bad, Dawn thought. Morpheus trusted him. 'Come on, you'd better show me where I'm meant to be.'

The crowd parted to make a path for them through the bustle. Once they were out of the courtyard it was easier to speak.

'What will happen to the old man?' Dawn asked.

'The sorcerer?'

'You don't believe that.'

The captain made a face that suggested he did. He cleared his throat. 'The performance of magic is banned. The accused has been brewing potions.'

'Magic potions? Magic doesn't exist. He's a scientist.'

The captain eyed her before replying. 'It will be up to the Lord High Marshall to decide the magician's punishment. He may be generous. I would have him beaten and locked in the dungeon with rats for company.'

'Would you?' Dawn stepped back. 'I'll find my own way. Where do I go?'

'The ladies' quarters are this way.'

The captain had no intention of letting Dawn wander off unaccompanied. She followed him under an archway and along a marble corridor without speaking. Morpheus kept close to Dawn's side, despite the captain making clicking sounds with his teeth to call the dog to him. They reached a secluded square with fountains carved in the shapes of fantastical animals. Dawn recognised a winged unicorn and a griffon, but wasn't sure what the three-headed giraffe was. She was about to ask when they were approached by two ladies smothered in green velvet and intricate lace.

'What are you doing here?' The taller lady poked a blackened finger at the captain.

'The Lord High Marshall has requested that this lady join him at the banquet tonight,' the captain stammered. He was poked backwards by the woman's finger.

'Has he indeed?' She turned to examine Dawn.

'It doesn't look like a lady to me,' the second woman said. She bore a strange resemblance to one of Dawn's work colleagues. So did the first woman, for that matter.

'What is your name, girl?' The taller woman was of higher rank than her friend and as such was the one to demand answers.

'Dawn.'

'We weren't informed you were coming, Pawn,' the second woman said.

'Dawn, with a D,' Dawn corrected.

'The Lord High Marshall met the lady at the fayre,' the captain said. He was answered by two soul-destroying stares.

'Guards,' the tall woman called. She turned to the captain. 'Knaves and dogs are not allowed here. You had better leave before they flay the hide from your backside.'

The captain paled. He saluted the ladies and scurried backwards from the yard, followed by Morpheus wagging his long, curled up tail.

'Come.' The first woman signalled to Dawn.

Dawn stood her ground. 'He won't be beaten, will he? I mean, he was only escorting me here.'

'It wouldn't do that rascal any harm,' the woman replied.

'Why? What has he done?'

'Nothing – that is the problem. He is the Lord High Marshall's only son, a spoilt wastrel. He thinks he can get away with anything…'

'…and usually does,' her friend put in. 'I wouldn't be surprised if his mange-ridden mongrel carried the plague.'

Dawn laughed at the woman's puckered face. The tall woman glared at Dawn then laughed too. 'You are an odd one, Dawn with a dee,' she said. 'I see why the High Lord finds you interesting, but you can't go dressed to the banquet like that. We must prepare you.'

Dawn looked at the clothes she'd spent the last two days and nights living in. 'I guess you're right.'

'The Lady Lisabet is always right,' her companion said.

'Thank you, Darcora.' Lisabet put an arm on Dawn's shoulder, but lifted it at once and rubbed her fingers. 'Come.'

Dawn followed the women to their chambers. Lisabet clapped her hands and Dawn was surrounded by maids. 'To the bath chamber,' Lisabet ordered.

Dawn felt like a dog that had rolled in dung and needed a dunking before being allowed in the house. In the bath chamber, five smooth pairs of hands undressed her and she sank into a pool of scented foam listening to airy music played by a young flautist. Her scalp was massaged by expert fingers and a glass of something sweet and alcoholic was placed in her hand.

Sinking into intoxication, she decided the banquet could not be as bad as she imagined.

VII

'Choose a robe.' Lady Lisabet displayed the garments as her friend stood wringing her hands. None of the heavy ball gowns took Dawn's breath away. After five minutes of holding them up and prodding the material, she picked a plain grey woollen dress.

'Not that one. It shouldn't be there.' Lisabet scooped the dress from Dawn and thrust it at Darcora.

'Not the grey,' Darcora tutted in agreement.

'I like it,' Dawn said.

'The Lord High Marshall's wife wore grey, poor soul,' Lisabet said. 'She drowned last year in a dress like that.'

'The purple one.' Dawn chose again, hoping not to make another faux pas.

'A handsome choice,' both ladies agreed.

Dawn emptied the pockets of her trousers and jacket – her purse, an old handkerchief and the ring she'd found in the snow – and stuffed everything into her handbag before she undressed. A maid picked up her discarded work clothes and took them to be laundered. She kept a tight hold of her bag.

'Shall I help you dress?' Another maid curtseyed.

'I've dressed myself since I was four years old,' Dawn said. She looked at the array of corsets, petticoats and undergarments laid before her. 'But I might need a hand.'

She stood like an ancient megalith while the girl wound

bandages round her stomach and encased her in whalebone before covering her in lace and velvet. The jewellery Lisabet picked for her was clunky.

'You do want to please the Lord High Marshall, don't you?' Lisabet argued.

Not particularly, Dawn thought.

'The Lord High Marshall.' She giggled. 'I can't call him that.'

'What do you care to call him?' Darcora snapped.

Dawn didn't answer. The maid finished her couture by spraying a musky liquid over her hair and pinning a white rose behind her ear.

'Ouch.' Dawn adjusted the clip and the rose flopped. Lady Lisabet looked to the ceiling and Darcora shook her head. 'I'm not used to dressing up,' Dawn said.

Lady Lisabet plucked a delicate gold pocket-watch attached to a fragile chain from her woven purse. 'We're late,' she said, without opening the casing.

'I'm ready.' Dawn grabbed her handbag from the chair she'd set it on while she was being mummified and swung it over her shoulder, narrowly missing Darcora's eye.

She wasn't used to walking in layers of bone and taffeta. While trying to avoid a stuffed bear standing sentry on the way to the banqueting hall, she nudged against an alabaster bust. It wobbled on its base.

'Be careful,' Lisabet warned.

'Someone has already knocked an arm off,' Dawn said.

'That is how the artist intended it to look,' Darcora replied.

'We're here.' Lisabet said as they arrived outside a pair of heavy oak doors, incongruous in the fairy-tale glassiness of the palace. She flung them open and stood back. Dawn was greeted by an open fire framed by a carved stone fireplace.

'That's an unusual coat of arms on the fire surround,' she said.

Lisabet looked blankly at her before peering at the stonework. Darcora leaned over to whisper something in her friend's ear and Lisabet gave a titter.

Dawn stepped into the room. Benches and tables were set in rows at right angles to the High Table and she swung her hips to manoeuvre round them. The other guests were already seated, drinking from stone goblets or golden chalices depending on their rank. Flaming torches lit the tapestries decorating the walls – hunting scenes and stylised battles, with little difference between them. In the corner a band of minstrels played a jolly tune on lyres, lutes, horns and harps. Dawn felt she had beamed into a television costume drama and expected to see cameras and stage lights suspended from the ceiling.

Lady Lisabet caught up with her and linked arms to guide her towards the top table, where the Lord High Abelard was munching on a hunk of bread and gesticulating towards his son. The captain was on his father's right, looking handsome in a gold and white tunic. He spotted Dawn, Lisabet and Darcora and rose to give them a bow. Lisabet scowled, but Dawn smiled back.

'You had better sit to the Lord High Marshall's left,' Lisabet whispered. 'I'll be next to you.' She turned to Darcora. 'You go at the end.'

Dawn shuffled past a group of guests throwing dice on the floor. The first player threw a double one.

'S… s… snake eyes,' Dawn said.

Lisabet frowned.

'Craps,' Dawn explained. Darcora tutted. 'I meant the game.' Lisabet and Darcora simultaneously lifted the ends of their noses an inch higher and Dawn assumed gaming wasn't for ladies of standing. 'The dice are loaded,' she commented to the losing player in passing. Two soldiers moved in to stop the ensuing dispute.

Abelard made room and Dawn bustled into place at the table, trying to sit down gracefully. She misjudged the train on her gown and Darcora stifled a snigger as the material tore on the chair leg. Dawn pretended not to notice and hung her bag on the end of the chair.

'Our fayre maiden,' Abelard guffawed between bites of bread. 'Have a beaker of mead to warm beneath your petticoats.'

Dawn put her hand over her goblet, but he had begun to pour and the liquid seeped through her fingers. 'What makes you think I am unmarried?' she asked.

'You are not wearing a ring,' Abelard answered. 'Besides, any sane husband who let you loose on your own would deserve a beating.' He laughed at his humour. Lady Lisabet smirked. Dawn wiped her mead-stained hands against Lisabet's gown when she wasn't looking.

'Waiter, we're starving, bring the roast,' the captain ordered.

A servant plonked a leg of something too large to be a chicken on the table in front of her.

'No plates, how modern,' Dawn muttered.

There was no cutlery either. Lisabet was stuffing what seemed like half a sheep into her gullet. Abelard set into his bird with gusto, carving chunks with an ornate hunting knife. Seeing her awkwardness, the captain leaned behind his father to offer her an ornamental dagger.

'Thank you.' Dawn accepted, but didn't use it.

'You're not eating,' Abelard observed.

'I'm not hungry.'

'What about a dance instead?'

The Lord High Marshall was on his feet. He dipped his fingers in a bowl of water on the table and wiped them dry on the waiter's sleeve. He held out a hand for Dawn to take. She hesitated until Lisabet gave her a nudge.

'I can't dance,' she said.

'There's nothing to it.' Abelard took her hand and dragged her into the middle of the floor. His palms were warm. Dawn felt a hundred pairs of eyes judging her as the floor was cleared. The minstrels played a dance melody and Abelard jerked his legs in a comical jig. Dawn tried to copy his moves, but tripped on her skirts and stumbled. Abelard caught her before she smashed her head on the ground. He let out a hearty roar. 'Indeed the wench has two left feet and a cow's behind.'

'I didn't come here to dance,' Dawn grumbled as Abelard accompanied her back to the table.

'What did you come for?' Abelard reached for the wine.

Dawn was about to remind him he had given the order, but thought better of it. 'I came to talk about the prisoner.'

She heard Lisabet suck in her breath.

'Which prisoner?' The Lord High Marshall cracked a hazelnut

between his teeth. Dawn noted the gold fillings – a bit tacky for Abelard du Niaull.

'She means the sorcerer,' the captain clarified.

'He's no more a magician than you are,' she retorted.

'We don't have coloured smoke billowing from our chimneys.' The captain demonstrated the fireplace. Dawn had already been disappointed by how ordinary the flames were. She spotted a bowl of salt and reached to take a pinch which she tossed into the nearest candle. The flame sparked a vibrant orange. The High Lord swore and pushed his chair back.

'It's High School science,' Dawn explained. 'The old man is a chemist.'

'He has a grey cat, a grimalkin,' the captain countered.

'You've got a grey dog,' Dawn said.

'You saw how it attacked the guard at the fayre. It is a devil.' 'You were going to burn it. It was terrified.'

'Enough.' The High Lord raised his hand. He turned to his son. 'Did you find evidence of wizardry in the house before you torched it?'

'Everything was destroyed,' the captain said. 'He knew we were coming.'

'He saw it in his crystal ball, did he?' Dawn mocked.

'Someone warned him.' The captain stared at Dawn. 'The magic papers and witchcraft books were burnt. The glass vials were smashed and their contents released into the ether.'

'But you found the sorcerer's ring?' the High Lord Marshall said.

The captain puckered his lips. Dawn felt for her bag and hoped there wasn't going to be a spot check.

'Not yet,' the captain admitted.

'No?'

'No'

'Then there is no evidence against the man,' the High Lord Marshall said. Dawn sensed from his tone that he was relieved.

'I'll find the ring. Give me time. The man is a necromancer of the worst order.'

'He's an innocent old man,' Dawn declared. The guests stopped talking and gaming to look at the top table and she realised her voice was raised.

Abelard lifted his hand to bring the discussion to a close. The captain played with his fingernails. Lisabet whispered something to Darcora, who stifled a snigger. The High Lord snapped his fingers and a guard appeared. 'Release the prisoner in the stocks and give him forty gold coins for his trouble.'

'Forty?' Darcora whined.

'Make it fifty,' the High Lord Marshall said. He turned to his son. 'You have been hasty in your arrest. You will apologise to the man in the morning.'

The captain's mouth fell open.

'Since you and your friends have destroyed his house, you will build a better one at your own expense.'

The captain was about to protest, but the High Lord Marshall hadn't finished.

'Finally, as you are responsible for losing the man's cat, you will give him your hunting dog in exchange.'

'I won't. You can't make me.' The captain rose from his seat, upsetting his wine.

'I think you'll find that I can.' His father spoke softly, but Dawn felt a shiver.

'And mind your language to your father, boy,' Lady Lisabet said. 'Or you'll be spending the night in the dungeon and your flea-ridden mutt will be drowned.'

The captain eyeballed his father.

'Sit down and finish your food,' the High Lord Marshall said.

The captain sat down, but he didn't eat. Dawn watched him spin the remaining dregs of liquid in his goblet. His face was darkening to a deep purple. He tore the leg from a chicken carcase and stood up. 'If you will excuse me, I have business to attend to.' Pushing his chair noisily against the wall he marched out, knocking a troupe of dancers against a table. A jester followed him out, mimicking his anger, to the delight of the revellers.

'That was harsh,' Dawn said.

'The boy needs discipline,' his father answered taking a gulp of mead.

'Not like that. Not his dog,' Dawn said.

'The beast stinks,' Lisabet said. 'I'll be delighted when it has gone.'

'It wasn't tactful to say you would have it drowned,' the High Lord Marshall rebuked her. 'The boy had it as a pup after his mother... died,' he explained to Dawn.

'You indulge him. The boy thinks too much of his mother. He will be twenty soon. He needs responsibility. He needs a wife.' Lady Lisabet plumped herself up. 'Lady Avril is of good stock and would breed strong grandchildren.'

Dawn looked to where Lisabet pointed. A plump girl with a pockmarked face was licking grease from her fingers. She let out a loud burp.

'Pity she's so plain,' the High Lord Marshall said.

'*So plain,*' Dawn thought. That's what he was thinking about her. It was definitely what Lady Lisabet and the awful Darcora were thinking – plain and common. The smoky atmosphere and tight corset made her sick.

'You will have to excuse me.' She stood up, remembering to lift her handbag. She tried to curtsey, but felt faint and teetered. Lisabet rose to aid her.

'I need to lie down. I've got a headache.'

'Lady Darcora is knowledgeable in herbal medicine,' Lisabet said.

The High Lord got to his feet and took her hand. He raised it to his lips and kissed her fingers. Dawn felt a pulse rush from her nails to her wrist, up to her shoulder then down her spine. It swirled around her hips before sweeping down to her legs.

'I have to go,' she said hoarsely.

Blues and yellows blurred into green as she squeezed past the drunken guests to the door. The closed-in smell of cooked meats and spices overpowered her. She imagined Lisabet and Darcora telling jokes about her to the High Lord Marshall and hurried out of the hall. Corridors branched off and she felt lost.

Which way had she come?

One marble corridor looked like another. She tried to find the statue she knocked, but failed. She was sweating in her layers of clothes and she was angry.

Angry, fuming, mad.

She circled the corridors three times searching for an exit into the courtyard. She needed water. She needed air. Clutching her aching head she sank to the floor. Two crossed swords hung on the wall above her.

'Are you all right?' Dawn heard a male voice offer concern.

'Fine,' she lied. Rubbing her eyes she realised it was the captain. He was still holding the chicken bone. 'Is that for Morpheus?' she asked.

'Yes.'

'I'm sure the old man will let you see him,' Dawn said.

'I don't socialise with sorcerers.'

'That's your misfortune.' Dawn put out a hand to push herself up, but it wouldn't take her weight. The captain gripped her wrist and helped her to her feet.

'You hate me, don't you?' she said.

'No. You're the sorcerer's friend; you stick up for him. That's what friends do.'

'Am I a sorcerer too?'

'Are you?'

'No, so how about showing me where the bathroom is?'

VIII

Dawn hadn't closed the curtains in her room and the morning sun woke her. The clamour from the courtyard couldn't be muffled by two pillows and a cushion. She didn't hear the knock and a maid entered the room while she was tussling with the bedclothes to free her feet. She wasn't wearing pyjamas, so she grabbed a shawl to cover her nakedness. The girl was immune to her embarrassment. She carried a tray with mulled wine, spiced nuts and a crystal bowl containing rose water, which she laid on the dresser.

'Do you have tea and toast?' Dawn yawned.

'I'm sorry, my lady?'

'Sausage and eggs, a slice of bacon with fried tomatoes?'

'I can ask the cook to roast duck eggs.'

'Never mind. I don't suppose you can find my clothes?'

The girl left and returned five minutes later with her blouse, jacket and trousers, washed, dried, pressed and smelling of jasmine. Dawn felt a twang of guilt. When the maid departed she splashed her face with the rose water, pulled on her clothes and straightened the sheepskin on her bed. She stepped back to admire her work.

Good; she was ready to leave the palace and find Sholto. She would say goodbye to the old man and check he was none the worse for his ordeal, but first she would try to remember the way to the toilets.

Crossing the main courtyard was like running in front of a Formula One grid on race day milliseconds after the flag. Dawn spotted a shepherd trying to lead a flock of nervy sheep to the gate. His path was blocked by two servants bargaining with a wine merchant. The animals bleated, the shepherd swore and the kitchen staff haggled with their carving knives aloft. Dawn looked beyond them to where four heavy horses were harnessed to a cart brimming with timber. The trader's papers were checked and one of the sentries lowered the drawbridge. Dawn made her way over, hoping to cadge a ride. She spotted the captain. It didn't look like he'd slept well.

'You stay with the load. I'll go ahead,' he said to one of his men. The soldier leapt onto the cart beside the driver.

Dawn waved. 'Any chance of a lift?'

The captain strolled over, with Morpheus padding behind. His doggy nose touched his master's tunic.

'Lady Dawn, you could hold Morpheus on the journey. I wouldn't want him to run off after rabbits.'

Dawn scrambled onto the back of the cart, perching on top of a sawn tree trunk. Morpheus jumped up next to her and squeezed his head onto her lap. A soldier brought the captain's horse and he mounted, riding ahead of the cart. Five soldiers marched behind carrying spades instead of swords.

The cart bumped along at a steady pace. The logs rattled, but there was no danger of the cargo dislodging. Dawn felt her eyes close as she bobbed up and down. She pictured herself dancing with the High Lord Marshall while Lady Lisabet stood wringing her hands. A jolt woke her. A dribble of saliva had christened Morpheus's head and she wiped it with her sleeve.

They had reached the village. The driver reined the horses to a halt and Dawn saw the old man beside the well, drawing water. Her legs were numb. She stretched and waited until the pins and needles sensation died before struggling to ease down. The captain was there to offer a hand. He took Morpheus and walked with slow steps towards the old man.

'I apologise for accusing you of being a sorcerer,' he said, without looking at the man. 'My men will rebuild your house. Here, look after him for me.' He thrust Morpheus's collar into the man's hands and turned away. Morpheus gave a whine. The captain signalled to his men to unload the wood.

Dawn stood beside the old man and they watched the guards clear the debris.

'He's not a bad boy,' Dawn said.

'He'll make a fine young man,' her companion agreed.

Dawn reached in her handbag. 'I have something I believe is yours.' She found the ring, trapped between the pages of *Nobody Loves Rose*.

'Where did you get that?' The old man's voice was harsh.

'I found it in the snow,' Dawn said offering him the ring.

'The book – where did you get it?'

'In the library.'

'Give it to me.' He reached out to take it, but Dawn held it fast.

'It's just a silly romance. I haven't finished reading it.'

'You've opened it?' The man pulled at his beard. 'And now you are here.' He paused to think, examining Dawn with X-ray eyes. 'It makes some sense, but be careful. Not everything is as it seems. The characters will change. They will try to deceive you.'

Dawn gave a laugh. 'I have read books before.'

'Not like this one… Ah, I see you've found my ring.' The man's voice softened. 'I must have lost it in the woods.' He let go of the book and took the ring, slipping it on the fourth finger of his left hand. Dawn felt a tightening on her ring finger.

'It was lucky you lost it,' she said.

The man gave a wrinkled smile. 'I don't believe in luck. I owe you my thanks, and also your strange friend. He is waiting in the woods.'

'I should go.' Dawn hesitated. She felt there was something she should ask, but wasn't sure what.

'I have something for you.' The man fidgeted in the pocket of his robe and pulled out a tiny glass bottle made to hold expensive perfume. The few drops of liquid inside were azure blue. He held the bottle still, but the liquid bubbled and danced. Dawn found it hard to take her gaze from it.

'I hope the stopper is tight,' she said.

'As tight as it needs to be. We wouldn't want to lose any. It is extremely precious. Use it wisely.'

'Oh?'

'It is distilled happiness.' He offered the bottle to Dawn.

'I can't accept that.'

'You must. It was brewed for you,' the man insisted.

Dawn took the bottle. 'Thank you.' The vial burnt in her palm, releasing a tincture of roses. She placed it into her handbag. 'Perhaps I should give a drop to the Lord High Marshall.'

'It is important to know what brings true happiness before using the elixir. Since his wife departed, the Lord High Marshall has been happy being miserable. A gallon of the potion would not help him.'

'Departed? I thought she drowned.' Dawn remembered Lisabet's words.

'The Lady Malia found it hard, being confined.'

'The brute locked her in the palace?'

'No, no, you misunderstand. Malia was a free spirit. Adalhard, the High Lord, respected that. They were truly in love, but being trapped in time and space crippled her. She had to find a way out.'

'She sounds like a selfish person,' Dawn said.

'She was my niece.'

'Sorry.'

'Perhaps the Lord High Marshall will be happier with the Lady Lisabet.' The old man's voice suggested otherwise.

'What about her son?' Dawn said, watching the captain dig a trench to mount the foundation posts. 'He must be your grandnephew.'

'He is not aware of our relationship. It is better that way.' The old man answered then laughed. 'I don't need a potion to make him happy. I am too old to look after a prize hunting dog. Perhaps you know a younger man who could.'

'That's kind of you,' Dawn said.

'I prefer having Katter.'

'Katter is back?'

'Not yet, but he'll fly back as soon as the walls are up and a new fire is lit.'

'Fly back?'

'A figure of speech.'

'A new fire, but no coloured smoke please,' Dawn warned.

The old man gave a creaky bow. 'It has been my pleasure to meet you. If you don't mind doing the honours...' He gestured towards Morpheus.

Morpheus walked ahead, pulling her to where the captain was resting on the handle of his spade, taking a swig of water from a leather pouch.

'Working hard,' Dawn said.

'It won't take long to finish. Alexis has gone for roof thatch.'

The captain and his men were the most efficient builders Dawn knew. It had been less than an hour since they started, but the wooden walls were built and plastered with mud and the roof beams were in position.

'Are you sure you haven't used a bit of magic yourself?' she teased.

'The house is rebuilt. The actual nuts and bolts of building it are unimportant,' the captain replied.

'I would rather have thought they were vital.'

'I was speaking...' Dawn's grin stopped him.

'My scientist friend asked me to tell you that he is too old to look after Morpheus. He would like you to do it.'

The captain stared towards the old man then knelt to take Morpheus's head in his hands. He ruffled the dog's fur and jostled him in a play fight.

'Goodbye,' Dawn said.

The captain looked up. 'Where are you going? I thought you were staying with father?'

'I can't.'

'Father hasn't been any fun since… He needs someone to look after him.' The captain spoke with a concern that made Dawn smile. He leant to mutter into Morpheus's fur. 'Someone nice, like you.'

'There is someone not unlike you waiting for me,' Dawn said. She looked past the well, towards the hills where a figure hid behind the trees.

'Father will marry Lady Lisabet,' the captain said. 'She hates me.'

'I'm sure that's not true,' Dawn lied. 'Can't you try to get on with her?'

The captain didn't answer.

'Talk to your father.' Dawn saw Sholto waving to her. 'At least you are talking.'

'He doesn't listen.'

Dawn had heard it before. 'Goodbye… I don't know your name.'

'Fulbright, son of Adalhard.' Fulbright puffed out his chest and stood tall.

'Goodbye Fulbright, son of Adalhard, and good luck.'

'I don't believe in luck.'

Dawn took a step away then stopped. 'Your father won't marry Lisabet.'

'Why do you say that? Can you foretell the future? Are you a sorceress?'

'No – she's just too plain and common for him.'

She leant over and placed a kiss on Fulbright's cheek. Leaving him smiling, she turned and skipped towards Sholto. As she neared him, Sholto was wiping his left cheek with his sleeve.

IX

'Slept well?' Dawn asked. A stalk of dried grass was poking from behind Sholto's ear, matching the couple of light hairs beginning to edge through the smooth skin of his chin. He was in need of a shower and a change of clothes. 'Where to now?' she asked, hoping he was tired with his show of petulance and was ready to head home.

Sholto pointed up the hill towards the pass.

Dawn agreed. 'With a fair wind we'll be home for tea.' Sholto furrowed his eyebrows. 'You are too young to be grumpy,' she told him. 'Come on.'

She took the first steps, but Sholto marched ahead, setting a military pace. She puffed her way behind him and it wasn't long before they were out of the trees. Green replaced white beneath their feet. Dawn's feet slipped in the slushy mud. Her throat was dry, but it couldn't be long before they reached the stream where they'd abandoned the ponies. The sun was up and she removed her jacket and slung it over her shoulder. Sholto's was wrapped around his waist. The temperature rose half a degree with every hundred metres they travelled. Palm trees and tropical plants appeared, as though they'd sprouted complete from the soil.

We've taken a wrong turn, Dawn thought.

The grass thinned and was replaced by sand that worked its way into her shoes and chaffed her heels. She hadn't been able to find new socks in the palace and her feet were unprotected. Leaning against a citrus tree, she emptied the sand. With his longer arms, Sholto reached to pick a ripe orange from the lower branches. He peeled the skin and tossed the rind over his shoulders. Juice dribbled on his lips as he stuffed slices of the fruit into his mouth.

'Don't I get any?' Dawn complained.

Sholto waved a finger at her, like a scolding schoolmaster. Dawn picked up an orange lying on the grass. Fallen fruit wasn't stolen. She peeled the skin, but the fruit inside was rotten. She thought she heard her sister's girlish laughter as she dropped it.

The path was leading somewhere, although there was no sign of houses. They were in the middle of a citrus grove with grapefruits, lemons and limes, as well as oranges and a turquoise fruit Dawn couldn't put a name to. The orchard had to belong to someone. The trees were pruned and healthy, generous with their fruit.

'What was that?' Dawn jumped, startled by a rapid movement between the trees. 'Hello,' she called. The branches rustled and she laughed. A shaggy grey donkey was munching on the windfall. Sholto didn't share her amusement. He picked up one of the turquoise fruits and threw it at the beast. The fruit burst in midair, puffing a purple cloud and giving a high-pitched squeak – no, that came from the donkey.

'Can't you behave?' Dawn gave Sholto a shove and he walked on, stopping at intervals to pick oranges and cram them in his pockets. They left the orchard and trekked through a desert of red sand dotted with brilliant emerald and topaz cacti. To the right, in the near distance, Dawn saw a red and white pagoda surrounded by a Chinese garden of ponds, sculptured rocks and miniature bushes. An echo of bells drew her to the garden. Intrigued, she stepped onto the path that forked towards it. Sholto seized her arm and jerked her back.

'I hate sand. If I see a lizard, I'll scream,' Dawn warned.

Sholto ignored her, but someone must have heard, because they arrived at a thick forest without Dawn having to sound alarms. She looked at the forbidding trees, their branches formed into barriers shading the darkness beyond. The Chinese garden was more appealing, but when she looked back their footprints had vanished – there was nothing to guide her back across the vast blanket of dusty yellow.

'Have you got your torch?' she asked.

Sholto twirled it through his fingers like a drum major's baton. An indistinct path opened to lead through the trees. Leaved fingers stretched towards them, knitting together once they'd passed to prevent retreat. Dawn held onto Sholto's shirt. After a while the trees parted to show a flight of stone steps leading down a bank to a river. Sholto jerked free of Dawn and skipped down the stairs three at a time. The stones were wet and Dawn edged her way down, choosing her steps like birthday presents for special friends. Sholto was untying a boat from a metal peg on the bank when she reached him. She supposed the leather, stretched over a willow frame, was a boat. It was oval, about five feet in diameter, with room for two slim people at a push. It wasn't designed for middle-aged spread.

'It's a…' Dawn struggled for the word. She snapped her finger '…a coracle.'

Sholto jumped in and beckoned her to join him. She didn't move. He picked up the paddle from the bottom of the boat and was about to push off when a roar sounded above them like a frightened lion.

Was that the donkey? It didn't sound like hee-hawing.

'Wait for me,' Dawn called. She stretched out a wavering leg. Sholto steadied the vessel as she teetered from the bank into the boat. It wobbled and Dawn fell against the side. Sholto struggled to stop the coracle upending. He frowned as she crushed opposite him. He was kneeling, but Dawn sat on her bottom with her knees prodding into her chin. The wood was damp and water edged up the seat of her trousers. She positioned her jacket beneath her to give protection. It was more comfortable at the football terraces her father forced her to go to. Men shouting and waving rattles like babies. Wilma had asked the team captain to sign her programme. Dad beamed. She had always been his favourite.

'Are we going far?'

Sholto stuck the paddle in the water and splashed her.

'They sailed away for a year and a day to the land where the bong tree grows,' Dawn recited.

The stream was calm. Dawn dangled her fingers in the warm water. She could see the river bed a few feet below and let out a small gasp as fish twisted between her fingers, their fluorescent scales leaving lines in their wake. Sholto was finding it hard to get up speed. He dug the paddle in and pushed towards the middle of the stream. The coracle caught a ripple and bobbed in the water.

'Do you want me to help?' Dawn said.

Sholto shook his head. The river widened and deepened and the water grew murkier. It dribbled into the boat as the vessel rose and fell. Dawn felt her nerves tingle as she held onto the side. She was facing backwards to the direction of travel and, although she wanted to see where they were going, turning would upset the balance. Sholto urged the boat faster.

'Slow down,' she said. 'We aren't late for the Red Queen's party.'

The boat circled like a fairground ride. Dawn's trousers were soaking, her jacket was ruined and her head was spinning faster than a whirligig. Sholto pushed the paddle hard in the water and the boat tipped. She clutched her handbag and her movement jerked the craft the other way. It tilted and took in water before righting.

Sholto stared at her. For a second she thought he might speak, but he looked away. She concentrated on keeping her balance and bailing out water. The backyard stream had become a major river joined by tributaries. Sholto stopped rowing and sat back, allowing the boat to flow with the current and pick up pace.

Dawn had been on pedal boats at the holiday camp they endured every year with her aunt, but her father steered them in when their number was called. This was more like white water rafting. She spotted rocks peeking from the surface of the water, but the significance didn't register until the coracle crashed into them. She was jolted forwards in a spray of foam, landing on Sholto's lap. The coracle shuddered. It circled, caught in an eddy of water where two streams met.

'Do something,' Dawn yelled.

Sholto struggled to free the boat, but he didn't have the strength. He handed her the paddle, slipped into the water and rocked the side of the boat.

'What are you doing? Are you mad?' Dawn felt seasick. She retched, but nothing came up.

It seemed the ever decreasing circles were about to suck the coracle and her into oblivion when Sholto succeeded in yanking them free. The boat danced and ran with the flow, darting downstream faster than Sholto could swim.

Dawn stuck the paddle in the water to act as an anchor, but she hadn't counted on the pull of the river. The wood was ripped from her hand. She sucked her finger where the paddle left a splinter. Sholto swam to the bank and hauled himself onto the side. The boat sped on and she watched as his figure got smaller. She thought about abandoning ship, but she couldn't swim fifty yards even with a rubber ring and arm bands. Staying in the tub and hoping to be drawn to the bank before they reached the estuary was worth the risk.

With Sholto gone the river calmed, as if his mood had been feeding the waves. The boat slowed to a pleasant bobbing and Dawn was able to stretch her cramped legs. The tingle was a delight. She wished she hadn't been premature in using and losing the oar. Her clothes were dripping, but the sun was high giving welcoming warmth on her back. A heron was perched on one leg, guarding the bank as she glided by.

'Who goes there?' she saluted.

A mother duck quacked, guiding her ducklings clear of the boat.

With feathers all stubby and brown. She closed her eyes and imagined she was the only survivor from the wreck of a luxury liner. Bedecked with the jewellery she'd saved, she floated in a life raft towards a tropical island paradise where her Man Friday was roasting dinner over an open fire. He turned to welcome her and it was Abelard du Niaull. She woke with a start.

What was going on?

A tanned arm reached towards her. The coracle was dragged onto dry land by two armed men – wearing skirts.

X

The men muttered in a language Dawn recognised, although it wasn't English. Rubbing her eyes, she saw the skirts were dusty red tunics reaching to their bare knees with metal breastplates and leather boots. They wore iron helmets with plumes and side panels and carried swords in their belts. Dawn chuckled. They looked like they had jumped from the pages of an ancient Roman history book. She wanted to say something in Latin, but the only words she could think of were Caesar's 'veni, vidi, vici', which didn't seem appropriate. She was disappointed when they spoke in English. Playacting could only go so far, she supposed.

'How come you are here, lady?' the first soldier asked.

She was in a boat, for goodness sake.

'I lost my paddle,' Dawn said. If her father were there, he'd have said she'd lost her marbles.

'What is your business?' the other man demanded.

'I'm looking for my friend, a young lad – tall, skinny, dark hair, freckles.'

The soldiers conferred. 'We haven't seen anyone. We need to inform the Magister of your arrival,' the second soldier said. 'Is he expecting you?'

'I don't think so,' Dawn replied, but she had a hunch that he might be. Sholto knew where the boat was berthed and he knew where he was heading.

'I know where he will take her.' Abelard du Niaull's words jangled in her head.

'You must come with us.'

It sounded like a request, but before Dawn could arrange her hair the younger soldier grabbed her by the arm and dragged her from the coracle.

'A Celtic craft,' the senior officer said, giving her boat a kick.

'It's not mine,' Dawn said.

'It belongs to the skinny boy?'

'I'm not sure.'

Sholto didn't bother about property ownership. The du Niaulls could afford to pay for what they took. Dawn thought about running, but felt a hand on her shoulder. She was marched along a path similar to the one through the citrus grove and she wouldn't have been surprised to see the donkey. She sensed someone or something was following them.

The soldiers didn't speak and Dawn didn't make conversation. They reached the gates of a walled town. Two sentries saluted by hitting their breastplates with their right hands. Dawn's escort repeated the action. The gate was opened.

'Inform the Magister that I have returned, bringing a stranger from Celtic lands,' the senior officer commanded. The sentry saluted and ran off.

'Wait here,' the senior officer ordered his colleague. 'I shall take the foreign woman into town.'

Dawn had been annoyed, but now she was curious. She eyed the officer as they marched. He had a nose like the eagle on his badge. 'Are you a Centurion?' she asked, remembering her school history.

'I am Cornelius, commander of the Twenty-second Century.'

That sounded more like science fiction than history.

They entered a poorer area of town where the houses rose three storeys. From the noises Dawn imagined several families inhabiting each apartment. She blocked out images of the sanitary provisions. A group of people stopped to stare.

'Get back to work,' Cornelius ordered.

The men were shopkeepers and traders. Their clothing demonstrated their social rank – stained tunics for labourers, coloured robes for merchants. Some led mules pulling loaded wagons, with children running between the wheels to pick fallen fruit. A clean-shaven man with dark, curly hair was standing at a street corner reading from a scroll. Nobody was listening. The crowd moved aside to allow Cornelius to pass. Dawn heard whispers in Latin. She made out the word 'Magister', followed by gasps.

Her toes were aching and the blisters on her heels were resurfacing as they moved into a more sedate district – bigger columns, larger mansions and fewer people. Cornelius slowed his pace to allow her respite. She raised her head to look at a twenty foot marble statue of a naked man about to throw a javelin. She looked away. The super-sized fellow must be a god, she decided.

'Jupiter?'

Cornelius didn't answer. She gave it another peek before they turned the corner. The face was familiar.

In the next street the villas were covered in white plaster and decorated with painted vine leaves. She squinted to see into a courtyard with fountains, mosaics and palm trees.

'Is this where the Magister lives?'

Cornelius glared at her as if she had a feather pillow for a brain. 'That is the house of the physician.' He pointed along the street. 'The Magister lives in the praepositus.'

'I should have known, the all singing, all dancing, biggest

house in town,' Dawn said.

As they approached the villa, a small, white terrier with a patch of brown on its tail rushed up and worried Cornelius's feet. He aimed a kick at its rump. The dog skipped to the side and barked at Dawn's heels.

'Cave canem,' Dawn said with a laugh.

Cornelius grunted. 'That dog should be strangled.'

'Here, Pluto.' A teenage boy in a plain brown tunic bent to take control of the dog. Dawn noticed the metal band biting into his left wrist. He looked about fifteen, but small for his age – shorter than Dawn. He was a servant, not the son of the house. She didn't see his face until he stood up.

'Sholto, what are you doing here play acting?'

He must have run fast to get here before her and change, not to mention having his hair cropped. He wasn't even out of breath.

'Is this the boy you are looking for?' Cornelius asked.

'I… I… I've n… never seen this woman be… fore.' The boy stood back. He moved with a limp and Dawn saw that his left foot was twisted.

'I'm sorry, my mistake,' Dawn said. 'My friend can't speak.'

Cornelius looked at her as if he would happily punish her for wasting his time – if she weren't so simpleminded. He turned to the servant boy. 'Where is your master, Servus?'

'In the atr… trium.'

Dawn felt mean, but she hoped Cornelius didn't have many questions for the boy. Cornelius handed a coin to the boy before ushering Dawn into the courtyard.

'Th… thank you.' Servus rolled it between his fingers and limped off with the dog.

The atrium was a marble hall the size of a school playing field, surrounded by the ubiquitous columns and statues. Dawn was beginning to tire of marble. The floor was covered in polished mosaic tiles depicting gladiators and lions, so realistic she was afraid to stand on them. The master of the house stood at the far end, dressed in a white toga with purple trim. He was reading from a tablet. Cornelius halted ten feet away and saluted. Dawn felt she should pound her chest too as a mark of respect, but he might think she was taking the mickey.

'Magister, we rescued this woman from a ship in the river.'

'It wasn't a ship and I didn't need rescuing,' Dawn said.

The Magister's eyes ordered her to be silent.

'She seeks a companion – a boy with freckles.'

'Freckles?'

'They are from Celtic lands.'

'Spies?' The Magister jerked his head. His golden hair fell in curly locks to his shoulders. Dawn noted his prominent chin and Roman nose.

'No, just lost,' Dawn said.

'Where were you heading?'

'Home,' she said, although she guessed Sholto wasn't heading back to Number 21 Collier Terrace.

'To Cambria?' The Magister asked.

Cambria? Did he think she was Welsh?

Dawn felt his blue eyes undress her and pick fault. 'Where am I?' she demanded.

'This is Abelardium,' Cornelius answered.

'Abelardium – you are kidding?'

'Why would I lie?'

'Cornelius's men will search for your friend.' The Magister signalled to Cornelius, who saluted and marched out. 'Until they find him, please make yourself at home in my humble abode.'

Dawn felt a now familiar tingle. The Magister didn't have matinee idol looks, but there was something attractive about power. There was vulnerability too. He made a show of being a hard ruler, with his erect stance and broad shoulders, but there was sadness in his eyes, like a romantic hero from her books. She thought of *Nobody Loves Rose*.

He could give Gideon a run for his money.

'You won't mind if I wash and change into more appropriate clothes,' she said.

'I would expect nothing less.'

Dawn sensed they were playing a game. Before she could work out her next move, the Magister produced a hand bell from the folds of his toga and shook it. Dawn wanted to laugh. Who carried a bell in their cloak?

Someone who knew it would be answered.

They waited a moment in silence. The Magister tapped his fingers on his tablet then stamped past Dawn to the entrance and rang again. Dawn heard hobbling along the tiles.

'Y... you called, m... m... master.' The Sholto look-alike was out of breath.

'I called ten minutes ago, you idle ass.'

'S... sorry I...'

'Don't start. We haven't all day to listen to your excuses. Escort this lady...'

'Dawn.'

'Escort Dawn to the ladies' chambers and instruct the maids to assist her in her toilet.'

'Y... yes s... sir.'

'Go.' The Magister waved him away. Dawn wiggled her finger, teasing the Magister, before she followed the servant out.

The boy walked ahead without speaking, but Dawn wanted answers. 'You must be good at your job,' she said.

'Wh... why? Because my m... master puts up with my st... stammer?'

'The Emperor Claudius had a stammer.'

'Who?'

Had they got to Claudius yet?

'No matter. How old are you? Fifteen? Sixteen?'

'F... f... f...'

'Fifteen.' Dawn pre-guessed, feeling the word wasn't going to come.

'F... f... four... teen.'

'That's young to be in such a position. The Magister is an important man and a rich one. He must pay well.'

The boy turned. 'I'm a sl... slave. My m... m... mother was captured when she w... was expecting me. She died when I w... w... was born.'

'I'm sorry,' Dawn said.

'D... d... don't be. One day my father will rescue me. He's a brave warrior in a f... far off land. He'll take his sword and...'

Servus made some swishing actions with his arms. Dawn parried the blows with a laugh.

'You fight well.'

'C... Cor... nelius taught me. I get s... sent to the m... m... market and he says I should be able to pr... pr... protect myself. I'm going to j... join the army.'

'I can't see your master allowing that,' Dawn said.

'I plan to r... r... run away.'

'Is that wise?'

'Bet... ter than b... be... ing a slave.'

'What about your father? You might have to fight him if he isn't Roman.'

Servus stopped play fighting and turned away. 'My father is d... dead.'

A group of maids giggled as they pushed each other through a doorway. Dawn was handed into their care and hustled into the room. In the distance she heard a bell ring.

XI

The bathtub was bigger than Dawn's bedroom. Bigger than the public swimming pool, although similarly tiled in terracotta. Fountains bubbled in the corners, with figures of naked demigods spouting water from the appropriate orifice accompanied by stone nymphs playing lyres. The bath water was milky and steaming, scented with lavender and geranium. She removed her clothes behind a screen and lowered herself in to what seemed like a massive cup of tea. Three maids poured warm water over her from porcelain jugs. Another stirred the water and every so often she leapt in the air with a soprano's top 'A' and scattered a handful of rose petals on the surface. Dawn held the side and pushed her legs forward, allowing the ripples to take the tension from her travel weary limbs. She closed her eyes. The aroma of cut flowers soothed her and, letting go, she floated to the middle of the pool.

'Girls from your background don't go to university.'

She heard her old headmaster's voice bubble below her.

'You can't marry. Who will look after father?'

Wilma's voice was shrill, but then her boss spoke over it.

'If you want a promotion, you must be willing to relocate to London.'

Dawn opened her eyes. Her feet were being pulled down. She splashed the water. The maids gesticulated from the side. One girl jumped into the pool and swam towards her. Dawn felt an arm around her shoulders and lashed out. The water turned red. She scrambled to the edge of the pool and pulled herself onto the tiles. Two maids circled her with steaming towels. The girl in the water was holding her nose. There was blood on her hands.

'I'm sorry,' Dawn said. 'I don't know what came over me. I thought I was drowning.'

She allowed herself to be led into a smaller chamber, where the maids attended to her. One girl manicured her fingernails while another painted her toenails. There was a girl to comb and dress her hair and one to prepare her clothes and jewellery. She chose a silk stola with a slim silver chain and adorned her with bracelets and necklaces.

'Any more and I'll fall through the floor,' Dawn joked.

The chief maid handed her a red rose. 'It is a gift from the Magister,' she said.

'Does he give all his guests flowers?' She accepted. Her hand was still shaking from her experience in the water and as she did so she scratched her palm on a thorn. The maid took a step back, holding her hand to her mouth. Her face was pale. Nicking your hand on a thorn was obviously a bad omen. Dawn's tummy chose that moment to rumble. 'Oops, pardon me.'

The maid laughed. 'It is time for dinner.'

'Where did I leave my handbag?' Dawn felt a moment of panic, but her bag was produced and she clung to it.

'This way, my lady.'

The leather sandals were comfy, cushioning her blisters and letting her bunions breathe after being imprisoned in her work shoes. She skipped after the maids to the dining room. The hall was sparsely furnished, with a low table in the centre. It was crammed with delicacies – grapes and olives, flatbreads and sweetmeats, small birds and fish with their salty eyes still accusing.

Two couches were set end-to-end beside it, with their arched heads touching. They appeared similar, but the one the Magister was reclining on was more masculine compared to the adjoining one. He was throwing dice onto the floor and Dawn saw that the legs of the sofa were shaped as wolves. The Magister had dispensed with his toga and was wearing a light tunic of red silk with a studded leather belt. The folds of the tunic were arranged to flatter his middle-age spread. He had hairy knees.

'You win,' Dawn said.

'I always do.' The Magister waved her to join him and she approached the table.

'You need a more challenging opponent.'

'Indeed? Do you play dice?'

'I'm afraid not. Oh, almonds – I love almonds.' Dawn bent to pick a handful.

'I have instructed a troupe of native dancers from Asia Minor to entertain us,' the Magister said. He signalled to the nearest maid. 'Bring the wine.'

Dawn positioned herself on the feminine couch, the body forming a curve. She tried to lounge in a ladylike fashion, with her hand supporting her chin the way she'd watched on the screen. She was close enough to her host to smell his garlic and sardine breath. He lifted a handful of green olives and chose a plump one to offer to Dawn, holding it to her lips balanced between his thumb and index finger. Dawn didn't like the bitterness of olives. She moved her head away.

'Bread would be nice,' she said, hoping he didn't pick it up for her. His fingernails were black.

'W... wine, my lady?' Servus had entered and was standing behind the head of the couches.

'Thank you.' She lifted a goblet from the table and held it for the boy to pour from the gold jug he held. 'That's plenty. I don't want to get tipsy.' She smiled at the Magister. 'I'm told I sing bawdy songs and dance on the table, but I can never remember.' She sniffed. 'Italian?'

'Of course. We have it shipped over.'

Dawn was about to ask where they were – it was too early

for the Romans to have established flourishing towns in Britain, although the correct timing of events didn't seem to be important in the reenactment – but the Magister was speaking and the conversation moved on.

'You got my rose.'

'Yes, thank you, Magister.' Dawn took a sip of the wine then laid the goblet on the table. 'Magister – I can't call you that.'

'Call me Ludo.'

'Like the game?'

'There are games we can play.'

Ludo stretched a greasy paw to grope Dawn's right breast. It was too soon for that lark. She jerked back, raising her arms. Servus was fussing around beside her and Dawn's wrist knocked against his leg. The boy stumbled. The jug of wine spilt. Dawn saw it in slow motion, unable to avert the outcome. The liquid spouted from the container like Etna erupting. It flowed through the air. Dawn put her hands over her dress to avoid the cloth being stained. The wine covered her palms and flowed onto the white silk. It looked for a moment as if she had slit her wrists and was bleeding red wine.

'You clumsy, pea-brained buffoon.' Ludo was on his feet. He grabbed the stunned boy by the ear and dragged him across the room, thrusting him onto the floor in front of the trembling maids. 'Hand me one of those.' He ordered.

The girl broke off a branch from one of the miniature willows in decorative urns that were placed along the wall. She handed it to the Magister and stood back, ushering the other girls into the corner. Dawn rose, wiping her dress with her handkerchief.

'Don't, please,' she cried as the Magister swung the cane and brought it down on the slave's legs. Servus bit his lip. He didn't cry. The Magister repeated the punishment. Blood oozed from gashes on the boy's calves. He squirmed as his master lifted the stick a third time.

'It was my fault,' Dawn said, approaching the Magister. 'Let him be, please Ludo.' She put a hand towards him.

'He's a no good lump of dog's dung that should have died at birth rather than his mother.'

'He's only a boy.'

The Magister held his arm in the air for a moment before dropping the stick. 'Get out of my sight.'

'Y… yes s… sir.' Servus struggled to stand. Dawn knelt to help him, but he refused her hand. His legs shook as he teetered towards the door.

'Tell the dancers to come,' the Magister ordered as Servus departed. He swaggered across to the table and reached for a leg of fowl. Dawn waited a moment before following him. She helped herself to grapes and they sat eyeballing each other until the dancers tumbled in to a rowdy beat.

The four male dancers, accompanied by their drummer, were dressed in animal skins with their bodies dyed. The animal skins didn't cover their lower regions and eyes were painted on their genitals. Dawn felt queasy and looked away as they writhed and gyrated. The drummer bounced close to the table, pounding a wooden stick against the stretched leather. A grey monkey was perched on his shoulder with its impossibly long tail wound round the man's neck like a boa.

It glared at Dawn then let out a screech, jumped onto the table and convulsed, knocking over dishes and sending olives scattering across the floor.

XII

It was too much for Dawn. Making excuses, she retired to her room and snuggled under the covers of her bed. It was hot, and she kicked them to the bottom. The scent of Roman chamomile wove its way into the room through the open window. She got up. The window looked onto the street. It was dark, with only the padding of passing paws on the pavement to tell her anything stirred. She wondered where Sholto was.

Had he eaten? Would he catch a chill from the river? She had to get him home. His father would be worried sick.

The room was lit by torches held on the wall by metal brackets. They gave an unpleasant odour of burning animal fat, but Dawn was afraid to extinguish them. The light flickered. In the humid heat, with her mind active, she knew she wouldn't get to sleep. She found her bag and reached for *Nobody Loves Rose*.

She was nearing the end. The story had moved on several years. A tattered postcard on the mantelpiece, postmarked Berlin, revealed to the reader that Gideon was involved in a cloak and dagger affair. Meanwhile a middle-aged Rose was swinging her hips to the Beatles on the radio in her mother's kitchen. She had accepted the offer of marriage from the local butcher, a man twenty years her senior with a permanent layer of pig's grease on his chin and a flatulence problem.

'You'll do nowt better than me, lass.'

Dawn groaned. She could write more convincing trash in her coffee break. She was about to turn down the top corner of the page, but stifled the urge. It was her pet hate. She had a blacklist of culprits who handed library books back with folded corners.

Rose couldn't marry the butcher. That was too mundane. It wasn't why she read books. The final page offered no relief. Instead the author had written an overly long poem about love and loss that didn't make sense or even scan.

There were several blank leaves to make up the numbers before the cover. Dawn found a pen in her bag. Gideon needed her help. She transformed him into a misunderstood philanthropist with piercing blue eyes and a noble nose, every bit the black sheep du Niaull. He had a son, of course, the result of a hurried liaison with a Polish Home Army fighter, who later died in a failed mission to disrupt Nazi supplies to the Eastern Front. The boy, Jakub, now lived behind the Iron Curtain.

Dawn's Rose stuck two fingers up at the dishes and her father's ironing. She stuffed her engagement ring into the snout of a pig's head in her fiancé's shop, took a ferry to France then caught an overnight express to Berlin. She blagged her way through Checkpoint Charlie to find her true love. Yes, he'd let her down, but that was because he wanted more from life. She understood and was full of forgiveness. With a flick of her imagination she was Rose, now a secret agent herself, freeing prisoners, taking photographs, asking questions:

Does anyone know where Jakub is?

Escaping assassins, waiting for the knock on the door – the uniformed police, the Stasi interrogation, betrayed by someone close, the bright lights, a pistol at her forehead…

I'm a British citizen.

Dawn was about to scribble her ending in the blank pages, but rested her pen. Defacing a library book was just too awful to imagine. She felt a trickle of sweat on her forehead. Her mouth was dry. She needed water. She wrapped a shawl round her shoulders before heading into the corridor. There were voices coming from the far end.

'Hello,' she called.

The voices fell silent. Dawn walked towards a statue of a discus thrower. She reached the end of the corridor and turned, but her way was blocked by the white terrier. It drew back its lips to show strong, white teeth.

'Where is your master?'

The dog gave a back of the throat growl. A door opened behind the dog and a girl emerged. Dawn was staring at her, but the girl didn't notice.

'Wilma?' Dawn choked. She felt a stab in her chest. It couldn't be. Her sister was dead. The girl hurried along the corridor, turned a corner and vanished. The door opened again and the Magister stepped out.

'What's going on?' Dawn said.

It wasn't the Magister. The man was dressed in a Sixties suit with a tweed Trilby and battered briefcase. He spotted Dawn and lifted a finger to his lips.

'Gideon?'

The dog barked and Gideon disappeared.

'Wh… what are you d… doing here?'

Dawn turned to see Servus. 'I need a glass of water.'

'There is a p… pitcher in your room.'

'I didn't see it. Who are the couple in that room?'

'Wh… what room?'

Dawn pointed to the wall. The room was gone. 'But I… there was…' Servus was watching her. He looked tired. 'Good night,' she said. She made her way back to her room and spotted the pitcher of water on the bedside table. Her hand was shaking as she drank then lay down. Within minutes she was snoring.

The sun was shining when she woke. The statues, mosaics and marble reminded her she was in a freak, Roman theme park. She'd better get dressed and leave before the Magister presented her with a twenty-first century bill.

A maid brought her a new stola. 'The Master is at breakfast, if you care to join him.'

Dawn didn't. When the maid left, she picked up her handbag and made for the main exit. When she reached the street, Servus was haggling with a tradesman. The bargaining didn't take long. The seller had better things to do than listen to the stuttering slave, trying not to finish his sentences for him. Time was money. The cart drawn by a familiar pony trudged away.

'Good morning,' she said. 'I found the water.'

Servus looked quizzical. 'Wh… at water?'

Dawn hesitated. She was sure she had seen her sister steal her boyfriend. It wouldn't have been the first time. If her sister wasn't dead and her boyfriend imaginary it would have sounded convincing. As it was she let the matter pass. 'Forget it. How are you feeling?'

'You sh… shouldn't be here,' Servus said, inspecting the string of garlic he'd bought.

'Where am I supposed to be?'

'W… with the oth… ther women.'

'How many "other women" does your master have?'

The boy rubbed his lower lip. He counted on his fingers, but miscalculated and started again.

'It was meant as a joke,' Dawn said. She didn't have time for his poor arithmetic. 'I need to find my friend.'

'You c… can't.' Servus moved to block her way. She could push him aside with one hand, but she spotted the red weals on his legs. He moved to conceal them.

'Why not?'

'You need per… mission from the M… master.'

Dawn smiled. 'You could get me permission, a clever man like you.'

'M… maybe.' He rubbed his chin. 'St… stay here.'

Dawn waited as the boy hobbled off. There was nothing to stop her leaving, but she strolled into the courtyard and made her way to the pool, where she wet her fingers in the cool water. There was something odd about her reflection. She looked younger, she was smiling and she had fair hair covering her face. There was the shadow of a man behind her. Dawn gasped and jolted forwards. The pool was a few inches deep, but she succeeded in soaking her dress.

'The M… magister says I've to acc… com… p… p… acc… comp…'

Dawn mouthed the word for him.

'…go with you.'

Dawn rose from the pool. She could lose him in the crowded streets if necessary.

'You're w… wet.'

'I'll dry in the sun,' Dawn answered.

Servus carried a leather satchel. He struggled to shift it onto his shoulder, but she didn't offer to help. He stumbled towards the stables and entered one of the stalls. Dawn heard the sound of agitated pawing on the straw.

'Oh no,' she laughed.

Servus came out dragging a long-eared, shaggy grey donkey. He had fastened the bag to her back and she wasn't happy.

'Meet F… Fidel… lia,' he said.

Dawn stroked the donkey's nose. 'What's in the bag?'

'N… nothing.' Servus picked a roundabout route into town. Dawn didn't recognise the landmarks.

Where was the naked god? She fancied another peek at that.

'Where are we going?' she asked.

Servus was as unforthcoming as Sholto. After ten minutes he slipped into a deserted cul-de-sac, positioned Dawn in front of him so no-one coming up the street could see what he was doing, and unfastened the bag. Dawn pictured the magician at her friend's eighth birthday party, producing blown-up animal balloons from an impossibly small case. She remembered the twiddle of his fingers before each plunge into the bag. Servus dispensed with any show as he drew out one of the Magister's robes and slipped it over his tunic, arranging the folds to cover his slave's band. He tucked up the bottom of the overlarge toga to prevent tripping and slung a gold chain over his neck. Dawn knew he was up to no good, but it took a minute to click. This was his escape bid. Dressed in his master's clothes, with the donkey and her, a slave girl, in tow, he could pass as a merchant visiting the city, and leaving it.

He could do with being a foot taller, but it might work. Then again, it probably wouldn't. Dawn didn't want to be a part of it, but she couldn't turn him in.

'W… we'll use the East G… gate. The guards will be pl… play… ing dice.'

'This isn't a good idea. Let me speak to the Magister.'

'He w… won't listen.'

They retraced their steps and Servus chose a road into a busier part of town, passing a multicolumned, public building. A crowd gathered outside. Servus waved at no-one in particular. Nobody gave them a second glance.

'Where is that?' Dawn asked.

'The temple to Aug… gus… tus.'

'I've heard of him.'

'He is the Emp… per… or.'

Dawn pointed to a circular shaped building that looked like a mini version of the Colosseum. She hadn't been to Rome and if Augustus was Emperor, the Colosseum hadn't been built. 'What's that?'

'The Cir… cus.'

'With lions?' Dawn asked. She had seen too many films.

'J… just one, but it has k… killed three men.'

'Gladiators or prisoners?'

'R… runaways.'

Ahead of them was the forum. Dawn had seen umpteen versions of it on telly, in documentaries, costume dramas and comedies. This was from a comedy, some zany director's idea of a forum. A whole world crushed into one square. Overlarge buildings housed overlarge people, in glorious Technicolor. A politician canvassed for support, senators and well-bred ladies looked on. While the hecklers catcalled, servants and merchants went about their business.

'W… watch out for th… thieves,' Servus warned.

Dawn tightened her grip on her handbag. A woman in the crowd watched her. She pretended to straighten her tunic, joking with a merchant, but she was looking at Dawn's handbag.

'Th… this way,' Servus said.

Dawn followed him past a row of shops. When they reached the end, she spotted the same woman, this time examining a wooden bowl.

'Who is that at the bottle stall?' She nudged Servus. 'I think she knows us.'

'Wh… o? Wh… where?'

The woman was gone.

'Out of the way, plebs.' A band of soldiers marched through the streets and one pushed Dawn into the gutter. Servus pulled the material of his toga over his face and turned away. Hardly inconspicuous, Dawn thought, but when the stench of rancid sweat and animal faeces hit her she decided covering her nose wasn't a bad idea. Fine war horses and down-on-their-luck mules shared watering troughs. Dogs wandered between legs or sat guarding their owners' possessions. A mangy looking beast growled at her and she moved back, afraid of rabies.

'We should m… ming… gle,' Servus said. He hobbled over to listen to the politician while Dawn inspected a jewellery stall. She moved from the cheap bracelets to finger the silk in a haberdashery. The shopkeeper was talking to a soldier in Latin. The end of his thumb was missing, like the grocer in her town. When the customer turned, Dawn dropped the cloth she was holding. It was Cornelius, the centurion. He would recognise Servus dressed in his master's toga and expect a better excuse than the slave could invent. Servus was too far away to alert to the danger without attracting Cornelius's attention. She buried her head in the merchandise, hoping he wouldn't see her.

'I'll be back tomorrow,' Cornelius said and left the shop. Servus had dragged his donkey to a drinking trough. He was dressed like a noble, but he acted like a slave, shoulders hunched and head bent low, expecting to be punished. Cornelius passed without noticing him. He joined a group of soldiers and they marched towards the Circus.

'Are you buying?' the shopkeeper asked in English.

'I've seen better quality rags in a dustbin.'

'Not at my prices.'

Dawn shoved the material into the man's hand and left the shop. She spotted Fidelia, nose to nose with a light coloured donkey stallion. Servus wasn't with her.

'Is this your beast?' the owner of the other donkey asked.

'Yes,' Dawn said.

'I'll give you five denarii for her.'

'She's not for sale.'

'Six, but she's worth no more.'

Fidelia brayed. Dawn took hold of her halter. 'She's not for sale.' She could feel the horse trader's eyes upon her as she dragged the donkey away from its beau. Where was Servus? As she searched the crowd, she felt a tug on her shoulder. A hand was on her bag.

'Oh no you don't.' Dawn swung her arm in the air.

'I need the book.' It was the strange woman.

'Who are you?'

'That doesn't matter. Give me the book.'

'It's a library book.' Dawn didn't like people lending library books to their friends. That was how they lost track of them.

'You must give me it now. You have written your ending. Someone else needs it.' The woman grabbed at the bag, but Dawn was too quick for her. 'If you want to do it the hard way…'

'What do you mean?' Dawn demanded, but instead of the woman, Servus was standing beside her.

'Th… th… this way. Hurry.' He scrambled down an alley lined with tenements. She followed, catching up as the donkey stopped to relieve herself. Servus's eyes were shining. He pulled the donkey's head and began walking. They were near the end of the lane. Turning sharp left Dawn could see the city wall and the East Gate.

'Ouch.' A stone hit Dawn on the ankle. Another landed in front of her. 'Who's there?'

A figure stepped from the doorway of the end building. His hair was uncombed and his shirt was ragged. He walked towards Dawn.

'Wh... who are y... you?' Servus let go of Fidelia and hobbled to stand beside Dawn. The man pushed Servus to the ground and grabbed hold of Dawn's arm. Servus struggled to his feet.

'It's fine,' Dawn said. 'This is the friend I was looking for. Sholto, meet Servus. Servus – Sholto.' She wondered if they would realise how similar they looked. Servus picked up a stone and brandished it above his head.

'She is c... c... coming with me,' he shouted.

'Don't be stupid, Servus,' Dawn said.

There was a wild look in Sholto's eyes. Dawn feared he would smash the slave's head against the wall without a thought. She put her arm on his shoulder. 'I'm coming. He's just a kid; leave him alone.'

Sholto turned his back and Servus threw the stone. It was a weak shot that bounced a few feet in front of him and tumbled to rest a yard from Dawn. Sholto twisted with the speed of a mountain lion and leapt at Servus, punching him on the chest and head with a neat one-two. Servus buckled and crumbled. He curled in the foetal position to protect himself. Sholto took hold of Servus's robes and lifted him in the air. Servus kicked out and Sholto thrust him down with a dull thud.

'Sholto don't, you'll kill him,' Dawn cried.

A group of citizens appeared from their houses.

'What's going on? A street fight?'

'It's a robbery. Call the guards.'

Nobody tried to restrain Sholto. He stood with his fists clenched, breathing heavily. Servus was slumped against the wall, blood oozing from his nose. Dawn wiped his face with her handkerchief, but he pushed her away.

'Stand aside.' Cornelius and his men pushed through with their swords drawn.

'Are you injured, sir?' The centurion approached. 'Servus?'

Servus looked up and swallowed. Cornelius struggled to understand.

'This is my friend,' Dawn said, but Sholto had scarpered. 'He was there.' She appealed to the crowd, but they were heading back to their houses, away from the soldiers.

'Explain yourself. What is going on?' Cornelius said.

Neither Dawn nor Servus answered. Servus was crying. Fidelia chose that moment to empty her bowels.

'I'll deal with this.' Cornelius spoke to his men. 'Return to the barracks.' The men saluted and marched off. 'All right lad,' Cornelius said, raising Servus to his feet with a strong arm. 'We'll see what your master has to say.'

XIII

Cornelius took a firm grip of Servus's shoulder and marched him down the street. Dawn followed pulling Fidelia. Sensing they were heading home, the donkey picked up pace and Dawn struggled to keep her in check. Cornelius avoided the forum, saving Servus from the taunts of the citizens. He relaxed his grip and slowed to allow for the boy's crippled leg. The slave walked with his head bent. The occasional sniff showed he was trying to stop blubbing.

The Magister made them wait, which didn't please Cornelius. 'I've army business to attend to,' he complained.

'The Magister is aware of your presence,' a slave replied.

'I don't mind waiting with Servus, if you have to go,' Dawn volunteered.

'You're in trouble too.'

Cornelius paced a figure of eight path round the topiary hedges. He was about to swipe the top off one when the Magister was ready to see them. Ludo was sitting on a carved chair, draped in too many clothes. There were beads of sweat on his forehead. Cornelius saluted and pushed Servus forwards.

'He's been in a fight,' Cornelius explained.

'Has he?' The Magister stared at his slave.

'It wasn't his fault,' Dawn said. The Magister ignored her.

'Why are you wearing my toga and chain?'

Servus didn't answer. There wasn't much he could say and his stutter would infuriate the Magister.

'Where were you going?'

Servus pulled at his fingers.

'Answer me, boy.'

'We were searching for my friend,' Dawn answered.

'Silence, woman. I didn't ask you to speak.' The Magister turned to Cornelius. 'Where was he found?'

'At the East Gate.'

The Magister rose and hovered over Servus. 'You were escaping.' He slapped the boy on the back of his head. 'You stole my clothes, you stole my mule, you kidnapped my woman and you were trying to flee. You are a thief, a liar and a runaway.'

'N… n… no, s… s… sir.' The words struggled to come out. Servus fell to his knees and fumbled to remove the offending clothes.

'You weren't trying to escape?' The Magister scoffed. 'You were helping this lady find her friend, dressed in my toga?' He turned to Dawn. 'What do you say?'

She felt her face burn. She felt sorry for Servus, but she couldn't lie. 'He told me he was leaving the city,' she said, feeling a lump in her stomach. 'To join the army.'

'He would make a fine soldier. Whoever heard of a lame legionnaire?'

'I'll take him outside and flay the skin from his backside. He can swill out the army latrines for the next month.' Cornelius put his arm out to steady Servus, who was about to faint.

'He is a runaway,' the Magister said. 'This isn't a matter of a simple beating.'

'Pl… lease… sir.' Servus's voice was weak.

'He'll be sent to the Circus and will face the lion.'

'He's just a boy,' Cornelius said. 'A foolish one, but…'

'I have given my orders.'

Cornelius didn't move. There was silence in the room apart from Servus's sobs.

'Do you intend obeying?' the Magister asked.

'Yes sir,' Cornelius said at last. He saluted and ushered Servus to his feet. Dawn watched them leave. There were a hundred things jumping in her head.

'He wants to find his father,' she blurted out.

'He doesn't deserve one.'

'That is a stupid thing to say,' Dawn snapped.

The Magister turned away, expecting her to leave.

'I want to be there.' The words were out before she thought what that would involve.

The Magister faced her. His features were set hard. 'Tomorrow afternoon. Be my guest.'

The rest of the day dragged. She wasn't allowed to speak with Servus and searching for Sholto was futile. She retired to her room and lay on her bed, remembering the woman in the market.

What had she meant by "doing it the hard way"? Was she responsible for Servus's predicament?

The Magister was calling everyone's bluff, surely? He wasn't a cruel man; he wouldn't go through with it. She hadn't seen a lion fight before. The only lions she'd seen were in the zoo and they were old, toothless lionesses. She'd seen films and documentaries, but this time there would be real blood and torn body parts. Servus wouldn't stand a chance with his crippled leg. One swipe and he would be down. She didn't want to watch, but she couldn't abandon him.

She rose, opened her door and called for a maid, although all the perfumed water in the villa couldn't wash the stench of the town from her. While she waited she thought about the Magister. Why didn't he have a wife or children? Perhaps he did. A man of his standing must have a consort, some long-suffering wife who tolerated his indiscretions. No children though. If he had an heir, he would make sure the world knew about it. He was that sort of man.

'Would you like a massage? Portia is skilled in the laying on of burning stones.' The maid, Julia, interrupted her thoughts.

'Oh, no thank you, a bowl of water will be fine.'

'Did I startle you? You seem troubled, my lady. You should seek guidance from the Oracle.'

'What's that?'

'A wise woman who lives in the catacombs below the city.'

'The sewers?'

'Ancient passageways cut out by Titans before the city was built. The Oracle is as old as the stone she lives in. I have not seen her, but it is said that she speaks prophecies from the gods.'

'I can't believe the gods care about my problems.'

'The woman has her own, earthly wisdom and potions to soothe the soul.'

'There is no harm in meeting her,' Dawn decided.

'I hope you are not afraid of the spirits in the catacombs,' Julia said.

'Spirits I can cope with. Rats are a different matter.'

XIV

'Should I take a torch?' Dawn asked. Julia hesitated before replying.

'The passage is lit as if the sun shines in on a June morning. It is unnatural, but not said to be harmful. You will reach a yellow door and you must knock four times. No more. When the door is answered you must say to the woman – a little milk and one sugar...'

'...that's all I ask.'

'How did you know? What does it mean?' Julia looked at Dawn.

'It means I'm closer to home than I thought. Wish me luck.'

'Here, you'll need this.' Julia handed her a willow cane. 'It's for the rats.'

Dawn accepted the stick and swished it in front of her for practise. The entrance to the catacombs was at the end of an alley behind the forum. Julia led her there, but didn't venture inside. Dawn took her time negotiating the uneven steps. She could always turn back before she came to the door. She didn't believe the sage could help, but lately her beliefs had been turned topsy-turvy. Julia had exaggerated the light levels – it was more like a cloudy November afternoon. She heard a scurry of paws and swept the stick in front of her, hitting the side wall. The corridor was dusky with the smell of wet jackets, old boots and cordite, reminiscent of a World War I trench, or so she imagined. It was too narrow for her cake-guzzling stomach and she had to edge sideways like a crab. Her foot crunched on something bony.

'Argh,' she screamed.

Argh, argh, argh, argh. The noise echoed along the stone.

Dawn tried to laugh. Only a nutcase would be scrambling in the sewers to find a mad woman who kept company with a caboodle of gods and spirits. She reached the door, a single thick plank of wood with no handle or knocker. It was impossible to tell what colour it was in the dim light. She raised her fist and knocked. The door didn't open and she remembered what Julia had said. Four knocks, no more, no less. She had forgotten to count.

O... pen... the... door. That was four. Perhaps she had only knocked three times. *Let... me... in.*

She waited a minute, debated whether to knock again, but decided she was justified in leaving. Before she could move away, the door creaked open. Dawn expected to see an unwashed old hag with grey hair covering her tattered rags, surrounded either by cats or snakes. She'd smell of garlic, gaze into a crystal and speak riddles in ancient Greek.

'Are you lost?' A girl was peeping from behind the door.

Dawn reckoned she couldn't be more than five or six. She was holding a battered teddy bear by its left ear. Its right ear was missing and it only had one glass eye. The girl was wearing a blue gingham dress with short sleeves that looked like a hand-me-down from an elder sister and had a daisy chain round her neck.

'I'm looking for the Oracle. Is that your gran?'

The girl giggled and instead of answering Dawn, she spoke to her bear.

'She's silly. As if gran would be here.'

The door was about to be closed, but Dawn stuck her foot in the gap. 'A little milk and one sugar, that's all I ask.'

The girl smiled.

'Where are your parents?' Dawn asked.

'They died many moons ago.' She opened the door fully and Dawn saw in. There was no altar or divining pool. Instead the room was fitted out with richly upholstered sofas and cabinets of solid wood. There were pieces of modern art on the white walls and what looked like a television in the corner. An empty mug had made a stain on the coffee table and a pair of men's slippers lay at the side. There was the whiff of lily of the valley, Dawn's favourite scent.

'What do you see?' the girl asked.

'It's like my living room, only better.'

'People see what they want to see,' the girl said. 'Would you like tea?'

'No, thank you. Should you be on your own?'

'I'm not alone.'

Dawn spotted a cat asleep on the sofa.

'I meant without an adult.'

Looking at the girl again, Dawn adjusted her opinion. She looked ten or eleven, still too young to live alone.

'You are not like the others. They ask questions about themselves. Will I find love? Who should I marry? Will I be rich? Is there a cure for my illness?' The girl performed a pirouette. 'Are you seeking a husband?'

'No.' The pair of slippers clicked together and disappeared.

'A lover?'

'You are too young to be asking. I'm wasting my time. I don't know why I came.'

'You want to help S… S… S… Servus,' the girl said in a voice older than her years.

'You know him?'

'How can I know him? He doesn't know himself.'

'That isn't helpful,' Dawn said.

'It takes a wise man to know who he is and a wise woman to know the truth about life.' The girl had grown. She was now in her teens and instead of a teddy bear she was clasping a mirror.

'Who are you?' Dawn said.

'Ask yourself, "Who am I?". When you find the answer, you will know what to do and who it is that needs your love.'

'You seem obsessed by playing matchmaker. There is more to life than marriage, which you would discover if you ventured outside into the real world. Goodbye.' Dawn turned to leave, but the girl reached a bony hand out to stop her.

'Can I see it?' the girl asked.

'See what?'

'What everyone who comes here seeks. You have it in your possession.'

Her bag was closed, but Dawn could see the potion of happiness bubble up in the vial. It changed from blue to yellow to green. The girl's eyes changed from blue to yellow to green as Dawn watched her. They were greedy eyes and Dawn was loath to show her the potion.

'It is not something to be kept locked away. It is useless unless you use it.' The girl was now a woman.

'Do you really talk to the gods?' Dawn asked.

'Yes. The gods are no wiser than we are; they don't have all the answers, but they see things from a distance.'

The words were bland, no more than a clever adage to be offered for money. The woman was ancient now. Cobwebbed slithers of hair dangled across her weather-beaten face, wrinkled and sad. Dawn felt claustrophobic. The flowery aroma she sensed earlier had changed to the odour of the sewers. She covered her nose.

'You should get out more,' she said.

The woman didn't answer. She hobbled to the television and switched it on. As Dawn stepped into the passageway she could hear the opening jingle to her favourite soap. She looked back and the face watching the television screen was her own.

The meeting with the Oracle hadn't taken more than fifteen minutes, but it was dark when Dawn stepped into the street. A man was scrutinising her from a doorway. He was smoking a cigarette.

'Having time out from playing a Roman?' she called across.

The man stamped out his cigarette and stepped from the shadow. He walked across and put his arms on her shoulders.

'Let go of me,' Dawn said.

The man's sharp eyes probed her. 'Hey, what's wrong?'

'I'm not who you think I am, that's what wrong.'

Two soldiers stumbled round the corner. The stranger glanced furtively round.

'We need to leave now,' he said.

'I can't leave. I have to help Servus.'

'I've come for you, like you wanted. Have you changed your mind? Is there someone else? Don't you love me?'

'I don't know you.'

'What's going on?' One of the soldiers slurred. Dawn could smell wine on his breath.

The stranger let go of Dawn and she noticed his left hand was crushed. There was a mole on his palm.

'Gideon.'

He blew her a farewell kiss as he scurried down the street.

The second soldier moved close. He put a hand on her stomach and slid it down her tunic. Dawn slapped it away. The first soldier laughed.

'I don't think the Magister will find your behaviour amusing,' Dawn said. The soldiers straightened up at once. 'Perhaps you could escort me to his villa.'

XV

'Whoever let the donkey loose can clean up the mess.' The voice outside her window woke Dawn the following morning. It was strange not to hear Servus's stutter above the clamour in the courtyard. She rose to look out the window. Two burly slaves were chasing a mule with sticks, but the animal was too clever for them. It kicked the first man, knocking him against his friend, and they both fell into a dollop of dung. Dawn had checked on Fidelia before retiring to bed. Had she shut the stable door behind her?

She dressed and ventured out to the gardens. Servus's dog watched her as she splashed water from the pool onto her face. It looked lost. She stretched to pat it, but it growled and ran off.

She didn't feel like breakfast, so she strolled outside. The street was jammed with people heading towards the Circus. She looked for Sholto in the crowd.

The young man with his back to her?

The lad bending to pick up a coin on the paving?

'What are you doing here?' The voice was shrill and Dawn jumped. A middle-aged woman with dyed red hair was standing beside her.

'Lisabet?'

'The Magister is expecting you in his box.'

'She doesn't deserve to be with the Magister.' The woman's companion was the image of Darcora. She had the same simpering voice.

'We must respect the Magister's wishes,' Lisabet said.

'I can hear you,' Dawn reminded them.

'Well hurry along, girl. He won't wait, you know.'

Dawn wanted to ask them who they were – Ludo's "other women" perhaps – but they marched off. She saw the back of Darcora's shawl as it pushed between two girls.

The guards at the Circus entrance had been given instructions and Dawn was escorted to the Magister's box overlooking the arena. He was drinking red wine from a goblet. She sat down beside him.

'You came.' The Magister offered her a lump of something red and sticky which she declined. He put a piece in his mouth and she guessed it was a sweet.

'I said I would,' she answered.

The entertainment had started and she turned her attention to the crowd to avoid the skirmishes in the ring. The chants told her what was happening. The sun was up and the atmosphere was close and sweaty. It was chock-a-block with testosterone.

'*Stick your sword in him.*

'*Chop off his head.*'

Rotten eggs and bashed fruit landed in the arena. The Magister clapped, but he wasn't watching the gladiators. He was staring at Dawn's chest. The man on his left cleared his throat and when that didn't work he gave the Magister a nudge. Ludo put his wine down before standing and raising his right hand. A drumbeat sounded and a group of soldiers marched into the ring. The wounded fighter was dragged out by his feet, leaving a trail of blood in the sand. The crowd hushed.

Cornelius entered the ring, dressed in full uniform with his helmet and breastplate polished. A small figure in a loincloth hobbled beside him, dangling a tiny dagger from his right hand.

Dawn had a deadlier letter opener at home. The knife would do no more than tickle the lion, and if Servus tried to dodge the beast he would trip on his lame leg. Cornelius saluted then stood back, leaving Servus in the centre. The crowd jeered as he stood rooted to the spot. Someone threw a chicken into the ring and the mob cheered. The chicken ran between Servus's legs, causing him to stumble. The Magister rolled his eyes and gave a sigh. He raised his left hand.

The drummer rattled a beat and a golden cage covered by a silk cloth was carried on poles by eight slaves dressed in the skins of zebras and giraffes. They stopped a few feet from Servus and lowered the cage to the ground. The cover was whipped off to reveal the lion. The spectators gasped. The beast was enormous. It reared and rattled the bars. Seven of the eight cage bearers scampered to safety. The last brave soul was charged with unlocking the gate. He stood back and slid the latch with a stick. The gate opened. The lion roared and pounced out as if stung by a scorpion. The cage door clanged shut. The beast swung round. A circle of armed soldiers prevented its escape, but to Dawn that seemed insufficient protection. The Magister sat back and reached for his goblet of wine.

'Don't worry, we're safe here,' he said.

Servus stood, knees shaking, with his dagger at his side. The lion didn't notice him until someone in the crowd threw a grapefruit that smacked it on the rump. It turned to face Servus. Dawn put her hands over her eyes, but splayed the fingers. She didn't want to watch, but she felt compelled to. The crowd expected carnage, but something wasn't right.

The lion padded round Servus, but instead of attacking it wanted to play. It poked a paw at the boy the way Billy did with his toy mouse at home. Servus raised his dagger and shook it at the lion.

'G... g... get b. ..back.'

Dawn couldn't hear the words, but could read the boy's lips. The lion shook its mane. Servus retreated and so did the lion. The crowd cheered. The Magister puckered his lips. The lion could easily kill Servus, but like a showman it was giving him a chance.

That was ludicrous.

She gave a gasp as the lion switched its tail against Servus's lame leg and he lost his balance. The Magister turned and the light caught the angle of his chin and his prominent brow. Dawn's mouth fell open. Why hadn't she seen it? Below the locks of curly hair, he carried the du Niaull profile.

'You're his father,' she said.

Ludo narrowed his eyes, but Dawn wasn't finished. 'His mother wasn't pregnant when she was captured. You took advantage of her.'

There was a cry from the spectators and the Magister looked back to the arena. Servus was on his feet, brushing sand from his face. The lion was backing off, neck bowed.

'I loved her,' the Magister said. 'He killed her.'

'She died in childbirth. You can't blame Servus for that.'

'The boy is a disappointment – a cripple who can't speak p... p... properly.'

'And you think it's funny to mock him?' Dawn felt her temper rising. 'He wants to impress you. Can't you see how brave he is?'

'Cornelius has shown him a few moves. I'd hardly call it fighting.'

'He's got a penknife to protect himself. What are you expecting, D'Artagnan and the three musketeers?'

'Who?'

'He's fourteen. A boy that age needs a father to teach him how to be a man.'

'Enough.' The Magister fixed his eyes on his son. Servus thrust his dagger at the lion. The beast threw a clawed paw and blood flowed from the boy's arm.

'You have to stop this.' Dawn grabbed the Magister's sleeve.

'Do I?'

'You'd rather watch your son die than admit you're the one to blame.'

'Tush.' The Magister shrugged her off and turned to speak to his aide. There was only one thing for it. Dawn reached in her handbag for the bottle the old man gave her. The lid was loose and the lining of the bag felt damp. Only one drop of the blue elixir was left clinging to the glass. As the sunlight caught it, the drop glistened and she saw Servus reflected in it. The lion roared and the crowd 'oohed'. Dawn didn't look down. She clasped the vial in her fist and poked Ludo.

'Look there.'

'What? Where?' The Magister looked where she pointed and Dawn slipped the last drop of the magic elixir into his wine. It skimmed round the surface like a palate knife smoothing the icing on a cake. The wine changed from claret to deep purple.

'It won't be long now,' the Magister's companion said, rubbing his hands. 'The lion is in for the kill. This will be its fourth victim.'

The Magister raised the glass and drank.

A thrill fluttered down Dawn's ribs as she watched his Adam's apple bob. It had to work. The Magister was a hard man, but there was no way he could be happy if he condemned his son to death.

Dawn waited. There was no flash of light or puff of smoke. The Magister burped. He called to the slave standing behind him. 'This wine is sour.' He handed his goblet to the man. Dawn couldn't stop the slave pouring the remains of the wine into the gutter.

The Magister stood up. The lion leapt and knocked Servus to the ground. For a dazzling blue second, time stood still. Servus was lying helpless on the sand with the lion poised over him as if waiting for the Magister's permission to make the final blow.

Thumbs up or thumbs down?

Ludo raised his hand. Thumbs up.

The crowd cheered.

A group of soldiers, led by Cornelius ran in, shooing the animal away from Servus. The beast gave a swipe at the Centurion, drawing blood.

'Oh no you d... don't.' Servus scrambled to his feet. Brandishing his dagger, he advanced on the lion, as if he was chastising his pet dog. The animal roared, but backed off. It circled the ring, taking its bows. The cage door was pulled open and it retreated inside. The gate was closed.

Dawn got the feeling she was watching a staged performance. She turned to speak to the Magister, but he had left. She saw him march into the Circus ring surrounded by four soldiers. Servus fell to his knees as his master approached. The Magister held out his hands and raised him to his feet. He placed an arm round his shoulders and addressed the crowd.

'Today, this man is no longer my slave. He is my son.' The crowd cheered. Cornelius handed the Magister a cloak and he put it round Servus. 'Henceforth he will be known as Primus.' Dawn saw Servus whisper something in his father's ears. The Magister laughed. 'The lion shall be returned to Africa and set free.'

Dawn felt tears welling. The lion gave a roar from its cage. She looked down and the animal winked at her. Of course, it was grey and shaggy like all the animals on her journey. There was no way it was going to kill Servus – and the Magister knew that. It was an elaborate game, but for whose benefit? There had been no need to use the happiness potion and she felt tricked. The Oracle should have told her.

She was trying to make sense of events when she felt a finger in her back and turned to see Sholto sitting next to her, dressed in a Roman toga.

'Salve, Sholto,' she said. Sholto didn't smile. He was watching the Magister parade his son around the ring.

'Thinking about your dad?'

Sholto screwed up his nose.

'He'll be worried about you.' Dawn thought of her father. How long had she been gone? Would he have eaten a hot dinner or survived on biscuits and stale bread? What if he'd fallen down the stairs or set the house on fire? 'It's time to go,' she said.

Sholto stood up and pushed past the man who had been sitting next to the Magister. He reminded Dawn of the greengrocer, or the cart driver, and she raised her hands like a rampant lion and gave a growl. The man started back. She laughed and followed Sholto out of the Circus.

XVI

They walked through a ghost town. Anybody who was somebody and everybody besides was at the Circus.

'High Noon,' Dawn said.

Sholto was walking beside her, but didn't respond.

'It's a film.'

Sholto mimed a cowboy drawing his pistols.

'You've seen it.'

They headed towards the East Gate. The guards were playing dice. Dawn gave them a chest salute, but they didn't look up. It wasn't as much that the soldiers didn't see them, Dawn thought, but that they weren't there, or they were in a different dimension. When they were out of town Sholto threw his toga into a bush. He was wearing his jeans, T-shirt and jacket beneath, freshly laundered. His baseball cap was stuffed in his back pocket. He tugged it free and put it on. Dawn couldn't remove her stola. Her clothes were in the Magister's villa. At least she had her handbag.

Sholto walked until the sun went down. The road had fallen into disrepair and degenerated into a boggy, cattle track. They passed ploughed fields, but there were no houses and no people. Dawn imagined she had been painted into a pastoral watercolour. The artist had gone for realism – she was sweating and her feet felt parboiled in water and ready for the fryer. Sholto took bread from his trouser pocket and offered her a chunk. She refused, not knowing where the bread had been.

'Where are we going?' She felt like one of her father's scratched 45s with the needle stuck in a groove.

Sholto made a rowing action with his arms.

'I'm not going back on that river.' Dawn tried to sound like her old form teacher. She stopped and scanned the horizon. Sholto copied her.

'That's not funny.'

He pointed left, right, up in the air, towards the ground then put his palms out in front of him and stood with his mouth gaping.

'All right, I don't know where we are or where home is, but I'll find it.' When her neighbours moved house they took Spotty in a basket in the car. Three weeks later he was meowing for food on their doorsteps with Billy hissing at him. Such stories were ten a penny in the feel-good magazines she read, but she suspected clicking her heels and thinking of home wouldn't help.

'We headed west from the farm, then north to the sorcerer's village.'

Sholto was looking at her, but he wasn't giving clues.

'After that we turned east along the river to Abelardium. Now we're heading south. We're going in a circle.'

Sholto raised his head and sniffed. Dawn caught the smell of salt sea air. Her house was sixty miles from the sea. There was a flavour of vinegar too. She closed her eyes to see memories of holidays by the sea with soggy banana sandwiches and pickled onion crisps.

When she opened her eyes they were standing in a clearing among a copse of hazel and birch trees. The ground was moist. Autumn leaves squelched beneath her, poking at her toes through her open sandals. Sholto had picked up a stick and was whacking nettles while she decided on a path.

'This way.' Dawn headed towards the sound of the waves.

Sholto followed and soon they were out of the woods and on a promenade beside a sea wall. The wall stretched for miles in both directions with steps down to the beach at regular intervals. To the left was a rocky shore. To the right the shingle became golden sand with holidaymakers enjoying themselves. Children were riding donkeys and jumping on trampolines. Teenagers had set up a net to play volleyball and surfers bobbed in the water. She made out the jingle of a carousel and her mouth watered as it tasted candyfloss and toffee apples. Sholto smiled and turned right.'I need to rest my feet,' Dawn said. 'I'll catch you later.'

Sholto leapfrogged over the wall. He landed on the beach a few feet from a black-backed gull, kicking sand in his wake. The gull took to the sky. Dawn looked out to sea. There was a boat on the horizon with green funnels. A life at sea appealed in her imagination, but not in real life. A pod of dolphins or porpoises (she wasn't sure of the difference) leapt out of the water in an arc to make synchronised swimmers' eyes weep. With a graceful flow they nosedived under. Dawn climbed down the steps and walked to the water's edge. She could almost reach out and touch the animals. They were too close and she hoped they weren't in danger of beaching.

As if reading her thoughts, the three larger dolphins turned to swim back out, but the smaller one lagged behind. It raised a flipper to wave at Dawn. She blinked. The dolphin winked at her. She was imagining things, but then she heard the noise. A whistle at first, but the notes softened into a melody with notes taken from the sea. Strings led the lilt and below them a single woodwind sound. An oboe.

She was alone apart from the gull that had returned and was preening its feathers. The dolphin was calling to her. It was spellbinding and sad. It drew her into the water. The song changed key and pulled Dawn further in. She waded out until the waves rippled against her knees then her thigh.

'Don't do it,' a woman's voice shouted. 'It's a siren.'

Woken from her revelry, Dawn felt the coldness of the water. The music rang out clearer. She turned to see a slim woman on the shore, her silver hair fluttering in the sea breeze. She held out her hands, urging Dawn back to land.

'It's just a dolphin,' Dawn said.

'That is one disguise. They seek brides and grooms for those lost at sea. They lure the unwary to their deaths.'

Dawn had heard of river dolphins in the Amazon who changed into handsome men. She imagined the woman was deluded, or researching a book, but she was the one thigh deep in water. As she looked she saw Wilma's plaits of hair surround the dolphin's face. The pointed nose shrank and the flippers grew fingers.

'Being a sea wife might be exciting,' Dawn said. 'Nobody else wants me. I'm a failure. Stupid and ugly. Nobody loves Dawn.'

'There are people in this world who need you,' the woman said.

'My father, but I'll never be what he wants. I'll never be Wilma.'

'There are others.' The woman smiled the most beautiful smile Dawn had seen.

Nobody smiled like that. She had fallen asleep and was dreaming. The water was cold. Couldn't she dream warm water?

The woman was standing in the water beside her. Dawn took her hand. It was hot. She pulled away. 'You're her, the person in the Roman town. You wanted my book.'

'Do you still have it?'

Her handbag was round her neck, safely above the water level. Dawn opened it and reached inside. 'Are you Rose?'

'Rose doesn't exist,' the woman said. 'You know that. Or rather, there are lots of Roses. The challenge is to find the one you are happy with. Not all changes are to be feared.'

Oliver Twist, you can't do this, so what's the use of trying?

Her sister's voice no longer came as a surprise. She shooed it back. 'Here, take the book.' Dawn held it out. The woman laid a hand on the cover then drew back.

'Someone is waiting for this book, but I was mistaken. You haven't finished it.'

'The story is done. The ending is boring details, tying off the threads.'

'There are no boring details in life unless you want them to be there. The story is not done until the final word on the final page. There is time for you to change the ending.'

While they were speaking, the dolphin dived below the surface. Dawn watched for it to surface, but it didn't appear. The lilt from the sea turned into the jolly jingle from the amusement arcade.

'It's gone,' Dawn said. She replaced the book in her handbag and allowed the woman to lead her from the water.

'Here is your friend,' the woman said.

Sholto jogged towards her holding a stick of pink candyfloss. His face was sticky from the sugar. Without speaking, the woman wiped his lips with her finger then kissed him on the forehead. She skipped along the sea wall towards the beach and was gone.

'Who was that?' Dawn asked Sholto.

Sholto looked to where the gull had returned to pick at the remains of a hamburger bun. She saw that his eyes were moist.

XVII

'I'm worried about my father. I'm going home,' Dawn said, surprised by the authority in her voice.

Sholto nodded. He led the way into the hazel wood, swiping at nettles with the stick from his candy. The ground was damp and a slither of seaweed stuck to the sole of her right sandal. Dawn didn't notice the tree root poking from the ground. Her foot slipped and she heard a snap as she fell, twisting on her right ankle. A stab of pain shot up her leg. She tried to move it, but couldn't.

Sholto rushed to her. He put his arms out to help her up, but she pushed him away. It was too painful. She shivered and Sholto removed his jacket and placed it over her shoulders. He gathered dead branches, removed the damp bark with his penknife and placed the wood in a pile. He had a box of matches in his pocket. The wood was slow to light. Dawn's handbag had fallen a few feet away and Sholto reached towards it. He drew out her library book.

'No,' Dawn cried, grasping feebly for the book. Sholto looked puzzled, but returned the book to the bag and handed it to her. He knelt down to light the fire. After five minutes of blowing on sparks Sholto got a flame going. He tended it until it grew. Dawn dragged herself nearer the heat. Sholto pointed to his chest then in the direction of the Roman town.

'Don't leave me here.' Dawn was suddenly afraid.

Sholto raised ten fingers.

Ten minutes seemed an eternity. The copse became a forest then a primeval swamp. Dawn shuddered. She imagined animal noises creeping towards her. There was a panting at her side and she screamed. Brushing against her sleeve, warming itself by the fire, was a large, grey dog.

'Morpheus.' She stroked the animal's head. A tear fell on her arm. 'Where have you been?' She nestled into the hound's fur and her eyes followed the flames as they made patterns on the wood. 'Sholto won't be long,' she told the dog.

The shock and pain from the fall made her dizzy. The smell of wild poppies anaesthetised her. The flames reached out. She swayed and closed her eyes. Morpheus gave a low whimper as she collapsed onto the fire.

Dawn sensed a light on her eyelids. Her head pulsated. There were voices. She strained to open her eyes. She was lying down and remembered falling. She was in bed, but it didn't smell like her own pillow. Two blurred figures were standing at the bottom of the bed. The room came into focus. The smell was disinfectant.

She had broken her leg and Sholto had gone for help. She was in hospital and in a private room. She couldn't afford that. Where was her father?

The voices became clearer. They didn't realise she could hear them.

'What's this? A trashy romance.'

'It's a library book. It's overdue.'

'The boy gets the girl and everyone has a happy ending. Thank heavens for real life.'

'Shh, dad. I think she's awake.'

Dawn pushed herself onto her pillow and was met by two wide smiles. Sholto was dressed in the uniform of one of the better private schools. His tie was loose and the top button of his shirt undone. His father held *Nobody Loves Rose*.

'You've been in hospital for a week,' Abelard explained. 'Your father knows you're here.'

'You fell in the fire,' Sholto added. 'You've burned your shoulder and arm. The doctor kept you sedated until it healed.'

The shock of hearing Sholto speak robbed Dawn of her own voice. She was getting her head round it when a white-coated man entered the room, stethoscope round his neck. He carried a small vial.

'I have medicine for you.' He grinned at Dawn.

Dawn rubbed her eyes. His beard was trimmed and he wore glasses, but she recognised the sorcerer from the mountain village.

'This is Dr. Weiss. He's been treating you,' Abelard said.

'Drink this.' The doctor offered the vial which contained drops of a blue medicine.

He held it to her lips. She drew back.

'It is for you,' he said as he tipped the cup. The drops fell on her tongue. She tasted a mixture of strawberries and pineapples, sherbet and ice cream. Medicine wasn't supposed to be delicious. The drops swirled from her tongue and onto her palate. They bubbled round her cheeks, fizzed and popped in her mouth like a firework show. Then the sensation faded.

'Make sure she rests,' the doctor instructed Abelard du Niaull before leaving.

Dawn lay back. Father and son were reunited, Sholto had found his voice and sense of responsibility, the doctor was well, but there was something missing. She sat up. 'Where is Morpheus?'

'Who?' Sholto asked.

'Your shaggy, grey dog.'

Sholto looked at his father. Abelard frowned.

'Mauritia had a dog.' He rubbed his chin. 'A wolfhound. My late wife loved animals. She had dogs, cats, birds, horses, a donkey, even a monkey when I first met her. We had to find homes for them. A local farmer took the dog.'

'I'd like a dog,' Sholto said.

'We can get it back. Now, I have to take you back to school.' He turned to Dawn to look at her with his sea-blue eyes. 'Your father will visit this evening.'

Sholto and Abelard left the room, but a moment later Abelard return. 'I forgot, this is your book.' He offered it to Dawn. His hand touched hers as she reached to take it and the tingle spread to encompass her entire body.

'It's a trashy romance,' she said. 'I wanted to write a better ending.' She opened the book at the back, suddenly believing that her words would be there, but the pages were blank. 'I wanted Rose to escape from her sensible life and marry Gideon.'

Abelard looked at the book. 'So who does Ross marry?'

Ross – there wasn't a Ross in the novel.

'*Nobody Loves Ross.*' Abelard pointed at the title. As he did, she saw he was correct. The cover had changed. The plane was on fire, the dog was there, but the broken China doll was an Oriental princess standing next to a pagoda with a glass tear in her eye.

'You will have to read it to find out,' she said, offering him back the book.

Abelard opened it and read. 'Princess Kyu hadn't smiled for five centuries.'

As if holding a shell to her ear, Dawn heard the whisper of the woman by the sea.

Unless you want them to be there…

'Books offer the escape we want, but they aren't real,' she said aloud and smiled.

'Mauritia had a beautiful smile, just like yours.' Their eyes locked for a second before Abelard looked away. 'I should be going.'

Dawn felt the happiness medicine bubble in her stomach.

'Wait.'

It was time to write the ending.

Lightning Source UK Ltd.
Milton Keynes UK
UKHW011302060821
388387UK00003B/968